Finding Felix

JO PLATT
Finding Felix

CANELO

First published in the United Kingdom in 2018 by Canelo

This edition published in the United Kingdom in 2020 by

Canelo Digital Publishing Limited
Third Floor, 20 Mortimer Street
London W1T 3JW
United Kingdom

A CIP catalogue record for this book is available from the British Library.

Print ISBN 978 1 78863 803 6
Ebook ISBN 978 1 911591 60 3

This book is a work of fiction. Names, characters, businesses, organizations, places and events are either the product of the author's imagination or are used fictitiously. Any resemblance to actual persons, living or dead, events or locales is entirely coincidental.

Look for more great books at www.canelo.co

Printed and bound in Great Britain by Clays Ltd, Elcograf S.p.A.

Friday 17 September 1999

I shoved the last bit of pasty into my mouth, tossed the bag into the litter bin at the end of the bench and checked my watch. It was almost seven, and we'd agreed to meet at six thirty so that we could grab a pizza before the pub. I looked around the largely deserted marketplace for any sign of Dot. Unsurprisingly, there was none.

Leaning back contentedly, I put my hand to my mouth, checking for crumbs and at the same time stroking the three days' worth of stubble I couldn't be bothered to shave off. I wondered if she might lecture me about that. It'd be pretty hypocritical of her if she did, seeing as her man of the moment, Johnny Depp, had looked very beardy, not to mention completely stoned, in the four magazine articles about him she'd shown me in the past week.

I rolled my eyes at the thought and dusted off the new jeans Mum had bought me for going to uni. She hadn't done badly this time actually. They were a little snug over my gut maybe – I patted my temporarily appeased stomach – but other than that they were OK.

'Oi, Felix! Mop head!'

I looked up, lifting my hair out of my eyes. It was Ian Watson, and he was with Chris Fry. Both were waving frantically to me from the other side of the road. 'What you doing, Mopper? Coming for a drink?'

'In a bit,' I called. 'Waiting for Dot.'

'OK. We're going to the Crowns. See you there?'

'We're starting at The Lamb, but yeah, maybe later.'

Ian gave me a thumbs-up and the pair of them headed off, crossing the road and walking towards the Brittox as a church clock chimed the hour. I closed my eyes, and relaxed back onto the bench. It was strange to think that by this time tomorrow I'd be nearly a hundred miles away and living with loads of people I'd never met before. Scary, but exciting.

'Oh my God, Felix. Am I late? I ran all the way.'

I opened my eyes at the sound of her voice and looked up to see Dot silhouetted against the evening sun, her head swamped by a large khaki bucket hat. 'Wow, are these new jeans?' she asked breathlessly, bending down and patting my knee. 'Cos I love them. And that sweatshirt. That's my favourite one of yours right now. You look really great.'

'Thanks,' I said casually, trying not to look too pleased while hauling myself to my feet. 'And I like your...' I looked her up and down. She was still channelling the sporty look between waist and neck, wearing a black running vest with white piping at the neck and a shiny green tracksuit top. But waist down she had gone for throwback grunge, with one of her home-made wraparound maxi skirts – the vivid orange one – and her precious DMs, which she had worn all summer, despite the heat. '... hat,' I said, plumping for the best of a typically chaotic job. 'Where did you get it?'

'It's Dad's. He wears it for fishing and Mum really, really, really hates me wearing it,' she grinned, patting her head. 'Kept telling me no one could see my beautiful brown eyes and that I needed to show off my auburn tresses.' She laughed and shook her head. 'Auburn tresses?' she scoffed, tugging at a long strand of hair which had escaped from under the hat. 'What planet is she on? And which century is she in?'

I tutted. 'Well, your eyes are brown and your hair is auburn and she's paying you a compliment. You should give her a break sometimes, you know.'

'She should give me a break,' she said, frowning. 'It's OK for you, you don't have to live with her, Felix. You don't know what it's like. She's always on my case about boyfriends and the magazines I read and what I wear and bloody everything.'

'OK, OK, let's just forget it,' I said, trying not to worry that Dot's mum and I seemed to agree on so many things. 'Do you want to go for pizza?'

'Have you eaten?'

'I had a snack,' I said. 'But I'm happy to have a pizza if you want one. You should probably eat something, you know,' I added. She was a bit of a lightweight when it came to drinking.

She shook her head. 'Nah, I'm fine. I had a Toffee Crisp on the way here. Let's just go.'

'OK, if you're sure,' I said doubtfully, but letting it go. 'I just saw Ian and Chris. They're off to the Three Crowns and asked if we were coming along.'

'Oh, OK, yeah. I'm cool with that,' she said, trying to smile.

'I told them we were going to The Lamb but that we might see them later.'

Her forced smile transformed into a genuine grin and she threw her arms around my middle, resting her head against my chest and giving me a squeeze. 'Aw… You sure you don't mind?'

'No… it's fine…' I gasped. 'I like The Lamb too. But let me go now, yeah? You're like a boa constrictor.'

She laughed loudly and let me go. 'I'm gonna miss you, Felix Davis,' she said, taking my hand and pulling me in the direction of The Lamb. 'I really, really am.'

3

Chapter 1

I looked across the hospital bed at my mother, her hand resting gently on top of Nanny Flo's, her head bowed. Dad, sitting to her right, offered me a brave smile, which I did my best to return.

'Are you OK, Dot?' he mouthed.

I nodded and turned my head towards my sister. Becca was sitting at the foot of the bed, staring at our grandmother, her expression glazed and unreadable. I wondered if she, like me, was remembering all the love and laughter we had shared with the usually vibrant eighty-six-year-old woman who was now lying in front of us, so pale and fragile. I turned back to Nanny Flo just as her closed eyes flickered. My father nudged my mother and all four of us leaned forward simultaneously. I reached out and took Nanny Flo's left hand.

'Hello, Mum,' said my mother gently. 'Can you hear me? We're all here: me, Donald, Dottie and Becca. All of us.'

My grandmother's brow furrowed slightly and then, after a moment, her eyes opened. 'Dottie?' she murmured. 'Our Dorothy passed away years ago.'

Mum bit her lip and looked at Dad. 'The doctor said she might be confused.'

4

I squeezed my grandmother's hand. 'Not your sister, Nanny. It's me, little Dottie, your granddaughter. I took the train to Exeter from Bristol to see you.'

Her head turned slowly towards me and she smiled weakly. 'Little Dottie,' she said.

I nodded rapidly, taking a moment to steady my voice before I spoke. 'That's right,' I smiled. 'And Becca, too. Look.' I pointed towards my sister. 'She's driven from Bishops Cannings.'

'Hello, Nanny,' said Becca, with impressive brightness in the circumstances, although I could see the enormous effort behind it.

'Have I missed… the christening, Becca?' asked Nanny Flo, pausing mid sentence to take a breath.

My mother sighed. 'It's not a christening, Mum,' she said. 'It's a wedding. Becca's getting married… to Mark. You remember Mark. He's a policeman.'

Nanny Flo's eyes closed. 'Lovely boy,' she said. 'Like Dixon of Dock Green.'

Dad laughed and my mother smiled even as a tear escaped and rolled down her cheek. She hurriedly brushed it away.

'You'll have to help choose the flowers for the bouquets, Nanny,' said Becca.

The rest of us nodded and murmured our approval of this plan, despite the fact that a doctor had gently intimated less than an hour ago that my grandmother's pneumonia meant that she might not see tomorrow, let alone my sister's wedding in three months' time.

'Becca can't decide between white roses and lily of the valley,' I said. 'I suppose she could have both, couldn't she?'

With what seemed like an enormous effort, Nanny Flo reopened her eyes. 'I had lily of the valley,' she said. 'Wonderful perfume. Will you have that at your wedding, Dottie?'

I smiled. 'I can't see me getting married any time soon, Nanny.'

Her expression darkened. 'You're not all on your own, are you?'

Surprised by her reaction and kicking myself for the thoughtlessness of my comment, I rushed to reassure her. 'I'm fine. I love Bristol and I've got lots of friends. I'm very lucky.' I looked at my mother, who nodded vigorously.

'Yes, Dot's not lonely, Mum,' she said. 'She has a very busy social life.'

My grandmother turned towards her. 'What about that lovely boy who's always calling round after school? The cuddly one.'

'Dot is thirty-six now, Mum,' said my mother. 'School was a long time ago.'

'Hair all over the place, like a young Ken Dodd,' murmured Nanny Flo. 'Likes his food. Washes up in the hotel at weekends. Nice boy. Perfect for Dottie.'

Mum looked puzzled and turned to Dad, who shrugged.

'She means Felix Davis, Mum,' whispered Becca, before looking at me and smiling.

'That's right.' I smiled back at her, thinking of Felix for the first time in years.

'Oh, of course. Yes, Felix,' said my mother. 'You're right, he was a lovely, kind boy. But he was the other way, Mum,' she said, raising her voice slightly. 'He wasn't after a girlfriend.'

Despite the circumstances, I couldn't help sighing at my mother's long-held and continuing conviction that any male friend who failed to show a romantic interest in me must be either *the other way* or *afraid of his feelings*.

Nanny Flo frowned. 'So he's not with her, Helen?' she said. It was as if I was no longer in the room.

'They were just friends, Mum, and they still are.' My mother looked up at me and widened her eyes, a clear warning not to contradict her. I frowned. As if I would.

'That's right,' I said.

'But who is going to look after her?' murmured Nanny Flo.

'I can look after myself,' I smiled.

Reminded of my presence, Nanny Flo turned her head slowly back towards me. She stared expressionlessly at me for a moment, saying nothing, and then, without warning, her face suddenly and unexpectedly crumpled, a single tear escaping from the corner of her left eye and trickling down her cheek before being absorbed by the pillow. 'You're alone,' she gasped. 'All alone.'

Appalled, I looked to my mother for support. Her hand was now over her mouth.

'Flo,' said Dad, stepping into the breach, 'don't fret over this. Dot is very happy.'

'She has no one,' she replied with a slight shudder, as if terrified by the thought. 'I do worry.'

'Mum…' began my mother, but she got no further. Her tears were now flowing silently but unchecked and she was clearly beyond words.

My grandmother uttered a low, prolonged moan and began to sob.

'Oh please don't cry, Nanny,' I begged. 'I'm very happy.'

'Dot is *so* happy,' echoed Becca, leaning forward, now also on the verge of tears.

'I am,' I insisted quietly, my heart breaking to see the three women I loved most in the world so distraught. 'I am.'

I looked at my mother. Her head was once again bowed, and she leaned against Dad as he gently pulled her towards him. Becca too had lowered her head, and Nanny Flo's chest heaved with the painful effort of taking the deep breaths required by her sobs.

I covered my face with my hands, despairing at the heartache I had caused, and desperate to put an end to the distress so carelessly kick-started. My grandmother was dying and I had single-handedly managed to make the most agonising situation my family had ever had to face even more unbearable.

And then suddenly, just as heartbreak, guilt and hopelessness threatened to overwhelm me, the solution became obvious. I lowered my hands and sat up. 'I've got a boyfriend,' I blurted. 'I haven't mentioned him before because we haven't been going out for very long, but it's going really well,' I continued, the words spilling out of me. 'Really, *really* well.'

Nanny Flo's sobbing ceased abruptly and she blinked at me through her tears. I waited for her to say something, but she remained silent, studying me, suddenly calm.

'There now,' I said, collapsing back in my chair and experiencing a wonderful sense of relief. 'That's better.' I realised that there were tears streaming down my own face, and I dabbed at them with the sleeve of my jumper.

8

'Dottie…' said my mother, sitting up. Her eyes were red and her mascara smudged, but she had stopped crying and her expression was now one of stunned wonderment. 'Dottie…' she repeated, but said nothing more.

'So who is the lucky chap?' asked Dad jovially.

I turned towards him. He was beaming and his eyes glistened. 'The lucky chap?' I echoed, completely unprepared for this continuation of the topic.

'My mistake. The *very* lucky chap,' he said. He laughed but was clearly as emotional as the rest of us and sounded choked.

I looked at Nanny Flo, who remained fully focused on me. 'It's… Well, he's… The thing… It's…' I began, stumbling over my words, casting around for a name. Should I simply claim to be back together with my ex? I glanced at my mother, knowing that mentioning Alistair at this moment was definitely going to make her feel worse not better. More importantly, I wasn't sure that Nanny Flo would be much comforted by the thought either. No, I needed a name with positive or – at the very least – neutral connotations.

A succession of names popped into my head and I rapidly reviewed each in turn. Mark? No, Becca was marrying a Mark; we couldn't both have a Mark. Roberto? No, he was the Italian doctor who'd just explained Nanny's condition to us. Felix – my old friend whom Nanny liked?

'Felix.'

I frowned in confusion, uncertain for a moment whether I had merely thought the name or actually spoken it out loud. But I didn't have to wait long for clarification.

'Oh my goodness,' gasped my mother, placing a hand on her chest. She looked at me, then at my grandmother, and then back at me. 'Not *the* Felix? The one we were just talking about a moment ago? Felix who was always so afraid of his feelings? Is it him, Dot?' she asked, her eyes now wide with excitement.

I looked at her for a moment and swallowed. 'Yes,' I said weakly, knowing that I now had no choice but to go with it. 'It's him. My friend… who Nanny liked… from all those years ago,' I added, nodding. 'It's Felix,' I concluded in a hoarse whisper.

'It's a sign,' said my mother, raising her eyes to the ceiling.

'So how did you meet him again?' asked Dad, displaying an uncharacteristic and, at this moment, very unwelcome interest in romantic detail.

'Well, I…'

'Was it at the school reunion in February?' asked Becca.

I turned gratefully towards my cooler, calmer and much more collected younger sister and nodded rapidly. 'Yes,' I said. 'I met him there and we got chatting. That's what happened.'

'Meant to be,' said my mother, clasping her hands together. 'Isn't that lovely, Mum?' I could feel her looking at me but was unable to make eye contact with her and instead focused on Nanny Flo.

'Are you in love, Dottie?' she asked. She edged her small, thin hand towards me and I reached out and took it. She gave my hand a barely perceptible squeeze and I leaned forward, kissing her forehead, desperate to make everything all right, desperate to make her happy. Nothing else mattered. 'I am, Nanny,' I nodded, sitting up.

'That's good,' she breathed. And then she smiled, closed her eyes and said nothing more.

–

Several hours later, Becca and I stood side by side in the hospital corridor, leaning against the wall of Nanny Flo's room. 'You OK?' she asked softly.

I looked up at her. She was fair-skinned and pale at the best of times, but today she seemed almost transparent. 'Just about,' I said. 'You?'

Her head drooped, her short light-brown bob falling across her face. 'No.'

'Me neither, actually. I was lying.'

She looked up and offered me a painfully sad smile as the door to the room opened and Mum emerged.

'I just…' she began, quietly closing the door behind her, before abandoning any attempt at speech and beginning to cry.

Becca and I hugged her simultaneously.

'Thank you, girls,' she said. 'Dad and I are so grateful for you. We love you both so much.'

'And we love you,' said Becca. 'And Nanny. If there wasn't the love, there wouldn't be the pain, would there?'

'True,' said my mother. 'That's so true.'

We let her go and she took a handkerchief from her sleeve and blew her nose. 'Well, I know it's a very sad time, but that's such happy news about you, Dot. About Felix, I mean. I remember him as a very lovely boy. And you were friends for such a long time. I always thought it was a shame that you lost touch.'

Becca threw me a sidelong glance.

'Mum, I need to explain—' I began.

'No, no, no,' she interrupted, delving into her brown leather shoulder bag and extracting a small plastic-wrapped packet of tissues. 'I will not have you apologising for not telling us. Your father always said I was far too interested in your relationship with Alistair. He said I put the pair of you under too much pressure, and he was right. It's no wonder you didn't want to mention Felix to me.'

I shook my head. 'Mum—'

She opened the packet of tissues and took one out. 'I actually think *not* telling us was the right decision. No point in saying anything until you're absolutely sure. Oh, but Dottie,' she placed her hand on my arm, her eyes shining, 'what a wonderful time to tell us. Do you have any idea how happy you made Nanny? And me? And your father?' She stood on tiptoe and kissed my cheek. 'Hearing about Felix in that desperate moment was like someone lighting a candle in the darkest room. I'm not sure what I believe in, but Nanny mentioning him and then you telling us you're seeing him… well, it makes me think there's more at work in this universe than we can ever understand. We couldn't be happier for you. And, of course, we'd love to see him after all these years. I remember when the pair of you were teenagers and he'd be round every other night for tea, wouldn't he? And then he'd go home and eat another one.' She smiled fondly at the thought. 'You must update us, but,' she paused and rubbed my arm, 'not until you're ready, and I promise not to pester. I shan't raise the matter again.' She turned to Becca and took her hand. 'You cannot imagine what a comfort it is to me at a time like this to know that both my girls are happy. Such a comfort.' She looked up at each of us in turn and smiled.

I tried to return the smile but was aware of an underlying sense of panic, kept in check only by the overarching sadness of the day. I wanted to say something, but nothing helpful came to mind, so instead I simply nodded dumbly. Becca meanwhile was looking at me with obvious concern.

'Thank you again, girls,' said my mother quietly and, after hugging and kissing us both again, she disappeared back into Nanny Flo's room.

I stared at the floor, overwhelmed by unhappiness. After a moment, I felt Becca's hand on my arm and looked up. 'I think you did the right thing, Dot,' she said.

I smiled uncertainly. 'I hope so.'

'You did,' she said determinedly, giving me another hug. 'You made things right for Nanny Flo.'

Chapter 2

Kate leaned back in her chair and, putting her feet up on the small conference table at which we were sitting, looked at me disapprovingly over the top of her large purple-framed glasses. 'So what you're telling me,' she said, pausing to sip her mid-morning coffee, 'is that you told a big – nay, *huge* – fib two months ago and now your chickens have come home to roost.'

It was a perfect summing-up of the situation.

'You have to remember that the circumstances were exceptional,' I said defensively. 'She was on her deathbed.'

Kate shook her head, her short red curls joining in and echoing her disapproval. 'She was on her *bed*, Dot,' she corrected. 'It wasn't her *death*bed, because Nanny Flo is not dead.'

'Well of course I know *now* that it wasn't her deathbed!' I exclaimed. 'But at the time I thought it was, and I didn't want her going to her grave miserable about my single status. She was distraught.' I was aware of a rising tension in my voice. Kate's undoubted ability to mercilessly cut through the crap and get to the essence of a problem was a quality which made our day-to-day professional partnership, and our two-woman graphic design company, a success. But the approach grated whenever she applied it to my personal problems – which she invariably did.

'You're thirty-six,' she continued, apparently unmoved. 'Lots of people are single or unmarried at thirty-six. And it's not like you're permanently on the shelf. You were in a long-term relationship until less than a year ago.' She took another sip of coffee. 'As you know, I didn't meet Fred till I was thirty-five. And we didn't get married until August 2015, by which time we'd been together…' her eyes flicked up and to the right as she performed the mental calculation, 'two years and seven months and I was thirty-eight. So I hardly think temporarily single at thirty-six is any big deal these days.'

'You're so right,' I said tonelessly. 'If only I could have provided Nanny Flo with a pie chart showing UK sexual and marital relationships by age, I'm sure that would have calmed her down just as quickly as pretending that I had a boyfriend.'

'You're upset,' said Kate. 'I can tell.'

'I'm just cross with myself,' I said miserably, picking up my own mug of coffee and blowing on it.

'But what I don't understand…' she continued.

I braced myself.

'… is why Nanny Flo still thinks you're going out with Philip…'

'Felix.'

'… eight weeks later.'

I sighed and put down my coffee. 'She's never once mentioned him and neither has anyone else. She was in hospital, intermittently delirious for a couple of weeks, and it was touch and go whether she'd make it. And then when she came out, he didn't come up again. You know how relieved I was when she began to recover.'

Kate nodded sympathetically. 'I do.'

'Well, that was my only focus,' I said. 'So I just forgot about the Felix thing – and it seemed like everyone else did too.'

'Even your mother?' asked Kate with undisguised scepticism. 'I find that hard to believe. She'd usually be scouting out wedding venues for you by now, wouldn't she?'

'With hindsight I can see that that was suspiciously out of character,' I agreed. 'But at the time she was totally wrapped up in Nanny Flo, wasn't she? Of course, I now know that she didn't ask me about it because she'd promised not to pry. She feels guilty because she thinks she scared Alistair off,' I added.

Kate raised her eyebrows. 'You don't think that, do you?'

'Well, the fact that she described every single one of our holiday destinations as *the perfect place for a honeymoon* didn't help,' I sighed. 'But no. Alistair and I just wanted different things. I wanted us to stay together – he didn't. Can't really blame Mum for that, can I?' I smiled ruefully. 'Anyway, she was determined not to ask anything about Felix, so it was all left to drift.'

'Like a room-clearing fart,' Kate said, shaking her head.

'I had other things on my mind.'

She looked at me but said nothing.

'And OK, so maybe there was a little bit of not wanting to think about it involved,' I admitted.

'Head buried in the sand,' she said. 'Typical Dot.'

I frowned but didn't feel able to challenge the statement. I knew she had a point. My tendency to refuse to confront personal challenges and consider their consequences until my nose was pressed up against them was undeniable. In my defence, it was an approach that on the whole seemed to work reasonably well. It cut down considerably on the amount of time spent worrying and stressing about things, and, nine times out of ten, a last-minute fix was just as good as a lengthy, considered and, in my opinion, tortured approach.

However, like it or not, I had to admit that this was not one of those times. This was definitely the one in ten.

'So, what does Becca say?' Kate asked, dragging me back to the matter in hand.

I heaved a sigh. 'Haven't had a chance to talk to her since Mum phoned last night. But I'm going to Bishops Cannings for a dress fitting tomorrow, so I'll tell her about it then. You know what she's like. She'll be lovely about it all whatever happens – whether it completely over-shadows the run-up to her big day or not,' I concluded despondently.

Kate shook her head. 'Now don't get despairing on me, Dorothy Riley. I can't stand it when you're despairing. Let's think rationally and constructively.' She removed her feet from the table and put down her mug, placing a thoughtful hand on her chin. 'I think you have three choices,' she said after a moment.

'Really?' I experienced a sudden surge of surprised optimism. Three choices were two more than I'd hoped for.

'Your first option is to fess up to everyone.'

I immediately felt my optimism begin to wane. 'Confess that I told Nanny Flo a mega lie on her deathbed? That'll go down well just before a family wedding.'

'Don't discount it,' persisted Kate. 'Becca already knows the truth, your dad would accept that you meant well and your mother…' She hesitated and pulled a face. 'Well, she's got a month to get over it.'

I shook my head. 'You know Mum. She'd never get over it. She's still upset about Dad saying he couldn't go to a ballroom taster class with her because he had to work late, when in fact he was hiding in the pub.'

'To be fair to your mum,' Kate smiled, 'I'd be a bit fed up if Fred pulled something like that. When did that happen?'

'June 1989.'

Her smile dropped. 'OK, so that is quite a long time to be cross.'

I shrugged. 'I could cope with her lifelong disappointment in me if I had to. My real concern is that Nanny's not exactly fighting fit and on top of the world these days. I just don't know how she'd take it. She's still very frail and I'm afraid that…' I looked up, leaving the fear unspoken. 'I don't want to put her through that, Kate,' I said quietly. 'I don't want her to know that I lied.'

She bit her lip and waved a hand. 'Fair enough, forget about fessing up,' she said with a slight catch in her voice. She paused for a moment and cleared her throat. 'So, moving on, option two is that you claim you and Philip have split up. But you tell Nanny Flo that you are still very good friends, that you both feel good about the decision and that it's all for the best.'

'It's Felix,' I corrected again, experiencing a slight twinge of annoyance that she seemed incapable of remembering my pretend boyfriend's name. 'And I would have gone with that option if I hadn't told Mum on the phone last night that we were still together and that things were good. And she had me on speakerphone so Nanny heard,'

I added, closing and then rubbing my eyes as I felt a headache coming on.

Kate didn't reply, and, after a moment, I reopened my eyes to find her staring at me expressionlessly. 'Now why on earth would you tell your mother that?' she asked quietly, her tone searingly to the point. 'Why would you perpetuate the myth when you had an opportunity to draw it to a believable conclusion?'

'Because I panicked,' I replied, taking a breath and attempting to remain unflustered in the face of her unblinking gaze and crushing rationality. 'Mum asked me, absolutely out of the blue, how we were and I said everything was fine. I wasn't expecting her to raise the subject after months of silence, and my aim was to dead-end the topic and move on. But then she said she needed to confirm the seating plan for the wedding, which was something I *really* hadn't seen coming. It hadn't occurred to me that she'd want him to come.'

'It hadn't occurred to you that she would expect your boyfriend, whom your whole family knew for over a decade as a child growing up, to come to your sister's wedding?' Kate's tone had now shifted to incredulous.

'She hadn't mentioned him!' I protested, throwing up my hands and abandoning all pretence of calm. '*No one* had mentioned him! He was off the radar... in the Bermuda Triangle of my consciousness. It was like he'd evaporated. Like he didn't exist. Which, of course, he bloody doesn't!'

'OK, OK,' she said, holding up a placatory hand. 'I get it. You were taken by surprise. Go on. What else did your mother say?'

I reclosed my eyes and took a deep breath. 'Well,' I began again, trying to keep my voice steady, 'then it was as if the floodgates had opened and she just kept going on and on about how happy the whole thing had made her and Dad and, of course, Nanny Flo. And then Nanny started shouting in the background that Felix had saved her life and that she couldn't wait to see him again after all these years.' I groaned and ran a hand through my hair. 'God, what am I going to do? I've ruined everything for everyone.' I slumped forward, resting my cheek on the conference table. 'They're all going to be so upset and let down and it's supposed to be the happiest day of Becca's life. It's a disaster.'

'Hush now,' said Kate comfortingly, standing up and leaning across the table to gently rub my shoulder. 'Don't be defeatist, and try to stay calm. Getting yourself all worked up isn't going to help, is it?'

I felt myself relax slightly as she continued to rub. 'I'm sorry for being shouty and panicky,' I mumbled, my face still pressed against the table.

'It's OK,' she said softly. 'I understand. It's a huge mess and the potential to hurt and disappoint the people you love the most is enormous. No one would want to be in your shoes right now.'

'What?' I exclaimed, sitting up and shrugging her off, my panic immediately resurging. 'You're supposed to be helping me, not buying into my despair. What about option number three? You said I had three options.'

'Well, I would have thought the third one was obvious,' she said, shrugging and sitting back down. 'Find Phil – or whoever. Track him down and see if he's up for it.'

I screwed up my face. 'Sorry, what?' I asked after a moment.

'Find him and ask him if he'll go to the wedding with you,' she repeated, her face and tone completely relaxed, as if this was the most reasonable suggestion in the world.

'I can't do that.'

'Why not?' she asked, appearing genuinely confused.

'Well, because he…'

'He what?' Her expression remained calm.

'Well, I haven't seen him in years. Over a decade. And it's such a big ask.'

She raised her eyebrows. 'You're inviting him to a party, Dot, not requesting a kidney. What kind of bloke was he?'

'Big and round,' I said. It was an instinctive reply. At school, and into manhood, Felix had been what Nanny Flo termed *cuddly*. In fact, I reflected, by the time he was twenty, he was six-two and probably a good three or four stone overweight. 'He liked pies and pasties. A lot.'

Kate blinked. 'Okaaay, but moving on from his physique and dietary preferences, what was his personality like? Kind? Fun? *Helpful?*'

I didn't even have to think about it. 'Yes,' I said immediately. 'He was all of those things.'

'Well then,' she said, 'he sounds like *just* the kind of guy who would give up a few hours of his day to help out an old friend.'

I was surprised to find myself nodding. She was somehow making the whole thing sound incredibly doable.

'When did you last see him?' she continued.

'God, ages ago.' I put a hand to my cheek and thought. 'It must have been our third year at university. I was in

London for the day and we met up with some other friends and went to the cinema. It was just before finals. Fifteen, sixteen years ago maybe.'

'And you didn't see him at all after that?'

I shook my head. 'His parents moved up north during his first year at King's, and Mum and Dad moved to Exeter with Nanny Flo. So neither of us went back to Devizes after uni. We were supposed to meet up before I went travelling, but that fell through. I think maybe he had a job interview or something. I can't remember. Then I was away for eighteen months or so, and I sent a few postcards but I didn't hear from him. It was just much harder to stay in touch on the move back then, wasn't it?'

'It was,' she agreed. 'And sometimes I think it was better that way. The pressure today to *share* and *stay connected* is ridiculous. I mean, I know we have to maintain an internet presence for work, but I honestly wanted to smash my phone yesterday when Tanya Matcham posted a picture of her new stove-top kettle. For God's sake! Women chained themselves to railings so that she could stop obsessing about kitchen appliances. She posts utter rubbish, day in day out. I mean, who the actual cares about her ruddy HRT patches falling off? You know, I'd love it if...'

I nodded along as Kate said something about wishing people would either unfriend her, lose their phones or die, but I had actually stopped listening and was instead now thinking about Felix.

We had been friends from the moment he stood next to me in the school choir at the age of eleven, giggling over Roger Chapman's complete inability to carry a tune. It was the beginning of a laughter-filled friendship which had continued for ten years, throughout our time at separate universities. And during that decade we had shared mountains of homework, dozens of cakes, one cigarette and considerably more beers and ciders – not to mention, on my part at least, innumerable teenage crises. I smiled at the memories and felt sure that Kate was right: Felix would, if he could, come with me to Becca's wedding. The question was whether I could track him down.

'The question, of course, is whether you can track him down,' said Kate, having apparently completed her social-media rant and refocused on the matter in hand. 'If you can, he just has to smile and nod. And then, after the wedding, *you*,' she leaned across the table and poked my arm, 'can begin to extricate yourself from the situation, in a slow and considered manner, causing minimal distress and disappointment to Nanny Flo.'

She reached into the biscuit tin, which sat open on the table between us, and took out a digestive. 'And if you can't find him, I suppose you could claim he went down with diarrhoea and vomiting on the big day. I guess that's option number four. But personally I think there'd be nothing more annoying than paying for a guest who doesn't turn up, and besides, now that your mother *has* started asking questions, I can't see her stopping any time soon, can you? Better to give her, and everyone else, a boyfriend for the day and then get him to ride off into the sunset. Maybe he can realise he wants to live in Australia, or that friendship was better than partnership, or something. It doesn't really matter what you say, so long as you stress to your mother that if she makes any attempt to get the pair of you back together, he'll top himself.' She bit into the digestive. 'I'd kill for a Hobnob, I really would. Why did you buy digestives, Dot? They're so peasant.'

I took a biscuit. Kate's proposal was sounding increasingly attractive. But wary of getting my hopes up regarding a potential solution to my problem, I began mentally listing all the possible impediments to the plan.

'He probably *already* lives in Australia,' I murmured. 'Or is away that weekend. A month is very short notice. Maybe he has a wife… or a husband… and two small children.'

Kate shrugged. 'Location and prior commitments could definitely be a problem, but a partner shouldn't be. It's only one day – or just part of a day, actually. I wouldn't have a problem with Fred doing it to help out.'

'But what about people at the wedding asking awkward questions?' I said, my thoughts leaping anxiously ahead to the event itself.

'Like who? Like what?' she asked. 'People don't dive in right away with questions about a person's dating history when they meet someone new at a wedding. No one is going to ask anything personal. It'll be: *Where do you live? What do you do? Isn't the weather great?* And your mother,' she continued, as if reading my mind, 'will be far too busy to grill him in any depth there and then. And if it gets tricky, the pair of you can just reminisce. How long did you say you were friends for?'

'About ten years.'

'There you go then. You've got loads to say about each other if pushed.' She opened her mouth to take another bite of her digestive, before suddenly pausing, her hand in mid-air, the biscuit just centimetres from her face. Then, without turning her head towards me, she looked at me out of the corner of her eye. 'Did you ever go out with him? Sleep with him?' she asked, her expression now serious.

I frowned at her sudden change of tack and tone. 'With Felix?'

'No, with the Pope.' She didn't smile.

I shook my head emphatically at the suggestion that I had dated Felix. We had enjoyed each other's company very much, and it was undoubtedly a close friendship, but that was all. In my pre-teens, and with my bedroom walls plastered with posters of Chesney Hawkes, I had sighed over anyone lanky with a mole. Later, I had transferred my affections to Ronan Keating, Robbie Williams and finally Liam Gallagher before, at the age of fifteen, primarily in an attempt to annoy my mother, tearing down my posters and going out with school ne'er-do-well Sean Dowse. He was the only boy in the school with a tattoo; one which he had created himself, on his left forearm, over a three-month period, using a safety pin and indelible markers stolen from the art block. It was supposed to be a panther arched over a dagger, and, although it actually looked more like a guinea pig hurdling a melanoma, it made my mother's lip curl. And at fifteen, that was enough for me.

As for Felix, his affections had been altogether more cerebral. He had spent most of our secondary-school years hankering after beautiful minds, in particular that of Caitlin Bruce, undoubtedly our year group's most intelligent female, before discovering in lower sixth that she was gay and making the bold decision to *save himself* for university.

'No, we never went out,' I said to Kate. 'He was really sciencey and mathsy and those were the girls he used to go on about.'

Kate's expression brightened. 'That's OK then,' she said.

'Why?'

'Because, thinking about it, I wouldn't want Fred going without me to a party with anyone he had fancied, snogged or slept with, even fifteen years ago.'

'I'd feel the same way,' I agreed. 'But there was nothing like that, and besides,' I adjusted my grey pencil skirt and white blouse, both of which currently felt at least half a size too small, and tugged at my shoulder-length hair, which was in desperate need of a cut, 'there's not a lot for anyone to be jealous of here these days, is there?'

'Oh for God's sake stop fishing,' said Kate impatiently. 'You know you scrub up well when you bother, so don't pretend you don't.'

'Hmm.'

'Anyway,' she said, once again looking at me over the top of her glasses, 'I should get back to work.' She checked her watch. 'But why don't you take twenty minutes to start scouring the internet for him? Your meeting with the restaurant isn't till two and you've prepared to the nth for that, haven't you?'

'I have, but I want to go over things one more time.'

Kate sighed. 'Ah, if only you were as focused and forward-thinking in your personal life as you are professionally.'

I didn't reply, and she reached out and pushed my coffee towards me. 'Actually,' she said gently, 'you'd probably be a right bitch and I wouldn't love you half so much.'

I smiled and picked up my coffee. 'I'll google him tonight.'

'Fabulous!' She clapped her hands, suddenly brisk again. 'I know it's a delaying tactic, highly deceitful and something I wouldn't usually approve of,' she said, causing my shoulders to sag slightly, 'but in the circumstances, I think it's your best bet.' She stuffed the remainder of her biscuit into her mouth and stood up. 'But do make sure you crack on with finding Phil... ix this evening. This is one thing you really can't afford to put off, Dot,' she mumbled, spitting crumbs and wagging a finger at me.

I rolled my eyes. 'For God's sake, Kate, what's your problem with his name? It's two syllables: Fe-lix.'

She stopped chewing and peered down at me. 'I've never associated that name with a human being before, that's all, only a cat. So it feels odd to say it. And besides, his name is Felix only because that was the first one to roll off your tongue at the time. I hardly think you can be precious about it, Dorothy Riley.'

I slumped in my chair. 'I know. Sorry.'

She smiled, bent down and patted my knee. 'That's all right,' she said. 'I know you're stressed. But don't be. I have every confidence in your ability to steer this situation to a happy outcome.'

'You do?' I looked up at her.

'Do you want me to answer that question with a lie?' she asked matter-of-factly. 'Or would you rather I buy into your despair?'

I didn't hesitate. 'I'll take the lie.'

'OK, well in that case, yes, I do,' she said, and then, offering me what I supposed was intended to be an encouraging wink, she headed back to her desk.

Chapter 3

'I'm going to have to let it out… again,' said Eileen, running a hand through her short grey hair and sounding unmistakably peeved. As well as being a very talented dressmaker, she was also a part-time teacher at the primary school of which my sister was deputy head, and, at that moment, she was making me feel like a naughty five-year-old.

To be fair to Eileen, I deserved the telling-off. It would be the second time that she'd had to alter my brides-maid's dress due to weight gain since my first fitting two months earlier. And the need for alteration hadn't come as a complete surprise to me. I had decided to weigh myself before setting off for Becca's that morning and had been horrified to discover as I stood on the scales, that I had put on two kilograms. And that was on top of the two I had gained before my last fitting.

'Sorry, Eileen,' I said shamefacedly. 'But look, why don't you hold off making any more adjustments and I'll make sure I lose those extra pounds by the time Becca walks down the aisle.'

Eileen looked uncertainly first at myself, then at Becca. My sister shrugged amiably. 'If you'd rather do that, Dot,' she smiled.

'I would,' I said determinedly. 'It'll give me something to aim for.'

'Well I don't mind what you do. I'll just edge those sleeves and leave the rest. But Rebecca,' continued Eileen, turning towards her, 'if she's bursting out of that dress on the big day, I want you to tell everyone that it's her fondness for doughnuts and not my ability to sew that's at fault.' She gestured wordlessly for me to step out of the dress and then bent down and began picking up her pins, ribbons and tape measure from the floor of Becca's bedroom. Becca widened her eyes at me and I pretended to nibble my nails in fear before beginning to undress.

'And don't think I don't know you're pulling faces, Dorothy,' said Eileen. 'I haven't been a school teacher for thirty years without the ability to know what's going on behind my back.'

'Sorry, Eileen,' I said quietly. 'Again.'

She looked up and laughed. 'Lose the pounds if you want to, but you'll look beautiful at any weight. So if you decide to keep the curves and have any last-minute panics, just give me a call.'

I smiled and gave her a hug. 'You're a gem.'

'And you're in your bra and panties,' she said. 'Get dressed.'

Becca laughed, passing me my shirt and jeans before helping Eileen to gather the remainder of her things and heading downstairs with her to the front door.

By the time she returned, I was dressed and examining myself critically in the full-length mirror inside her wardrobe door.

'Your BMI is just fine,' she said, walking over and poking me in the side.

'I know. But I have gone up a dress size since Alistair, and I don't want it to be the start of a slippery slope. I'll lose some of it before the wedding.' I turned to look at her and was surprised to find her expression anxious. 'Is everything OK?' I asked. 'Everything going to plan?'

She sat down on the bed. 'Everything's fine.'

'What's Mum done now?' I asked.

She looked up at me and smiled. 'She's very excited and looking forward to everything.'

'And demanding constant reassurance that everything is in hand?'

Becca nodded wearily. 'I had two phone calls late last night: the first about the photographer and the second about the cake. And then this morning she asked for a floor plan showing the number and location of the toilets in the reception venue, because Sheila is fretting over Colin's IBS.'

I wanted to laugh but fought the urge as she was clearly stressed. It was something I had rarely seen, as she was, without doubt, the most laid-back person I knew. I regularly blew a fuse with Mum, but for Becca to be even mildly irritated was practically unheard of. Mind you, if anyone could wind a person up it was our mother, and I could see how the organisation of her daughter's wedding might create the perfect storm of all her anxieties and expectations.

I sat down next to Becca and placed an arm around her shoulders. 'Deep breaths and don't let it spoil things,' I said. 'And if it carries on, just stop picking up the phone. Do you want me to talk to her?'

She shook her head, and, as I felt her sigh, it occurred to me that I was currently far more likely to be part of the problem than the solution. 'She's hassling you about Felix, isn't she?'

Becca looked at me sadly. 'Not hassling exactly. But he's on her list.'

'I'm so sorry,' I said. 'She didn't mention him to me until a couple of days ago, but I should have realised the issue hadn't gone away.'

'It's OK,' she sighed. 'It's barely registered amongst all the other stuff.'

I gave her a squeeze. 'Don't worry. I'm going to call Mum the minute I get home and tell her that I'm now handling all wedding-related enquiries.'

'But you don't know any of the details,' she said.

I shrugged. 'I'll make it up, and then the *actual* arrangements can be a wonderful surprise for her on the big day.'

She smiled and leaned her head on my shoulder. 'Thanks, Dot.'

She said nothing more, and after a moment I said, 'You're so restrained.'

'About what?'

'Well if it was me, I'd be rattling you to tell me what you were going to do about Felix. We're so different.'

She sat up. 'I know you'll sort it out,' she said, looking up at me. 'I have confidence in you.'

The statement, which I believed to be both sincere and one hundred per cent misplaced, caused me to bite my lip. 'Thank you,' I said quietly, before clearing my throat and adding, 'I do have a plan, actually. But it's a bit mad and I don't want to worry you.'

She said nothing but looked at me questioningly.

'I'm going to try and find him and bring him along,' I said, now feeling a lot less confident about the proposal

31

than when Kate had put it to me so matter-of-factly just twenty-four hours earlier. 'I started looking for him last night, but he doesn't seem to be on any social media and none of the Felix Davises I found on Google were the right age. But I've only spent an hour or so on it so far, so fingers crossed.'

She smiled.

'You think it's an insane plan, don't you?' I asked.

She didn't reply, but instead turned and opened the top drawer of her bedside cabinet, taking out a small brown envelope.

'He's an accountant and living in Cheltenham,' she said, handing me the envelope. 'In there are his business address and phone number.'

I stared at the envelope. 'How...?'

'Mark looked him up,' she said. 'You know, just in case,' she added, nudging me mischievously.

'And how long have you had this?' I asked.

'Oh, a while.'

I nodded. She was so calm, considered and forward-thinking. I wondered, not for the first time, whether one of us was adopted. 'Right, well, I'd better get on with it, hadn't I?' I said, attempting to mask fear with feigned practicality.

'You had.'

I opened the envelope and removed a white A5 card. On it was scrawled in Mark's handwriting: *Felix Arthur Davis, DOB: 26.01.81, Bailey and Davis Chartered Accountants*. Underneath was a Cheltenham address and phone number.

I stared at the card. Felix, a chartered accountant? I struggled to imagine him, laughing and wild-haired, squeezed to bursting point into a smart suit and trying to take life seriously.

'I can't quite see him as an accountant,' said Becca.

'Me neither.' I returned the card to the envelope and popped it into the back pocket of my jeans, a renewed optimism and curiosity now combining to ease my anxiety. 'But I can't wait to see him.'

Chapter 4

As it turned out, I had to wait to see Felix whether I liked it or not. Because when I phoned his office, with Kate standing over me, at 9.05 a.m. two days after Becca had handed me his phone number, I was told by his secretary, Linda, that Mr Davis was out of the office all week and that the earliest available appointment to see him would be the middle of the following week.

I explained to Linda that I was an old school friend, and that the visit was social not professional, but this made no difference. She advised that she did not manage Felix's social diary, but that I was most welcome to leave my phone number and she would ask him to call me on his return. I did this, but then, concerned that my details might get shoved to the bottom of a post-holiday pile, I asked if I could perhaps have his mobile number or personal email address. Unsurprisingly, this request was refused and I was told, now with more than a hint of impatience, that I should instead email Felix at the office, although I was warned that all emails were automatically forwarded to his business partner, Kevin Bailey, as well as to Linda herself. And so it was, with a sense of defeat and disappointment, that I was forced to accept a 2.30 p.m. appointment to see Felix at his Cheltenham offices on Wednesday 19 July.

But although I had been disappointed by the delay, it was still with an undeniable sense of fear and trepidation that I at last found myself seated in the reception area of the tall white Regency building in which the offices of Bailey and Davis were located, waiting for Felix to come down from the second floor to collect me. Because, despite having left my phone number, I had still had no direct contact with him. I tried to tell myself that his failure to call must be because Linda hadn't prioritised the matter to him. I was almost certain that had he been directly handed my name and number, he would have been as eager and intrigued to talk to me as I was him. But this argument wasn't quite enough to settle my nerves entirely, and the situation left me far more uncertain of his reaction to my wedding proposal than I ideally would have liked before a face-to-face encounter.

Adjusting the beige culottes and sleeveless white shirt I had chosen with great care that morning, I shifted my position on the firm black leather sofa in order to scan the somewhat clinical reception area. I had been waiting for Felix for almost fifteen minutes now, with nothing to distract me but several very dry magazines provided for visitors, and the intermittent phone calls taken by the receptionist, to which she responded in a tone which could be best described as homicidally hormonal.

I was just plucking up the courage to ask her if she could double-check that I hadn't been forgotten, when the lift doors on the far side of the reception area opened to reveal a tall, and exceptionally round, man. I felt my pulse unexpectedly quicken as he ran a hand through his dark, slightly wavy but thinning hair and adjusted the collar of his open-neck shirt. He then exited the lift and began to walk hurriedly towards the receptionist, before catching my eye, veering towards me and breaking into the broadest of grins. 'Dorothy Riley,' he exclaimed, with just a hint of a query in his voice. 'I am so sorry that you've been kept waiting.'

I smiled back at him, using the moments it took him to cross the floor to adjust my eyes to this new, older Felix. So the wild hair had all but gone – that was a bit of a shock – but the easy smile, the dancing blue eyes and the slightly bouncing stride were just the same, and, of course, he was still *cuddly*.

I felt myself relax and, stepping forward, without thinking enveloped him in a hug. 'Felix Davis,' I laughed, 'I've waited over ten years, so another ten minutes doesn't matter. It's just so, so lovely to see you again.'

I sensed only the slightest of hesitations before he lifted his arms and returned the hug, adding a pat on the back for good measure. I continued to smile, uplifted by the reconnection and feeling instinctively that our relationship was, despite the intervening years, unchanged. After a moment, I released him and took a step back. 'Now, let's have a proper look at you.'

Starting at his feet and working my way upwards, I nodded appreciatively at his smart brogues, well-cut dark grey suit and pristine white shirt. 'You look fabulous!' I exclaimed, laughing. '*And* you haven't changed a bit!' I added, pointing at his reassuringly rotund tummy.

But on raising my eyes to his face, I discovered that his expression was now one of combined confusion and terror. It was difficult to know which emotion had the upper hand, but at that moment I had the distinct impression that, had he been several stone lighter, he would without hesitation have legged it into the street.

My hand went to my mouth and I felt myself blush. 'I'm so sorry, Felix,' I said, aware that I had completely misjudged the situation and spoiled things from the off with a presumptuous hug and an inappropriate reference to his size. 'I was just so pleased and excited to see you after all this time.'

Still flustered, and now with an unmistakably sweaty sheen to his balding brow, Felix nevertheless managed a wobbly smile and waved a hand. 'Not at all, not at all,' he said breathlessly. 'Just a misunderstanding.'

I nodded. 'It's just that I've been thinking about you rather a lot over the past week – you know, remembering the laughs and feeling nostalgic about our schooldays. I was forgetting that it's all much more unexpected and out of the blue for you.'

He looked at me for a moment before removing a handkerchief from his trouser pocket and mopping his forehead. And then, his composure apparently recovered, he laughed. '*Completely* unexpected and *totally* out of the blue,' he agreed, the broad grin now back in situ. 'Because, you see, I'm not actually Felix.'

Chapter 5

As we waited for the lift, Kevin Bailey – the man I had so enthusiastically embraced and body-shamed – explained that he had been Felix's friend for just over six years and his business partner for three. They had, he told me, worked together for several years in a large London accountancy firm, before deciding to go it alone in Cheltenham in early 2014.

I nodded along thoughtfully to this information, wondering, in light of their decision to relocate together, if perhaps Kevin and Felix were more than just friends and professional partners. Felix had claimed to have dated a couple of girls whilst at university, but he had never really talked about them or introduced them to me – or to any of our mutual friends so far as I knew. Nor had he ever produced any photographic evidence of them. So maybe, I mused, my mother had in his case been right. It was a theory which was certainly lent weight by the effusive manner in which Kevin spoke about him. Felix was, he said, the most reliable of friends and the perfect work colleague. I agreed wholeheartedly with the first assertion and was delighted to discover that Kevin's opinion of him was so in line with my own.

In all his conversation, Kevin reinforced my first impression of him as both good-natured and good-humoured. He was clearly intrigued and amused that I had known Felix at school, and I was grateful for his ability to quickly shake off the awkwardness of our first encounter, and also for his kindly attempts to help me to do the same.

I had the opportunity to assess Kevin, and to form all these opinions, thanks to what felt like an interminable wait for the lift to the second floor. And something else I concluded about him, after twice suggesting that we perhaps take the stairs, was that – just like Felix – he wasn't a fan of walking when there was the possibility of a ride. It was therefore a good five or ten minutes before we finally stepped out of the lift and he genially ushered me through the doorway of Bailey and Davis.

'Just take a seat here, Dorothy,' he said, as we entered a small outer office. 'Felix should be free at any moment.' He pointed towards four grey-cushioned chairs positioned along one wall next to a large, rather chaotic-looking pot plant. Immediately opposite the chairs was a desk, on which sat two in-trays, a pot of pens, a telephone, a keyboard and a computer, the screen of which was currently blank. 'I'm afraid Linda, our secretary, has flu so isn't with us today,' he continued sadly. 'That's one of the reasons you were kept waiting for such a long time. She's been off since last Wednesday, and I won't lie, it's been a struggle. We had a temp in yesterday and I think we'll have to get him back tomorrow.'

'Oh no, so I'm dropping by when you could really do without the bother,' I said, feeling suddenly guilty.

He shook his head and laughed. 'A potential new client is never a bother, Dorothy.'

I felt myself redden at this and was just debating whether to break it to Kevin that this particular visit was one hundred per cent social, when one of two white doors adjacent to Linda's desk opened and a woman and two men emerged. The group were mid conversation and didn't acknowledge either Kevin or myself.

'I'll talk to Nigel Fort in the morning,' said the woman. She was petite and blonde and was cradling two box files in her arms. I watched as she listed slightly to the right in an apparent attempt to maintain her balance whilst adjusting a laptop bag which was slung over her left shoulder. Neither of the two men seemed to notice, and I frowned at them, disappointed that they didn't offer to help.

The older man, grey-haired and not much taller than the woman, nodded and said something about assets. The other, who was younger and towered over his two colleagues, lowered his head and made a comment about European liabilities.

Having zero interest in their conversation, I peered inquisitively through the open door of what I assumed to be Felix's office, wondering whether he was going to come and fetch me or if I was expected to go straight in. I checked my watch. Well over an hour had passed since my train had pulled in to Cheltenham Spa, and despite my nerves, I was now increasingly impatient to see him.

'Is it OK for me to go in, Kevin?' I asked quietly, nodding my head towards the office.

He glanced into the corridor at the departing group of three, who were continuing their discussion in a series of murmured exchanges whilst waiting for the lift. He nodded and smiled. 'Of course. And if I don't see you before you leave, it was great to meet you. And I hope to see you again soon,' he added, before opening the other white door and disappearing from view.

I watched as he closed the door behind him, and then, taking a deep breath and experiencing some unexpected last-minute butterflies, I positioned a smile on my face, walked towards Felix's office, tapped lightly on the door and peered gingerly inside.

I found myself looking into a small but light room. The magnolia walls were bare, save for two certificates, which I was unable to read without my glasses, and an aerial view of what I assumed to be Cheltenham. A desk was positioned facing away from one of the sash windows which fronted the building, and a filing cabinet, a small conference table and three chairs were the only other items in the room. Felix himself was nowhere to be seen.

My smile dropped momentarily, before it occurred to me, somewhat bizarrely, to check behind the door, just in case he was planning to leap out and surprise me. I smiled at the ridiculousness of the idea, but decided to look nevertheless.

I leaned slowly forward, craning my neck and inching my way around the door. 'Felix?'

'Dorothy.'

I gasped at the sound of my name and turned to discover the younger of the two men I had seen walk to the lift now standing just a few feet from me and looking puzzled. It took me two blinks and a second sharp intake of breath to realise that he was Felix.

I put a hand to my chest and laughed in a mixture of delight and relief. 'Oh my goodness, Felix.' I wagged a finger at him and rolled my eyes. 'You gave me such a shock. I didn't realise you were you! You are so...' I looked him up and down, taking in the dark blue suit, honed physique and short dark hair, which was so completely – and, in my experience, uncharacteristically – under control. I laughed again and was about to complete my sentence with 'gorgeous these days' and perhaps a playful nudge, when we made eye contact and something in his expression, and a recollection of my unfortunate initial encounter with Kevin, caused me to reel myself in and say, 'Wow, it's been such a long time, hasn't it?' instead.

'It has,' he smiled, gesturing for me to enter his office. 'Have a seat.' He pulled a chair away from the conference table and placed it in front of his desk. 'Can I get you a tea or a coffee?'

'Er… no, no, I'm fine, thank you,' I replied, taking the seat he had positioned for me.

He nodded, walked to the other side of the desk and sat down, tapping a sheet of paper to his right. 'Linda tells me that you're working in graphic design and have been running your own Bristol-based company in partnership with Katherine Morgan since 2013,' he said, reading from the sheet. 'That's great. Bristol is a beautiful city, isn't it?'

'Yes, yes, it is.' I smiled uncertainly at him, slightly thrown by Linda's internet research and feeling suddenly uneasy – far more uneasy than when waiting with Kevin for the lift, in fact. I had spent the week since calling Felix's office thinking a lot about this moment. I had wondered what his reaction to seeing me might be and had guessed alternately at surprised, entertained and amused, but always, ultimately, delighted.

But what I now realised, as I took in the well-groomed professional sitting opposite me, was that every one of those imagined encounters had been with a younger, rounder Felix: a Felix thoroughly unconcerned by his appearance or what life might throw at him; a Felix who protested and partied with equal relish; a Felix whom I could read like a book and knew inside out. I had never once pictured meeting a well-presented thirty-six-year-old accountant, burdened by quarterly deadlines and a lack of secretarial support. Most significantly, I was stupidly unprepared for meeting a man with a decade and a half of life experiences behind him of which I had no knowledge and in which I had played no part whatsoever.

I looked at him, searching his expression for something familiar and relatable – for a starting point. He was still smiling at me and there was no hint of awkwardness or nerves about him, but I couldn't help feeling that that was due to professional confidence, rather than any sense of personal connection. As far as he was concerned, I thought, my own smile fading slightly, this was an appointment, not a reunion. And although I just about physically recognised the slick corporate type sitting opposite me, there was no sign of the friend I had grown up with.

I cleared my throat, deciding, in the absence of feelings, to stick to the facts. 'Felix, I hope there hasn't been a misunderstanding, but I came here today to see you socially, as an old friend, not as a prospective client.'

'Oh,' he said, maintaining a smile but clearly surprised. 'I must admit I had thought maybe it was a mixture of both.'

'I'm sorry, that's entirely my fault. I should have waited until you got back from holiday and then spoken to you on the phone first, but I was in a bit of a hurry to see you because...' I hesitated. Nine days ago, inviting him to spend a Saturday with me had seemed a reasonable proposition, on the basis that we would pick up exactly where we had left off fifteen years earlier. But as I sat opposite the accountant, with my Felix nowhere to be seen, the purpose of my visit seemed increasingly ridiculous.

He looked at me, his smile now a little fixed, with perhaps just a hint of impatience as he waited for me to complete the explanation regarding the timing of my visit. I took a deep breath. 'I was in a bit of a hurry to see you because I wanted to invite you to come to Becca's wedding with me in Devizes. And it's only three weekends away, on the fifth of August. So, as I say, I was in a bit of a… hurry.'

I whispered the conclusion to my sentence. The idea sounded even more preposterous out loud than it had in my head, and I said nothing more. Having no clue what his reaction might be to the invitation, or how I might influence it, I reasoned that there was no point in wasting my breath on any attempts at persuasion or mitigation.

He frowned and his cheeks went a little pink. 'Becca's wedding?' he queried. 'You mean Rebecca, your sister?'

I nodded.

'Well,' he said, shifting in his chair and offering me an anxious, and now quite clearly forced, smile, 'that is a very kind offer, Dorothy, and thank you for thinking of me, but, er, I'm afraid I'm actually away that weekend. Nevertheless, as I say, thank you. I'll be sorry to miss the day, but do send Rebecca and her partner my very best wishes.'

I nodded, deciding that, on reflection, I could have guessed his reaction after all – namely one of suppressed alarm as he attempted to manage the obvious fruitcake sitting opposite him.

I waved a hand. 'Don't worry, I realise it was short notice. And I know the invitation might seem a little weird,' I added, attempting to explain, 'but I was inviting you because I told my grandmother that we were dating.'

I paused, wondering if that might qualify as the worst attempt ever at trying to persuade a person who thinks you're mad that you're not mad after all. And I knew without a doubt that if there was a panic button under Felix's desk, he was now pushing it madly with his knee.

Above desk, he was still smiling, whilst at the same time nodding slowly, manfully feigning comprehension.

'I thought she was dying, you see,' I continued, focusing on the window, now resigned to the doomed nature of the visit and feeling strangely free of any sense of consequence, 'and I didn't want her to die unhappy, and she was unhappy at the thought of me being single, so I told her that we were a couple. Then she recovered and I should have told her that we weren't a couple any more, but instead I told my mother that we were still very happy together. And Nanny Flo overheard me telling my mother that, and so now she thinks you'll be at Becca's wedding in two weeks' time. I'd like to be able to tell her the truth, but the problem is that she's still very frail and I'm worried about what might happen if I now spring it on her that I lied about going out with you. So my idea was to take you along to the wedding and then later, when she's stronger, to tell her that we'd split up. But now I'm here, I realise…' I shrugged and shifted my gaze to the framed certificates hanging on the wall, not wanting to finish the miserable sentence.

'Why me?' he asked.

I returned my attention to him, surprised to hear something at last recognisable in his tone. The forced smile had disappeared and he was now frowning.

'She remembered you and asked after you when I saw her in the hospital,' I replied quietly. 'And so then I just said you were my boyfriend without really thinking,' I added.

'That's nice,' he said.

It was an immediate and straight-faced response which fifteen years earlier I might have laughed at as a typical example of his dry humour. But today his expression indicated that it was merely a polite comment on the fact that Nanny Flo remembered him.

I nodded. 'Yes.'

'Well, I'm sorry I can't help,' he said with a sigh, placing both hands on his desk and pushing his chair back slightly. He was clearly, and unsurprisingly, anxious to wind things up. 'But as I say, I'm away.'

I nodded again. 'No problem,' I said. 'And it was good to see you. Sorry I descended on you during working hours.'

'And I'm sorry that I'm so short of time today,' he said, standing up. 'But call me next time you're in Cheltenham and we can catch up properly.'

'I will.' I suspected that we both knew that my acceptance was as smilingly insincere as his invitation.

I stood up and together we exited the office, with Felix walking just inches behind me, his arms open slightly, as if to corral me and prevent any attempt on my part to dash back inside.

On reaching the lift, I pressed the button and we waited, Felix checking his phone and me pretending to look for something in my bag. When the lift failed to arrive within ten seconds, I gestured towards the stairs. 'I'm going to walk,' I said. 'I was just being lazy.'

He smiled. 'Good for you. I always try to take the stairs these days.'

'It shows,' I said, smiling. 'I hardly recognise you, Felix.'

He didn't reply, but as I looked over my shoulder and walked towards the stairs, I saw him briefly hold up a hand in an oddly dismissive mid-air salute, before turning and walking back into the outer office.

I sighed to myself and began to descend the stairs in a determined daze, reluctant to acknowledge the sadness and disappointment lurking within me following my briefer-than-brief meeting with Felix, and equally reluctant to think about what on earth I was going to do next.

Two flights of stairs later, I crossed the soulless communal reception area and with both arms extended, pushed wide the large glass doors which opened onto the street. Stepping outside, I headed for a bench on the opposite side of the road, which I had spotted on the way in and which was now bathed in full sunshine. On reaching it, I sat down wearily and closed my eyes. Lifting my face to the sun, I decided to allow myself just a few moments of counterfeit peace of mind before confronting my problems and coming up with an inevitably inadequate and unsatisfactory plan of action.

Several minutes later, the sun had rather symbolically just gone behind a cloud when the sound of a harp alerted me to an incoming text. Wondering if it was Kate seeking an update, I opened my eyes, delving into my shoulder bag and taking out my phone. The text was from a number I didn't recognise, and I opened it with only mild interest, having already decided to call Kate for a pep talk.

> Dot, I've double-checked my diary and see that I am free on the Saturday of the wedding after all. You can email me details at fdavis@baileyanddavis.co.uk or I'm in Bristol for a morning meeting on 3 August if you would like a coffee. Felix

I glanced up open-mouthed at the window of Felix's office and then back down at the screen, frowning as I reread the text slowly and out loud to make sure that I hadn't misunderstood what he was saying. But no. There was no doubt about it. Felix Arthur Davis, the accountant, was offering to save my bacon. And what was more, he had called me Dot.

Chapter 6

'So Felix can't come to dinner with us tomorrow night?' My mother's voice was heavy with disappointment.

I tensed, my grip on the phone tightening involuntarily. 'Nope. Still can't come. Just like I told you yesterday. And the day before that,' I said with feigned brightness, before adding, 'And the day before that actually,' under my breath.

'*Such* a shame,' she said. 'And you said it's because he's working too late to come up that evening?'

'Yes,' I said. 'That's right. Well remembered. But anyway, how are things? All good?'

'Yes, apart from the fact that we won't see Felix the night before the wedding,' she sighed. 'But of course, his work must take priority.'

I placed the receiver on the desk in front of me while she continued to talk, and looked despairingly at Kate, who was smiling broadly at me from her desk.

'Stay calm,' she whispered.

It was good advice, which had become increasingly difficult to put into practice since I had told my mother that if she had any wedding-related logistical enquiries she was to call me rather than Becca. I was tactful enough not to reveal that this was because she was driving my mild-mannered sister to the point of matricide, telling

49

her instead that I simply wanted to be more involved in everything. She had been delighted by this and it had resulted in multiple daily phone calls ever since. The ones to my mobile I could dodge or defer, but she had quickly twigged that whenever the phone on my desk rang, I would, if I could, pick up.

Her calls were on a variety of topics, most of which required no actual knowledge of the wedding arrangements on my part, just an ability to keep my cool while I calmed her down. Today's call was regarding the width of the chairs at the reception, as cousin Elaine's glands were *playing up again*.

I had thrown some fantasy chair facts at her, which she had accepted without question before moving on to the subject which was the common theme, and I suspected the real purpose, of every one of her phone calls to me: Felix. After such a long period of self-imposed silence on the topic, she now loved nothing more than to talk about him, at length, and would find any excuse to do so.

For my part I hated it, feeling guilty about gilding the fake lily with additional fictional information about the relationship. Most of the time I managed to head off her enquiries, but this took determination and a lot of effort, and I occasionally buckled in the face of her dogged persistence and simply made up answers to the more straightforward questions, such as which football team he supported and what kind of music he liked to listen to. But I felt awful deceiving her even more than I had already, and our conversations invariably left me irritated by her persistence and, more justly, irritated with myself for the situation I had created. It was one of the main reasons I preferred to deal with her calls in the evening, when I had access to alcohol and when my father was at home and able to check her curiosity, which he did by removing the phone from her hand mid conversation and proceeding to ask me how work was going.

'Dot? Dottie? Are you there?' My mother's voice rose with tinny anxiety from the receiver. Reluctantly, I picked it up.

'Sorry, Mum, I missed that. The line went fuzzy.'

'I was just saying what a shame it is that Felix isn't an usher,' she said, sounding disappointed all over again. 'But I was thinking that maybe you could call the florist and request a special buttonhole for him to match your bouquet. That way everyone will know you're a couple.' I pressed my lips together in order to stifle a groan. 'What do you think?' she pressed.

I closed my eyes. 'I think that's an interesting idea,' I said quietly. 'If it's not too short notice for the florist.'

'Oh, of course it won't be.' She laughed dismissively. 'And while I've got you, I wanted to ask if Felix—'

'Sorry, Mum, can I call you tonight?' I interrupted, deciding that I could take no more. 'Kate…' I opened my eyes and looked at my partner, mouthing the words *help me* as I did so. She tapped her watch and mimed drinking a cup of coffee. I gave her a thumbs-up. 'Kate has just reminded me that Felix is actually dropping by for coffee in a moment and there's a call I have to make before he gets here.'

'Oh my goodness! How romantic!' The delight in my mother's voice, coupled with the recollection of a meeting I wasn't exactly looking forward to, made me feel worse than ever.

'He's in Bristol on business, Mum. I'm just a quick stop-off.'

'Nonsense,' she laughed. 'He clearly doesn't want to miss out on an opportunity to see you, even when you're going to be spending the whole weekend together. That's true devotion, Dottie. Nanny will love that.'

I placed a hand on my chest, experiencing a sensation which felt like the literal sinking of my heart. Felix had told me he had a fifteen- to twenty-minute window in between a morning meeting in Clifton and a lunchtime one in Harbourside, and had suggested a coffee to run over the arrangements for the wedding, which, until that point, we had discussed only by email.

My immediate reaction to his proposal had been one of relief. He was clearly committed to the weekend and had an organised approach, which gave me renewed hope that things could pass off without a hitch. But after our first awkward encounter, and a series of emails which had done nothing to change my impression of him as unwaveringly businesslike, no matter what the topic under discussion, I couldn't claim to be looking forward to spending another five, let alone twenty, minutes in his company. And the knowledge that my mother was going to portray our brief coffee in a Romeo-and-Juliet light to my grandmother wasn't helping.

'I'll ring you tonight, Mum,' I said.

'That would be lovely, Dot,' she sighed, 'although your father can be so annoying, can't he, interrupting our girl talk all the time?'

'I'll call about seven or eight. Bye. Love you.' I put down the phone and slumped back in my chair.

'A little abrupt at the end there,' said Kate, her eyebrows arching disapprovingly.

I didn't reply.

'Well, I just wish your mum was my mum,' she persisted.

'You do not,' I said flatly.

'I do! I know she crowds you, but at least she's interested, Dorothy. My mother couldn't give a damn whether I'm winning the Nobel Peace Prize or sleeping in a box under a bridge.'

I sighed. Kate had made it to where she was in life despite, rather than because of, her family, and it wasn't the first time I'd been made to feel bad for complaining about my own. 'Sorry.'

She smiled and shook her head. 'I know it's tricky. But things will be easier after Saturday, won't they?'

'I suppose so, but I just wish I could one hundred per cent look forward to the wedding and I feel awful that I'm being even a little bit grumpy about it.' I turned towards my screen. 'I mean, I couldn't be happier for Becca. Mark's great – perfect for her. I'm just not enjoying Mum asking me about Felix all the time. And I've got to spend the entire evening with her tomorrow.'

'If she brings him up, just say that the evening and the weekend are about Becca,' she suggested. 'And why not call your dad this afternoon and tell him you want Becca to be the focus and that you really *don't* want to be grilled about Felix. He'll understand, won't he?'

I looked over my shoulder at her and smiled. 'Yes, he will. I'll do that.'

'Great,' she said, now focusing on her own screen. 'And the day itself will be such a laugh. I love weddings. Fred's friend Anthony's was the best. He married a Scot and all her relatives wore kilts and one of them did cartwheels across the dance floor. I have never seen anything like it before or since.' She shook her head at the memory. 'I was genuinely worried some of his bits would fly off,' she added absently.

I laughed. 'You've got me hoping for a kilt or two now.'

'You'll have a great time,' she smiled.

'I know I will,' I agreed. 'And I tried the dress on again last night and if anything it's a bit loose now. When I checked, I'd dropped three kilograms.'

'Do you think it's nervous weight loss?' asked Kate. 'If so, you've got your mother to thank for that.'

'True.'

'And you're OK about this coffee with Felix? You know what you're going to say?' She was still facing her screen and asked the question with a casualness bordering on indifference, but I knew she was as eager as my mother for details, although for different reasons. Her enquiry wasn't to satisfy rampant curiosity, but rather to make sure that I was on track and had every angle covered. 'Did you find him somewhere to stay?'

I turned my chair towards her. 'He found somewhere himself. I guess it's not like he doesn't know the area.'

Kate gave up the pretence of work and looked at me. 'When did he tell you that? Have you chatted on the phone?'

I shook my head. 'Nope, because he never picks up. I sent him that grovellingly grateful and apologetic email I showed you, and then another one confirming all the time and location details. I kept it all light, saying maybe we should linger a little on Sunday and pop into The Lamb, which is where we used to hang out in sixth form. But he just replied telling me he'd be driving up on Saturday morning, had arranged overnight accommodation and had to get back early Sunday. And that was it. I then offered to pay for travel and accommodation, but he said no.' I finished the update with a smile.

'That's all the logistics sorted then,' said Kate. 'You can use today to laugh about the good old days.'

I nodded whilst trying and failing to picture slimline Felix laughing about anything at all. 'It'll be fine,' I said with determined positivity, 'and the wedding will be fine too. Becca steered Mum towards putting Felix on a table with Mark's work friends, so he's not going to be inter-rogated by anyone who knows me during the meal. And there's nothing to stop him shooting off early if he wants to. Everybody loses track of everybody else at the evening reception, don't they?'

'They do. Sounds like you've really thought this through and got it all covered, Dot. I'm impressed.' She smiled, offering me an air high-five to which I responded with one of my own.

'I'm a bit sad that Felix isn't as relaxed as he used to be when we were younger,' I said. 'But he's helping me out. So that's a tacit acknowledgement of our past friendship, isn't it?'

Kate maintained a smile, but I thought I saw a hint of doubt behind it.

'What?' I asked. 'Please don't tell me you're worried on my behalf. I'm just about OK with everything.'

'No, not at all,' she said, looking surprised. 'I always told you it was no big deal.'

'Then why the nervous look?'

Her mouth twisted slightly in a rare expression of awkwardness. 'Well, I…' She hesitated. 'I just wondered if Alistair was still coming, or whether there'd been a change of plan.'

'Oh… no… he's still an usher,' I said, my stomach lurching at the thought. 'Mark offered to disinvite him and Alistair offered not to come, but they've been friends for such a long time it wouldn't be fair. It's Mark and Becca's day, not mine.'

Kate smiled sympathetically. 'Well, it was good of Alistair to offer to opt out,' she said gently. 'And even better of you to insist that he come. I think—' she began, only to be cut short by the buzz of the intercom.

'Oh God, it's him,' I groaned, hauling myself to my feet.

'I'll get it,' said Kate, standing up and hurrying towards our small lobby and the front door of the office. 'You stay sitting down and try to look professional and sane. He hasn't seen that side of you yet.'

I tutted but acknowledged the point by straightening the new blue linen dress in which I had invested the previous day, and opening some images from a recent project of which I was particularly proud, angling my screen to make it visible to anyone approaching my desk. Then I leaned to my right, straining to listen to Kate's effusive but indistinct welcome, and to Felix's calmer, but equally indistinct, responses. A moment later, she led him into the office.

'It's Felix, Dot,' she said needlessly, placing a hand on his back, pushing him gently towards my desk and taking a step back. Her eyes widened slightly and she mouthed, *Ooh*, whilst inexplicably drawing a curvy feminine outline with her hands to indicate her appreciation of his physique. 'I wouldn't have recognised him from your description. She'd be hopeless in a police line-up situation, Felix,' she added, laughing. 'The woman couldn't tell Rod Hull from Emu.'

I did my best to ignore her and stood up, grabbing my bag and glancing at Felix as I did so. 'Let's go and get a coffee. The cafe next door is great.'

'OK,' he said, checking his watch and then looking over his shoulder at Kate. 'Are you joining us?'

'I'd love to.' She paused teasingly and grinned at me. 'But I'm afraid I have to stay here and hold the fort, don't I, Dot?'

'You do,' I said, already on my way to the door. 'Because there's no rest for the wicked, Kate. And you're very wicked indeed.'

Chapter 7

I placed two cappuccinos on the small table situated in the window of the cafe and sat down opposite Felix. He glanced up at the outsized Roman-numeral clock, which hung above a counter laden with various cakes under Perspex domes.

'Are you OK for time?' I asked.

'Yes. And thank you,' he added, picking up his coffee.

I shook my head. 'Thank *you*. I know asking you to come to Becca's wedding with me was a strange request. And believe me, I don't like misleading anyone. I was wrong to let assumptions drift the way I did.'

'Assumptions?' He replaced his coffee cup on its saucer.

'I mean I shouldn't have let everyone carry on thinking we were dating,' I explained. 'I should have sorted things out before now.'

'But did people make assumptions? I thought you specifically *told* your family that I was your boyfriend.'

'Er...' I shifted slightly in my seat as he looked at me impassively, awaiting a reply. 'Well, yes, I did tell them that. So I suppose in that sense they weren't assumptions.'

'Or in any sense?'

I smiled uncertainly. 'Well...'

'You told your father, mother, grandmother and sister that we were dating and they believed you. Isn't that what happened?'

I looked at him and wondered whether he was deliberately torturing me, or if it was accidental.

'I just want to be clear about what you told them. So that I know what the situation is when I meet them,' he added.

So the torture was accidental, then. Not that that made it any less excruciating.

'I see,' I said, taking a deep breath and deciding that there was no option but to respond to his brutal, to-the-point questioning with the ugly, unvarnished truth. 'Well, of course you're quite right. There were actually zero assumptions. I just told lots of lies and my family, because they trust me implicitly, believed them.'

'Great,' he said, seeming satisfied.

'One good thing,' I continued, managing a smile and picking up my coffee, 'is that Becca *didn't* actually believe me. She and Mark know that we're not dating, so we don't have to pretend in front of them.'

'That's good to know,' he said, 'should the four of us find ourselves alone in a room at any point on Saturday.'

I looked up from my coffee to find him again checking the clock.

'Anyway,' I said, 'you're on a table with Mark's friends, not my relatives, so hopefully you'll be able to relax and enjoy the day. My mother will probably accost you at some point, and Nanny Flo will want to say hi, but they'll both be in demand and I can help you if things get awkward.'

'That's very reassuring,' he said, looking down as his phone buzzed in his briefcase.

'Do you want to check that?' I asked.

He shook his head. 'It's Kevin sending some figures I need for this afternoon.'

'He seems so lovely,' I ventured, seizing the opportunity both to change the subject and to delve a little deeper into his relationship with Kevin. 'The two of you are obviously very good friends, as well as business partners.'

He nodded. 'Like you and Kate?'

'Yes, except that Kate is married,' I said, before immediately regretting the response.

He looked up and frowned. 'I don't understand what difference that makes.'

'I just mean…' I paused, trying to come up with an alternative to *Are you and Kevin lovers?* 'I just mean that Kate is married and I'm single, so we don't socialise together in the same way that you and Kevin might socialise if he's single and you're single, or if he's not single and you're not single.' I was aware of sounding slightly flustered but didn't judge the explanation to be a complete disaster.

'OK,' he said calmly, before returning his attention to his coffee and offering no further insights into his sexuality.

I took a deep breath and tried again. 'So much has happened to us both since university,' I smiled.

'Of course,' he said.

'We've both got our own businesses.'

'We have.'

'That's a turn-up for the books, isn't it?' I forced a laugh. 'I think the last time I saw you, I couldn't think beyond trekking round India and maybe doing an art course, and you… What did you want to do?'

'I can't remember,' he said. 'It was probably something to do with pies.'

I laughed again, genuinely this time, but he didn't join in, instead reaching for his briefcase as his phone buzzed for a second time. 'I'd better take a look,' he said. He opened the case, taking out the phone and frowning at whatever notification was onscreen but making no move to open the message.

'All OK?' I asked.

He slipped the phone into his jacket pocket, closed the briefcase and returned it to the floor. 'It's nothing,' he said, while looking and sounding like it was definitely something.

I sighed to myself. This was proving to be possibly the longest fifteen minutes of my life, and I wondered why, if he was so pressed for time, he didn't just leave. I wished he would. But since he had now picked up his coffee again and was showing no sign of going anywhere, I decided to have one last go at engaging him in conversation. If after that he still refused to chat, then I would buy myself a Bakewell slice and entertain myself with that instead.

I cleared my throat and, deciding that I might as well make the exchange a useful one, asked. 'Do you have any questions about the wedding, Felix? I know we covered all the logistics by email, but is there anything else?'

He looked up from his coffee, blinking slightly as if he'd forgotten that I was even there, before looking thoughtful. 'Will there be many of your close friends at the reception?' he asked. 'Anyone who might think it's strange that you haven't mentioned me – or who I might be expected to know? Like Kate, for example.'

I raised my eyebrows in surprise. It was actually a very good question. I thought for a moment and then shook my head. 'There'll be a few cousins, but none that I'm in regular contact with. I know some of Becca's friends, but only through her; no one I know in my own right.' I smiled. 'Anything else?'

He shook his head and fell silent again, and I had just turned towards the cake counter and was wondering whether I would find a raspberry and white chocolate muffin more entertaining than a Bakewell slice, when a thought struck me. 'Oh, hang on,' I said, turning back to Felix and holding up a hand, 'my ex-boyfriend will be there.' Felix nodded but said nothing, and I felt a sudden awkwardness, as well as a need to take an extra breath, before adding, 'His name is Alistair Burgess. We were together for two years and split up about eleven months ago. He won't think it's odd that I haven't told him about you because we...' I cleared my throat. 'Well, we don't have that kind of conversation. I mean, everything's fine, but we're not in touch very often. But you should probably know about him.'

'Probably,' agreed Felix.

'As I say, everything is fine,' I repeated, forcing a smile. 'It was mutual, all very amicable. You won't have to deck him or anything.' I turned away and looked at the cake counter again, despite now having no interest in either slices or muffins. 'Those cakes look nice, don't they?'

He didn't reply, and when I turned back around, he had taken his phone from his pocket and was looking at the screen, checking, I assumed, the recently arrived figures.

Feeling inexplicably hurt, I stood up. 'Thanks for coming, Felix. I know you're really busy. It was great to have a chance to talk before Saturday, but I'll let you get on with that now.' I nodded towards the phone in his hands.

He had the decency to look a little embarrassed but made no apology. Instead, he glanced in what seemed to be mild frustration at the phone, placed it face down on the table and then he too stood up. 'I'll see you at the church on Saturday,' he said.

'You will,' I replied, hoisting my mouth into a smile. 'And thanks again.'

'What are friends for?'

I looked up at him, resisting an urge to ask him whether he genuinely felt that we were still friends. 'I can't remember seeing *pretending to be your boyfriend at your sister's wedding* on the job description. So this is really above and beyond.'

His response was a polite smile, but as his eyes flicked downwards towards his phone on the table, I could tell he wasn't really listening.

'See you Saturday then,' I said, unsure whether it was the company of my former friend or the conversation about my former boyfriend which had so suddenly flattened my mood to the point of tears.

'Saturday,' he echoed absently. Then he sat back down, picked up his phone and started to text.

Chapter 8

'And here's Becca in her Hawaiian outfit at the school fete. Do you remember that, Becca?' My mother passed the photograph to my sister, who was sitting to her left.

Becca laughed. 'How old am I here? Four?'

'It was 1989, I think. So you're five,' said my mother, leaning towards her to peer again at the photograph. 'It took me hours to make that crêpe-paper hula skirt and all those flowers for the lei and the headdress.'

'It did,' agreed Dad. 'And then just three minutes for heavy rain to turn everything to mush and leave Becca in nothing but her vest and pants.' He laughed loudly and I joined in, reaching for the photo.

It had, against all my shameful expectations, been a lovely evening with my parents and Becca. We had met in the lounge of the Bear in Devizes marketplace for drinks at six thirty, before moving through to the cosy wood-panelled restaurant at seven. Mum told us that she had booked early so that we could all get our beauty sleep, although as I was actually staying at the Bear that night, I knew I could be in bed within fifteen minutes of waving them off.

Mark was spending the night with his best man, and my sister had, quite valiantly I thought in light of my mother's pre-wedding nerves, insisted that Mum and Dad stay with her. I was invited to stay too, but, as I wasn't quite as valiant as Becca, I had declined, instead booking myself in for an extra night at The Bear.

I smiled down at the glossy 6x4 picture of my little sister and then up at Dad, feeling grateful for his suggestion that Mum bring along the photographs she hadn't found room for on the wedding reception storyboard. The snaps had been viewed between courses, prompting memories and anecdotes which had kept the evening firmly focused on Becca, which was just what I had hoped for.

'You were beautiful from the off,' I said to Becca, returning the picture to her. 'And you'll be at your most beautiful tomorrow.'

She sighed. 'I just hope I can make it down the aisle without tripping.'

'It's me you've got to worry about,' said Dad. He reached out and took her hand. 'But together we'll make it,' he added a little emotionally.

There was a short pause, during which my mother murmured, 'Oh Don,' and dabbed at her eyes with her napkin.

Becca looked at me across the table, offering me an affectionate eye roll.

I cleared my throat. 'Come on then,' I said to Mum. 'Show us the next picture. Dessert will be here soon.'

'Ooh, yes,' she said, returning her attention to the pile of photographs sitting next to her on the table. 'Here you are on top of Cat Bells, in the rain, in the summer of '91,' she said, handing one to Becca. 'And swimming in Derwent Water, in the rain, in '92. And waiting for the launch at Hawes End, in the rain, in '93.' She paused, putting a hand to her mouth and giggling. 'And oh my goodness, I'd forgotten I'd found this one. Just look at that, Becca!' She laughed again, but my sister, although smiling, didn't seem to find the picture quite so funny.

'What is it?' I asked, smirking and holding out my hand. 'It's not Becca's Hawaiian costume post-downpour, is it?'

'No, no, it's you, darling,' said Mum. 'You and Felix in the school play.' She turned it over. 'It says Christmas 1994.'

'Oh.' I stopped smirking and took the picture from her as she held it out to me.

'Yes, just look at him. There he is. Such a sturdy boy.' My mother leaned forward and tapped the picture. 'Didn't he make a marvellous Christmas pudding? And there you are, the candle, a good four inches taller than him, right next to him. See? You'll have to show him that tomorrow.'

'I will,' I said quietly, extending the long list of false-hoods told to date, whilst retrieving my handbag from the back of my chair and slipping the picture inside without looking at it.

When I looked up, my mother was still smiling broadly at me, increasing my sense of guilt.

'I've forgotten what I'm having for dessert,' I said. 'Did I go for the torte or the cheesecake in the end?

'That was the only picture of him I came across. But I wasn't really looking and you've probably got lots of him now, haven't you?' My mother looked at me expectantly. 'On your phone,' she added, nodding her head towards my bag, which was still on my lap.

'I have a few,' I said, wondering what number lie that was. I decided that I must have hit the high nineties by now.

'I think you're having the torte, Dot,' said Becca. 'I'm having the cheesecake.'

'I'd love to see a picture of what he looks like now,' said Mum, pointing at my bag.

'You'll see him in the flesh tomorrow, Helen,' said Dad.

'I know, Don, but I may not recognise him if he's very changed, and how embarrassing would that be? Apparently he looks quite different now, doesn't he, Dot? Shorter hair and less sturdy.'

I experienced a sinking feeling. She actually had a valid point. 'My phone is dead,' I said desperately, and waited with grim resignation for her to insist that I check.

But she didn't. Instead, she looked over my shoulder towards the entrance to the restaurant, her eyes narrowing and her lips thinning. It was the kind of look she used to give me as a teenager whenever I mentioned Sean Dowse's DIY tattoo in front of her sister-in-law, my Auntie Dawn, with whom she was fiercely competitive. I glanced at Becca and together we turned and followed my mother's gaze.

I saw Alistair just as he saw us.

He smiled in surprise and then waved hesitantly. My father was the only one of us with the wherewithal to respond. 'Alistair,' he said, standing up and holding out a hand as my ex walked uncertainly towards us.

'Hi, Don,' he said, shaking Dad's hand. 'Helen, Rebecca, Dot,' he added, smiling at each of us in turn.

'Hello, Al,' smiled Becca.

My mother folded her arms. 'Good evening, Alistair,' she said coldly.

I frowned at her before turning back towards him. 'Hi,' I said, trying to keep my voice light. 'Are you here for a drink?' I looked at Becca. 'Is Mark coming here?'

Alistair answered for her. 'No, I'm meeting Mark in the Three Crowns at...' he checked his watch, 'just about now, actually. But I need to check in first.' He gestured with his thumb over his shoulder while smiling down at me. I nodded and tried desperately not to miss him.

'You're staying here?' asked my mother unsmilingly. 'That's interesting, because so is Dorothy.'

'Oh?' Alistair's eyebrows raised slightly as he nodded his acceptance of the fact.

'Yes. And so is her *boyfriend*, Felix,' continued Mum, repeating an assumption which, for obvious reasons, I hadn't bothered to contradict. 'He's a lovely accountant with his own business and he is completely smitten with her.'

I closed my eyes briefly and heard my father murmur, 'Helen,' and my sister, 'Mum,' simultaneously.

When I opened my eyes, Alistair was still smiling. 'That's great, Dot,' he said, and to my devastation, he sounded like he meant it. 'I take it he hasn't arrived yet? Or is he having a drink with Mark?'

'He doesn't get here till tomorrow,' I said quietly.

'OK, I'll look forward to meeting him then,' said Alistair. 'And now I'll leave you to your meal, but I'll see you all at the church tomorrow. Especially you,' he added, pointing at Becca. 'Don't keep the man waiting.'

'I won't,' laughed Becca. 'He had just better turn up.'

'He'd have to be mad not to,' smiled Alistair. 'Right,' he checked his watch for a second time, 'I'd better run.'

'Good to see you,' said Dad. 'Hope we'll have a chance to talk tomorrow.'

Alistair's smile broadened and my heartache increased. 'I'd like that,' he said, and, after offering us a general wave, he left the restaurant and headed back to reception.

Dad reached out and patted my arm. 'Well done, Dottie,' he said, meaning well, but making me want to yell at him and sob on his shoulder in equal measure.

'Oh for goodness' sake!' exclaimed my mother. 'She doesn't give a fig about him, do you, Dorothy?'

'Mum,' said Becca gently, 'Alistair is Mark's friend. I'd really like you to try and be nicer towards him.'

'I was nice,' protested my mother, turning to Dad for support. 'What did I say that wasn't nice?'

Dad said nothing but looked disappointed.

'Well, he broke my daughter's heart,' said Mum, her voice wobbling slightly but her chin jutting defiantly. Dad still didn't speak, and, after a moment, with a tear escaping, Mum added, 'And that breaks *my* heart.' I reached for her hand across the table, while Dad put an arm around her and Becca kissed her cheek.

'I love you very much, Mum,' I said, squeezing her hand. 'But it would actually be easier for me, as well as for Becca and Mark, if you were nice to him. He didn't do anything wrong. It just wasn't meant to be.'

Mum bit her lip and nodded as my father reached into his trouser pocket and passed her a handkerchief. 'Sorry, everyone,' she said quietly. 'I promise to behave myself tomorrow.'

'Good girl,' said Dad, patting her shoulder. 'None of us believe you, but good girl for saying it.'

'Oh you,' said Mum, laughing through her tears and flicking him with the handkerchief. 'I've said I'll behave and I will. And besides, I probably shan't even notice him, and neither will Dottie, will you?' she added more brightly. 'Not with Felix around.'

'That's right,' I said briskly. 'I won't even notice him.'

And that, I thought to myself as the waiter finally arrived with our desserts, was probably my biggest lie to date.

Chapter 9

I awoke the next morning not to my alarm, but to the sound of an incoming text. Deciding not to read it immediately, I instead lay completely still, enjoying the quiet calm of my cosy, quaintly furnished hotel room as the light leaked in through the heavy floral curtains. Today was Becca's wedding day, and, if the forecast was to be believed, it was going to be a sunny one. I smiled at the thought and, propping myself up on two of the four large white pillows on my bed, retrieved my phone from the small, round bedside table.

It was 8 a.m., half an hour before my alarm had been due to go off. The wedding was at two, and I had told Becca that I would be with her by ten thirty, by which time Mum and Dad would have left to pick up Nanny Flo from Dad's brother and sister-in-law, Uncle Geoffrey and Auntie Dawn, in Avebury. From there, Mum, Dad and Nanny Flo would travel on to Shieldhill Manor, the reception venue, where they had rooms booked for the night, and where Mum and Nanny Flo would change into their finery. Dad had told me with a knowing wink that they would stop for a bite to eat in Avebury and so wouldn't be back with us until one thirty, just in time for collection by the wedding cars. We all knew that the less time Mum had to cry and fuss around Becca, the better.

I sank back onto the pillows and opened my texts to discover that there were three awaiting my attention: one each from Felix and Alistair and the most recent – the one which had woken me up – from Becca. The text from Alistair was the biggest surprise and the one which I was, quite pitifully, most desperate to read. But with my finger hovering over his name on the screen, self-respect, together with a sense of indebtedness to Felix, caused me to give his text priority over Alistair's. I tapped the message.

It was a photograph and had been sent at midnight, without comment, in response to my own text, requesting a recent photo in which he was easily identifiable, and explaining that Mum was worried that she might not recognise him at the church. However, as I now stared at the picture he had sent, I frowned in disbelief and mild despair.

He was easily identifiable; I couldn't fault him there. And I knew that the photo was a recent one because his appearance was identical to that during our coffee two days earlier, even down to the same immaculately tailored grey suit. So that was another ten out of ten. Where Felix *had* fallen down in his approach to the task, however, was that the photograph also featured an attractive blonde in a silver top and black leather trousers. She was laughing, her right arm draped around his neck, her head resting against his chest and her left hand raised as she saluted the photographer with a cocktail. Felix was also clutching a drink, although his, I noted, was held at a lower, less attention-seeking level.

I rolled my eyes and began to compose a reply.

Hi, looking forward to seeing you in a few hours' time. Sorry to be a pain but do you think you could send another picture with just you in it? Otherwise my mother will be asking all sorts of awkward questions about

I hesitated, uncertain how to describe the woman in the photograph: *your friend? Your girlfriend? Your work colleague?* I supposed she could be his secretary, Linda. In fact, it was perfectly possible that Linda was both his girlfriend *and* his colleague; after all, she had been extremely reluctant to give me his phone number. I zoomed in. They were clearly very relaxed together, and I now saw that his left arm was wrapped around her, his fingers just visible on her leather-clad hip. But if she was his girlfriend, why hadn't he mentioned her before? And why hadn't he thought to explain who she was when sending the picture? And who in their right mind would judge it an appropriate photograph to show to the mother of your supposed new girlfriend?

I sighed and told myself, not for the first time, that I simply had to accept that the current Felix was a very different person to the one with whom I had grown up. And I also had to accept that the new version was a bit of a moron.

I looked at my unfinished text, and then, deciding against prolonging what was turning out to be a surprisingly painful process, I saved the photograph and began editing it to cut out the woman – whoever she was. As Felix's chin was touching the top of her head, I eventually had to crop out everything except his face in order to remove all trace of her. The resulting picture was undoubtedly less than ideal, with a distinct head-on-a-plate quality to it, but I saved the edits and sent it to my father anyway, along with the word *Felix*, followed by an exclamation mark and a smiley emoji.

I then opened Alistair's text.

> Hi, just back from drinks with Mark. He was on good form, and, in case your mother asks, he stuck to Coke and headed home with Tim just after 10? I checked the bar for you when I got back to the Bear but I assume you'd hit the sack. Very sensible and just about to do the same myself. Will look forward to having a drink with you and Felix tomorrow. A x

The text, I thought to myself, was typically Alistair. To a casual observer, it might have seemed like a simple hi-how-are-you, but actually it was very carefully constructed, subtly clearing the air and paving the way for a smooth social encounter.

Firstly, there was the fond, playful acknowledgement of my mother's caring but judgemental nature, designed to reassure me that he hadn't been offended by her behaviour towards him in the restaurant. Then he had been sure to reconfirm that he was completely at ease, not only with me but also with my new relationship, by suggesting a drink with us both. His aim, I knew, was to avoid any awkwardness at the wedding and to make it clear that he expected, and looked forward to, an introduction to Felix.

All very sensitive and sensible, I reflected; just like his new girlfriend, no doubt. The same girlfriend whom he, in a very sensitive and sensible manner, was *not* bringing to the wedding. His invitation had, of course, been a plus-one, but Becca had told me that he hadn't so much as hinted at bringing her along.

I had mostly been relieved by this decision, but a tiny bit of me was undeniably disappointed at missing out on an opportunity to scrutinise the new woman and guess at what she had that I didn't. I knew it wasn't youth – Becca had told me that she was a year older than Alistair, which made her three years older than me. And in the photograph of her and Alistair I had spotted on the Facebook page of a mutual friend, she had looked attractive – nice smile, face-framing hair, trim figure – but not intimidatingly stunning.

On my better days, I convinced myself that Alistair hadn't upgraded and that his new relationship was simply a sideways move. But occasionally, at moments such as when sitting all alone in a king-size hotel bed, about to attend a wedding with a fake boyfriend because I hadn't managed to come anywhere near to acquiring a real one in the past eleven months, it was hard not to feel insecure.

'We're just so different, Dot,' was how Alistair had put it, the night he had told me that we needed to talk – the night before he had moved out. And I hadn't disagreed with him. I had known that we were different from the outset of our two-year relationship. He had a detailed five-year life plan on his laptop – I had week-ahead Post-it notes stuck to the fridge; his taste in decor was expensively minimal – mine was cosily cluttered; he went through life anticipating problems – I fought fires as required. I had recognised all this and had thought that we balanced and completed each other in a wonderfully yin-yang kind of way. What I didn't know was that while I had spent two years celebrating our differences, it turned out that Alistair had been generously overlooking them and hoping that I would change.

I sighed, deleted his text and, with some relief, finally opened my sister's. It was a short but sweetly enthusiastic invitation to the day, and I smiled at her unerring ability to say just the right thing, at just the right time.

I gazed at the screen and, taking a deep breath, willed myself to share her texted sentiment.

'Bring it on.' I murmured, reading her written words out loud. 'Bring it on.'

Chapter 10

I had never been a bridesmaid before, my other most likely opportunity having been scuppered when Kate and Fred decided upon a registry office wedding, with minimal fuss and fanfare. I hadn't been at all disappointed at the time, but the fact that I had never undertaken the role before left me completely unprepared for the amount of manhandling and general abuse which I quickly discovered went with it.

First of all, I was stabbed with pins and scolded by Eileen for losing too much weight, as she made some eleventh-hour alterations to my dress. And then I was tortured with curling tongs, tweezers and eyelash curlers by someone called Kayleigh who, having been born five centuries too late to participate in the Spanish Inquisition, clearly got her kicks from inflicting pain in the name of beauty.

And just when I thought I might be able to relax into the day, following the mustn't-put-a-foot-wrong formality and emotional intensity of the wedding service itself, I was set upon by a succession of my parents' friends and relatives, many of whom I hadn't seen for years, and all of whom were keen to get a picture with 'little Dottie'.

However, there was a significant upside to all this wedding-related activity, namely that I was fully focused on my sister and the day, rather than on any lingering sadness over Alistair, or peripheral, niggling doubts about Felix and whether our plan would come together or disintegrate faster than Becca's tissue-paper hula skirt in the rain.

Unfortunately, my carefree attitude regarding Felix eventually went a little too far and I became so carefree as to forget about him altogether. And it wasn't until I spotted my mother pushing Nanny Flo in a wheelchair up the cobbled path towards him as he stood alone, hands in pockets, in the doorway of the church, that I remembered that I actually had a plus-one at this wedding.

Letting out a gasp, I immediately extricated myself from the photo call in which I was at that moment involved and, hitching up my lilac gown, ran as quickly as was possible in heels on cobbles towards Felix, desperate to reach him before my mother and grandmother did.

I managed it with two seconds to spare, grabbing his arm and gasping, 'I'm so sorry. Don't worry, I'm here now, I'll handle this,' just as my mother came within calling distance.

'Oh, hello, darling,' she beamed. 'We couldn't see you in the melee, but Nanny spotted Felix here all on his own and wanted to come over and say hello.'

I nodded, still a little breathless, and bent down to kiss Nanny Flo, who was at that moment extending her arms upwards towards me. 'Hello, Nanny. How are you? I keep being grabbed for photographs.'

'Not one bit surprised,' she said unnecessarily loudly, whilst poking a finger into each ear. 'You're looking so beautiful. Isn't she beautiful?' She smiled, gazing up at Felix. He looked at me and laughed. Not quite the response I would have liked, but, I decided, better than an outright denial. I managed a weak smile in return.

'These things aren't working again, Helen,' continued my grandmother over her shoulder, removing two hearing aids and passing them to my mother, who sighed despairingly. 'Load of old rubbish.'

My mother shook her head. 'Did you put the new batteries in, Mum?' she asked, bending forward, her mouth stretching and pouting to the max as she slowly enunciated each word in an attempt to help my grandmother to lip-read.

'You look like a fish,' laughed Nanny Flo. 'Doesn't she look just like a fish, Dottie?'

'Yes,' I answered absently, a response which caused my mother to tut loudly. And then, anxious to get the long-awaited introduction over with, I lowered my head, speaking directly into Nanny Flo's left ear. 'Nanny,' I said, raising my voice to compensate for her deafness, 'this is Felix, my…' I hesitated, feeling a need to take an extra breath before completing the lie, 'my boyfriend.'

My grandmother rolled her eyes. 'I know that,' she said, still at maximum volume. 'My body might be in a wheelchair but my brain isn't in a jar yet, you know.'

'Felix said hello before the ceremony,' explained Mum, smiling.

'Oh, I didn't realise,' I said, taken aback and turning to Felix. 'Well done.'

He looked at me for a moment, then said, 'Thank you,' with a slight bow.

'Yes, and it's a good job he did introduce himself,' continued my mother with a disapproving sigh, 'because none of us would have ever recognised him from that dreadful man-in-the-moon picture you sent to your father!'

'Man in the moon?' queried Felix with a frown.

'It's just your face, Felix,' explained Mum. 'Dorothy didn't even get your neck in the shot. I don't know what she was thinking.' She looked down at my grandmother. 'I'm just saying about that picture of Felix, Mum,' she said, pointing at Felix's face, circling a finger and puffing her cheeks out.

'I know! I wouldn't have recognised him in a million years, would I, Helen?' my grandmother bellowed up from her chair. 'I said to your mother, "That's never the little fat lad our Dottie used to bring home."'

My mother coloured slightly and cleared her throat. 'Well, we all grow into ourselves, don't we? And I always thought—' she began, but my grandmother didn't pause for breath.

'And your father said, "He's been on a diet, Flo." And I said, "Some diet, Don." I mean, he used to be almost as big as our Elaine over there.' She gestured in the direction of my mother's cousin, who was standing a few metres away with her back to us. Elaine didn't turn around, but, to my horror, I thought I saw her stiffen.

'It's glands with Elaine, Felix,' said my mother conspiratorially, leaning forward and placing a hand on his arm. 'Eats like a bird, poor thing. Terribly, terribly sad.'

I closed my eyes and, to distract myself, raised my bouquet of lily of the valley and white roses to my nose and inhaled deeply.

'And I thought Felix must have had one of those elastic bands fitted, like the woman who used to be on that daytime television programme. You know, the one who was very good on *Strictly*, with Bruce, God rest his soul,' continued Nanny Flo before pausing. 'But I asked Felix and he says it's all down to eating less and running around a bread mill. Isn't that right, Felix?'

'It's a treadmill, but yes, that's right,' I heard him reply. He sounded unperturbed, but I didn't feel moved to open my eyes and check.

'And then I told him how he saved my life,' concluded Nanny Flo abruptly, her voice cracking slightly.

I opened my eyes, lowered my bouquet and bent down, taking her hand in mine and focusing on it, unable to look directly at her, or at anyone else involved in the current conversation for that matter. 'I love you, Nanny,' I said.

She smiled and pressed my hand to her cheek. 'I love you too. And this is my very best day in a long time,' she added.

I gave her a hug and there was a pause before my mother said, with a slight tension in her voice. 'Oh look, Dot, your Auntie Dawn is coming over. How lovely.'

I released Nanny Flo and stood up in time to see my mother's sister in-law advancing up the path towards us. Mum raised a hand and offered my auntie what Becca and I called the Posh Smile. It was the one she reserved for anyone with whom she wasn't completely at ease, and Auntie Dawn definitely fell into that category. It wasn't that they disliked each other, and they were in many ways remarkably similar: chatty, well-meaning and devoted to their families. It was just that neither could resist pouncing on any opportunity to outdo the other. It was a mutual compulsion which their respective families found highly entertaining, but I suspected that today I might find it less so than usual. I waved to Auntie Dawn and braced myself for whatever was to come.

'Oh Dorothy, you look beautiful,' she beamed as she approached, her eyes flickering distractedly between Felix and myself. 'And I love your hat, Helen,' she said, turning to my mother, her eyes moving upward to the latter's large cream number, which had a twist of pale blue tulle around the base of the crown. 'I noticed it from simply *miles* away. Oh dear me,' she laughed, putting a hand to her mouth and glancing up at Felix, 'now I'm making it sound like a lighthouse rising from the sea, aren't I?'

My mother twitched. 'Thank you, Dawn. It's from House of Fraser. Not in the sale and it cost an absolute fortune, but Don insisted that I treat myself. And yours is very nice. Is it from that lovely little hire shop you always go to down by the wharf here?'

Auntie Dawn's head snapped round as I glared at my mother and quite literally stepped in, forcing my way between them and gently pivoting my auntie back towards Felix. 'Auntie Dawn, I'm not sure whether you've met Felix, my...' I cleared my throat. Clearly this was going to be a recurring problem. 'My partner.'

Felix held out his hand and smiled. 'Great to meet you,' he said.

I was by now used to Felix's new appearance and largely unimpressed by it, paired as it was these days with all the charm and personality of a spreadsheet. But even I had to admit that when he smiled, he was unequivocally good-looking. Auntie Dawn clearly thought so too, as evidenced by her slightly flushed and breathless response. 'Well, Felix, how lovely.'

My grandmother laughed and pointed up at Auntie Dawn. 'She's blushing!' she boomed.

My auntie went puce but managed a smile. 'It is a bit hot out here,' she nodded, fanning her face with an order of service.

'Felix and Dottie grew up together and he is now an extremely successful and handsome accountant,' said my mother proudly, clearly delighted by Auntie Dawn's reaction. 'We're so pleased to have him here with us today.'

'And I'm even more delighted to be here, and, of course, to be surrounded at this moment by so many beautiful women,' smiled Felix.

'Oh, you.' My mother beamed and playfully tapped his arm. 'You're so naughty,' she added, reaching out and taking my auntie's hand as the pair were suddenly united in their appreciation of Felix. 'He had Mum and me in stitches earlier, Dawn.'

'Really?' I murmured, feeling my face contort in confusion as Auntie Dawn and my mother melted into fits of girlish giggles. I stared up at Felix. Did he reserve his charmless self just for me? I wondered. Because right now, Mr Dull-As-Ditchwater seemed to have this particular audience in the palm of his hand.

He turned to look at me and I quickly rearranged my bemused features into a smile and attempted to join in the giggling, producing a noise which unfortunately sounded more like machine-gun fire than genuine laughter. Felix offered me a look which I couldn't pinpoint but which seemed to hover somewhere between disdain and amusement.

'What did he say, Helen?' shouted my grandmother.

'He's flattering us, Mum,' said my mother slowly, bending down to place her face in front of Nanny Flo's, her rubber lips back in play. 'He said that we are beautiful women.'

'Ooh, did he now?' whooped my grandmother as she looked up at me and added her own giggles to the chorus.

I laughed loudly, as I felt I should, but the situation had actually begun to take on a distinctly surreal quality for me. And I was just beginning to fear that my continued fake guffawing was in danger of being replaced by genuine, but maniacal, laughter, when my mother pulled herself together and said, 'Oh, I think the photographer might want us now.' She pointed towards Mark as he beckoned to us from a small cluster of trees to one side of the church. 'Come along, everyone,' she said brightly, taking hold of the wheelchair and getting ready to push.

I looked at Felix. 'Do you want to come over?'

'What kind of question is that?' asked Mum, rolling her eyes despairingly at me. 'Don't you know how weddings work? Felix is your boyfriend, Dorothy. He's got to be in the formal photographs too.'

'Oh yes, of course,' I said, my heart sinking at the prospect of creating a photographic record of the deception, just in case my brain ever decided to take pity on me and permit selective amnesia. I reached for Felix's arm, but he was already walking towards my mother and taking the handles of the wheelchair from her. 'Let me push, Mrs Riley.'

My mother stepped back from the chair and beamed. 'Oh, you are lovely, Felix,' she said, squeezing his hand. 'But for goodness' sake, call me Helen. We're practically family now.'

Chapter 11

'Only the best for my girls,' said Dad as he placed four glasses and an ice bucket containing a bottle of champagne on the table in front of Becca, Mum, Nanny Flo and myself.

'Oh Don.' My mother sighed in faux protest. 'Didn't I just tell you a moment ago that I was going to stick to water from now on?'

'Well I'm not,' said Nanny Flo, her hearing aids now fully functional, thanks to two new batteries. 'So someone better hurry up and pop that cork.'

Dad laughed and picked up the bottle.

It was 8.15 p.m., and having just kicked off the disco with her new husband, my sister had retreated with us to the large adjacent bar to, as she put it, *take a little breather from being the centre of attention.*

Being the focus of the day was something which I knew would not sit comfortably with someone as self-effacing as Becca. But as I looked at her across the table, smiling up at Dad and still resplendent in her sleek, cream silk gown, I knew that the fact that the day was giving so much pleasure to others would, for her, outweigh any of its more difficult aspects.

Dad popped the cork to a cheer and hand-clapping from Nanny Flo, and then poured each of us a glass. 'Now,' he said, as he presented me with the final flute, 'I'm going to go and find Geoff for a quiet half-pint somewhere, so I'll leave you ladies to it.'

'Well, just be sure not to hide away anywhere I can't find you,' said my mother, grabbing his arm as he made to leave. 'I know what you're like for avoiding the dance floor, and that DJ has solemnly promised me some proper music later on. I don't want to be a wallflower like I was at Geraldine Mitchell's sixtieth, when you went to the toilet *for one hour and forty-five minutes.*'

My father bent down and hugged her, planting a gentle kiss on her forehead. 'I shall be sure to remain within screeching distance, my beloved,' he said, and then, having received a kiss and a smile in return, he headed off to find his brother.

'Cheers!' said Nanny Flo, raising her glass to us before taking a first sip. 'Ooh, that's lovely, that is.'

'How many have you had, Mum?' asked my mother, sounding slightly anxious.

'Don't know, don't care. I'm already sitting down,' said Nanny Flo, tapping the arm of her wheelchair, 'so I won't fall over. The worse that can happen is that I fall asleep.'

'I, on the other hand...' I smiled, raising my glass, 'might well fall over, so keep a careful eye on me.'

'I don't think there's any need for us to do that these days, Dottie,' laughed Mum. 'Not when there's someone else keeping such a careful eye on you.' She nodded her head towards the bar, where Felix stood with a group of Mark's friends, showing no sign whatsoever of keeping a careful eye on, or indeed anywhere near, me.

We had, much to my relief, barely had to interact all day. I had thought once or twice about going over to see how he was getting on, but each time I had spotted him he had been mid conversation and seemed to be genuinely enjoying himself – and far more animated than he ever was in my company – so I had left him to get on with it.

As I looked at him now, I realised that one friend of Mark's in particular, an attractive policewoman named Rosie, seemed to have been a pretty consistent satellite all day. She was standing next to him again now, gazing up at him and blinking slowly, either in admiration or inebriation, I wasn't sure which. He, meanwhile, was listening to some anecdote or other being delivered by another colleague of Mark's. As the teller ended the tale, all members of the small group nodded sombrely, until Felix said something which prompted raucously loud laughter.

'That boy is such a card,' said Nanny Flo, and I turned to realise that I hadn't been alone in watching the group.

'A card *and* a catch,' said Mum.

I didn't respond, instead picking up my glass and taking two large gulps.

'I had such a lovely chat with him after lunch,' continued my grandmother. 'I told him that I knew he had loved our Dottie from the very beginning, even when they were both little.'

I tried to smile but couldn't quite manage it, so instead took another sip of champagne and a deep breath.

Becca reached out and squeezed my hand. 'Ooh, careful, Nanny,' she said. 'You'll make Dot emotional.'

My grandmother took my other hand and kissed it. 'Becca's right, no more romantic talk from me. And besides,' she added, turning to my mother, 'I need the toilet.'

'Again?' exclaimed Mum. 'You went not half an hour ago.'

'Well if you will keep forcing alcohol down me,' said Nanny, pointing at the ice bucket. 'I'm not even sure I should be drinking at all at my age and in my condition, you know.'

Mum rolled her eyes and I stood up. 'I'll take you, Nanny.'

'No, no,' said my mother wearily, getting to her feet. 'I actually need to go anyway. You stay and finish your drink with Becca. We won't be long.'

She took the handles of the wheelchair and rotated it towards the exit, walking past the double doors which led to the disco just as they opened and Mark emerged, a few notes of the Scissor Sisters escaping with him. I watched for a moment as he crouched down to talk to my grandmother, before returning my attention to Becca.

'You OK?' she asked anxiously.

'Oh for goodness' sake, yes,' I smiled, upset at the thought of concern for me clouding her enjoyment of the day. 'I'm having a lovely time, and all that,' I jerked a thumb over my shoulder in the general direction of Felix, 'has been absolutely fine.'

She nodded. 'He's a lot more fun than I was expecting,' she said. 'More like the Felix I remembered than the one you described really.'

'I know,' I agreed. 'Maybe it's the company. Maybe I'm the dampener,' I added ruefully.

'Don't be silly,' said Becca, nudging me. 'It's more likely that you're gradually bringing him out of himself.'

I smiled at her. 'Your capacity for positive spin is endless.'

'Skivers!'

Becca and I turned simultaneously at the sound of the accusation to discover Mark standing behind us grinning, his dark blonde hair in slight disarray and his boyish face pink and shiny with sweat.

'So far, I've danced with two women and one bloke who all claim to be cousins of yours,' he said with obvious scepticism to Becca. 'Plus I've led a very early conga. Although I'm not sure it counted as a conga as there were only the four of us – me and the "cousins".' He drew the inverted commas in the air. 'But I'm keeping the energy up in there all by myself. Come and give us a hand, will you?'

Becca laughed and looked at me. 'Fancy it?' she asked.

'You go on,' I said, finishing my first glass of champagne and pouring myself another half. 'I'll be in just as soon as I've finished this.'

'I'm going to wait for Dot, Mark,' said Becca.

I stood up and hoisted her to her feet. 'You are not, you shirker,' I said, pushing her towards him. 'Now get back to the disco and stand by your man. I'll be in in two minutes to execute some spins with Nanny Flo. She'll love that.'

Becca looked at Mark uncertainly.

'Actually, I could do with a sit-down,' he said. 'I'll stay here with Dot for a bit while you go and have a bop.'

'That sounds good,' she smiled.

'You two are unbelievable!' I exclaimed, laughing. 'I have champagne and a comfy seat. Can I please just enjoy those two things – in peace – for a few more minutes until Mum and Nanny get back, and then I promise, hand on heart, I will come and do the Macarena.'

Mark nodded. 'Deal,' he said, with the sense of a man who knew when to end a conversation. 'Now come on, Becs,' he said, taking his wife by the hand and leading her away. 'You've procrastinated long enough.'

I watched them go, smiling to myself, before sitting back down and reaching for my drink, genuinely looking forward to a conversationless interlude in a day which had otherwise been nothing but chatter.

But it was not to be.

'Can I join you?'

I sighed internally before looking up a little wearily to discover Alistair smiling down at me, his cravat gone and the top button of his shirt undone. I stared up at him for a moment, picturing him taking my hand as he told me that he had realised he couldn't live without me.

'I'll take that as a no, then, shall I?' he asked.

I shook my head. 'Oh no – it's not a no. I just thought you might be someone I had to make an effort with, and I'm a bit pooped.'

'Please,' he said, raising a hand and sitting down, 'I wouldn't want you to make any effort on my account.'

I smiled. 'Having a good time?'

'I am,' he nodded. 'I managed to catch up with your dad earlier, which was great. You?'

'I'm really enjoying the day. I'll admit that the pampering required to get to this point was a bit painful.' I pointed towards my hair and face. 'But I couldn't be happier for Becca.'

'The pampering was well worth it,' he said. 'You look very…' He hesitated and picked up the half-full beer glass he had brought with him. 'The pampering was well worth it,' he repeated.

'So, how are you?' I asked. 'I don't really know what you've been up to.'

What I actually meant was, *Tell me all about your new relationship*, and I was pretty sure he knew it.

'I got to talk to Felix earlier. Just briefly.'

I nodded. It was as if he knew that I needed reminding that I had a boyfriend. 'That's… good,' I said uncertainly.

'It was,' he confirmed. 'I didn't realise you'd known each other as children. He talked a lot about when you were younger.'

Because there's nothing else to say, I thought ruefully. 'Yes, we go way back,' I said.

'And here's the man himself,' said Alistair, looking up and to my left. I turned my head.

'Hi again,' said Felix, smiling at Alistair. He looked down at me. 'What was it you wanted?'

I frowned up at him. 'What do you mean?'

He pointed over his shoulder. 'Helen said you wanted to talk to me.'

I looked towards the bar, where my mother was now standing with Nanny Flo in her wheelchair. She beamed and waved at me, in response to which I narrowed my eyes and pursed my lips, and then watched as she quickly turned and pushed Nanny Flo through the double doors and into the disco.

I returned my attention to Felix, who was still looking at me questioningly. 'So?' he asked.

'I've forgotten,' I said with an apologetic shrug. 'It was quite a while, and a few drinks, ago.' I pointed at the bottle of champagne.

'Oh, OK,' he said, his face now expressionless.

'Have a seat,' said Alistair jovially.

'Yes, sit down,' I echoed, working hard to make the invitation sound enthusiastic, desperate for Alistair to envy me my new relationship as much as I envied him his.

After the minutest of hesitations, Felix sat, and I casually extended my left arm to rest along the back of his chair. He glanced at it whilst fidgeting slightly in his seat.

'I was just saying to Dot that I had no idea you two were friends as children – until you told me,' said Alistair.

'Yes, and through university,' said Felix.

'Quite a relationship,' smiled Alistair.

Felix nodded. 'It was.'

'You mean it *is*,' laughed Alistair.

Felix looked towards the group at the bar. 'I think I've left my drink over there.'

I noticed Alistair's smile falter slightly.

'Get it in a minute, Felix,' I smiled, placing a hand on his arm. 'Stay and talk. I've barely seen you all day.'

He looked down at my hand and then up at me and then back down at my hand. He wasn't smiling and I felt myself tense, suddenly and unexpectedly afraid of what he might be about to say.

'Oi! You lot!' I turned, never more grateful to see Uncle Geoffrey. He was sashaying towards us, beckoning and laughing as he came. 'Becca says we need you to get people up and dancing,' he gasped, reaching our table and flopping down next to me. 'They're sitting round the edge of the dance floor and Becca said, "Get Dot in here. She'll get them on their feet."'

I laughed, more with relief at the get out from my currently awkward social situation than at the prospect of dancing the night away. 'Sure, I'll come.'

'Good girl,' said Uncle Geoffrey, hauling himself back onto his feet. 'And grab yourself a partner,' he added, placing a friendly hand on Felix's shoulder. 'It's all hands to the deck and feet to the dance floor, Felix.'

Felix smiled up at him. 'Can't wait to catch your moves, Geoff,' he said.

Uncle Geoffrey laughed, did a twirl and then headed off back in the direction of the disco. 'I'll tell them you'll be along in a moment,' he called.

I sighed and stood up. 'Do you want to come too, Alistair?'

He smiled and shook his head. 'Maybe later.'

I looked at Felix, who had now taken his phone from his pocket and appeared to be texting. 'Come on,' I said, smiling and punching him lightly on the arm.

He started slightly. 'Sorry, what?'

'Come and dance.'

'Oh.' He shook his head and returned his attention to his phone. 'No thanks. I'm fine here.'

I stared at him and punched him a second time. 'Becca needs bodies on the dance floor, and I'm not going to dance on my own.' I managed a light laugh.

'I'm sure somebody will dance with you,' he said absently, still focused on his phone. 'What about your uncle? Or I bet Alistair will, won't you, Alistair?' he murmured.

Alistair cleared his throat. 'Er, well, of course.'

Felix glanced up at me. 'There you go. Perfect partner.'

Aware of Alistair's obvious discomfort, I continued to stare at Felix because I didn't know where else to look.

Eventually he glanced up a second time. 'Sorry, what did you say?' he asked.

I shook my head. 'I didn't say anything.'

'OK, well, you two enjoy yourselves,' he said, smiling and standing up. 'I'm going to go and retrieve my drink and I'll see you later, OK?'

Alistair raised his pint towards him, while I remained silent.

'Great.' Felix offered us a general wave, then, apparently forgetting about his drink, walked straight past the bar and through a door which led into the main entrance hall of the manor.

I took a deep breath and picked up my glass.

'Do you want to dance?' asked Alistair.

I turned to look at him, and his expression of pity mingled with concern said it all: I was a woman on the rebound who had hooked up with the first available shit she had trodden in. And just when I thought I couldn't feel any more humiliated, he helped me to peak with an extra dollop of kindness and consideration. 'Or would you prefer to talk?' he asked gently.

I attempted a smile, although I suspect what I achieved was more representative of the agony of childbirth. 'Thanks, but it's OK. I'm just going to pop to the loo and then go and get motivational in the disco.' I felt my lower lip wobble as I came to the end of the sentence, and pressed my champagne flute to my mouth in an attempt to control it. 'I'll just finish this,' I mumbled into the glass, draining its contents for the second time in twenty minutes.

And then, without another word to Alistair, I went in search of Felix. Because no matter how much I needed his cooperation, I had had enough.

Chapter 12

I exited the bar through the same door as Felix and, after a moment's indecision, headed first for the men's toilets. But after my increasingly loud and aggressive enquiries through the outer doorway elicited no response, save for a very timid and elderly-sounding, 'I'm not Felix, I'm Leonard,' I returned to the entrance hall and, with hands on hips, considered the possibilities.

The hall was about fifteen metres square, with a wide, sweeping staircase rising up from its centre and forking off into two landings at the top. These, I knew, led only to bedrooms. So unless Felix had got lucky with Constable Rosie and she had a room booked, I reasoned that he was unlikely to have gone up there.

I glanced to my right, and out through large wooden and glass-panelled double doors, wondering if he had perhaps opted for an evening stroll around the manor's rather impressive gardens. But noticing that it was now raining, I discounted that possibility too.

So that left a choice of only two other doors, both situated on the rear wall of the hall, underneath the staircase. If Felix wasn't behind either of those, I would have to resort to scouring back corridors and kitchens for him. But I was ready for that. However long it took, I was determined to find him and have it out.

Now feeling slightly unsteady on my feet, due to a combination of pent-up emotion and one too many units of alcohol, I removed my heels and walked barefoot towards the first door. Opening it, I discovered a small room, empty save for two wooden desks and a dozen or so metal clothes rails on casters. Sighing, I closed that door before opening the one next to it and stepping inside.

I found myself in a large but cosy lounge, in which sofas, armchairs and various lamps effectively divided the space into four small seating areas, one of which had an enormous stone fireplace as its focus. The walls were painted a soft green, rising to meet an ornately corniced ceiling and hung with large portraits depicting, I presumed, former residents of the manor. It was a beautiful room and for a moment I was distracted and fascinated by the fact that none of the other guests had yet stumbled upon it. It was only after my alcohol-dulled brain reasoned that its door was all but hidden from view by the staircase, and that no one else would have felt a need to go in search of anywhere but a quiet bar or booming disco, that I realised the room wasn't in fact entirely empty. For in the far corner, with his head of dark hair visible above the back of a leather Queen Anne armchair, sat Felix – and he clearly hadn't heard me come in.

I closed the door quietly behind me and, taking a moment and a deep breath to steady myself, walked to the other end of the room to confront him.

'Hello, Felix,' I said, as I drew level with his chair.

To my satisfaction, he started slightly before looking up from his phone. I resisted an urge to rip it from his hands and dash it against the nearest wall.

'Oh, hi,' he said, looking at first surprised and then, I thought, a little irritated. 'Did you remember what you wanted to talk to me about?'

'I did, actually,' I said stiffly. 'But maybe now isn't the best time?' I pointed at his phone.

He heaved a sigh – which made me want to punch him – before turning the phone over and placing it face down on a low coffee table next to him. 'No, it's fine,' he said, interlacing his fingers and resting his hands on his lap. 'You carry on.'

'Do you even like me?' I asked my pre-planned question without hesitation, congratulating myself on my steely and steady tone.

He had been staring blankly at his phone but now looked up at me, clearly confused. 'What?'

'Do… you… even… like… me?' I repeated, pausing between each word for emphasis.

He studied me for a moment. 'Why would you ask me that?'

'Because you don't behave as if you like me, or remotely enjoy my company,' I said simply. 'And yet you seem to have a marvellous time with absolutely everyone else.'

'Is that so?' he said, sounding bored.

'Yes, it is so, *actually*,' I continued, irritated by his tone and unable to keep that irritation from my voice. 'You're more than happy to spend all day flirting with that female policeman in the bar, aren't you? And all night clubbing with sexy Linda and her cocktail hanging around your neck…'

'That all sounds intriguingly gender fluid and exotic, but I have no idea who either of those two people are,' he interjected calmly.

'... but when it comes to me, you're about as much fun...'

'You don't mean Linda our PA, do you? Because she's sixty-two and has never hung around my neck.'

'... as root canal work. And I just want to know why.'

He looked at me and shook his head. 'Why what? I genuinely don't know what you're talking about. Are you drunk?'

'No I am not drunk!' I exclaimed, losing what little cool I had left. 'I'm pissed off and hurt.'

He shrugged. 'OK, but I can't see what that has to do with me.'

I glared down at him, wanting to take him by the lapels and rattle him. 'What's happened to you?' I snapped, pointing at him. 'You're not Felix.'

He frowned and stood up, so that he was now looking down at me as we stood just a few feet apart. 'And why would you think that?' he asked. 'Because I've lost four stone, had a haircut and am no longer at your complete beck and call?'

I blinked, feeling suddenly uncertain and under-prepared for this exchange. I had expected him to apologise and agree to try harder. Felix going on the offensive was not a scenario that I had worked through. 'What? No. That's not what I meant.'

'Isn't it? Because maybe *I* could say that now you've acquired some dress sense and lost all consideration for the feelings of others, you're not Dot.'

'How *dare* you say that *I've* lost all consideration for people's feelings?' I exploded. 'Especially when you...' I paused, feeling both emotionally and physically wobbly and desperately trying to pull myself together, 'when you have just *deliberately* humiliated me in front of my ex-boyfriend.'

He held up his hands. 'And once again, you've completely lost me,' he sighed. 'So why don't you go and drink lots of water, Dorothy, and we'll continue this conversation when you've sobered up. Or preferably never,' he added in an undertone, bending down to retrieve his phone.

'No!' I grabbed his arm and pulled him upright. 'We're having this conversation right now, because I want to know what I've done to deserve being treated like that.'

'Like what, for God's sake?' he asked impatiently, shaking me off.

'Like refusing to dance with me and telling Alistair to dance with me instead.'

He appeared confused for a moment, and then his expression cleared. 'Oh, is Alistair your ex?'

'Of course he is,' I seethed. 'As you well know.'

He shook his head. 'Nope. I did not know that.'

'Yes you did!' I protested. 'I told you all about him when we went for coffee on Thursday. And yet just now, out there,' I pointed towards the door, 'you behaved as if you couldn't wait to get away from me, and then you told the man who no longer wants to be in a relationship with me to dance with me because you couldn't be arsed. You actually called him my perfect partner. Do you have any idea how embarrassing that was? How much that hurt? Of course you don't, because you,' I continued angrily, prodding a finger against his chest, 'whoever you are, are completely devoid of feeling and compassion. I've got a fridge at home that's warmer than you.'

Until then, he had been looking at me with something approaching mild amusement, but now his face darkened. 'So let me get this straight,' he said quietly. 'You're in here yelling at me and looking like you want to kill me because I didn't recall that Alistair was your ex?'

'You—' I began, but he held up a hand.

'Shut up. It's my turn,' he said before continuing without pause. 'Do you know how many people I have been introduced to, and introduced myself to, today?' he asked, the irritation in his voice rising steadily. 'Do you know how many hours of conversation I've participated in? How much information I've been bombarded with? How many personal facts I've attempted to absorb and retain? All with zero support from you, and all the while trying not to do or say anything which might alert your grandmother, your parents, your extended family and your friends to the fact that you've been lying to them.'

I stared up at him, momentarily struck dumb by the list of witheringly rhetorical questions.

He smiled humourlessly. 'You don't know? Well that's OK because I don't either. But what I do know is that *you*,' he jabbed an index finger towards me, causing me to take an unsteady step backwards, 'deserve none of the effort that I have gone to. And neither do you deserve your family and friends because, quite frankly, they're all too good for you. You are ungrateful, disinterested and self-centred. You complain that I'm not Felix. But how the hell would you even know? Have you asked me anything about myself?'

I maintained my increasingly ashamed silence.

'Have you?' he pressed.

'I think I did ask you some...' I began uncertainly, now actually unable to recall asking him even one direct personal question. 'I mean I'm pretty sure I at least tried. It felt like I tried.'

'Well, not hard enough for me to notice,' he replied angrily. 'You turned up at my office, after fifteen years of silence, suddenly wanting to be friends again. And why? Because you wanted something. That was the only reason, wasn't it?'

'It wasn't just that,' I said, my voice now little more than a whisper. 'I was really looking forward to seeing you and was interested in—'

'Sure you were,' he interrupted scathingly. 'So interested that you didn't even ask me if I had a partner. You came along, asked me to go to a wedding with you and didn't even wonder whether that might be inconvenient to a current relationship.'

I hung my head. 'I did wonder but I didn't know how to ask. I just assumed you'd say if it was a problem.' I mumbled my feeble defence at half volume.

'Well it doesn't matter anyway,' he snapped, snatching up his phone, tapping it and then thrusting it towards me. I focused and saw several text messages, together with a picture of the same blonde who had been draped all over him in the nightclub photograph, except in this particular photo she was make-up-free and wholesome: a glowing Gwyneth Paltrow lookalike. 'It doesn't matter because she'd already dumped me three months before you came along. It's all very amicable, of course,' he said, with obvious bitterness. 'She texts me several times a day and sends me lots of happy photos to make sure I realise that everything's great between us, but she's still shagging someone else.'

'Oh no, that's awful. I'm so sorry, Felix,' I said, staring at the picture and putting a hand to my mouth. 'I didn't know.'

'No, you didn't,' he pushed his phone into his jacket pocket, 'because you're too wrapped up in getting what *you* want, focusing on *your* worries and *your* needs and making sure that no one screws anything up for *you*. It's all about you, isn't it? But then it always was.'

'What?' I asked weakly, looking up and feeling a tear escape. 'What do you mean? We were best friends. I would have done anything—'

'God, I'd hate to have been one of your lower-tier mates!' He laughed humourlessly. 'All you did to me was ignore my letters and then ask me to back up your lies fifteen years later. What did you do to them? Have them stuffed for use as footstools?' he concluded, turning and walking away.

'Felix,' I said, reaching for his arm but missing and stumbling forward. 'What letters? I didn't get any letters.'

'I'm going to sort a cab,' he said, neither stopping nor turning round. 'Tell your family I'm sorry but I'm unwell, and if they get in touch I'll say the same.'

'Felix, please don't go. I understand why you're angry. But let me explain,' I began, hurrying after him. 'You looked so different in Cheltenham. And I know that might seem shallow, but it threw me. I hadn't expected you to be so professional and serious and I couldn't seem to find the person I knew and I didn't know what to say or how to say it. I felt silly. I was intimidated.' I rattled the sentences off at speed and without pause for breath. At the end of my little summing-up for the defence, I heaved a sob, no longer having the energy or the will to suppress it. 'I'm just so sorry,' I whispered.

He paused with his back to me and his hand resting on the handle of the door. 'You and me both,' he said quietly. And then, roughly pulling open the door, he left.

–

I lay full-length on one of the sofas in the lounge and gave myself a good ten minutes to calm down before heading upstairs to my parents' room, for which I had a key card. Once there, I raided my mother's make-up bag, doing my best to disguise my tear-swollen eyes and, more importantly, not to think any more about Felix.

I had already decided that I would call him the next day and apologise for the selfishness upon which he had so devastatingly shone a spotlight. But perhaps most of all, I wanted to tell him that I hadn't ignored his letters all those years ago, but simply hadn't received them. And also, for what it was worth, that I had sent him postcards while on my travels. It wasn't much, I knew, but at least it would show that I hadn't forgotten him the moment I had set foot on the first plane.

But although I was desperate to attempt to right all wrongs done to Felix, past and present, I was equally desperate not to spoil my sister's wedding day. So, having done my best with my mother's cooling eye cream and under-eye concealer, I hurried downstairs to fulfil my long-overdue promise to get people dancing.

I re-entered the bar to delighted cries of 'There she is!' from my father and grandmother, who were now seated, with Alistair, at the table I had vacated half an hour earlier. I smiled as brightly as I could manage and hurried over to them.

'Sorry, everyone,' I said on arrival. 'I felt a bit green and went upstairs to splash my face with cold water. I think it was a combination of the heat and drinking that champagne too quickly. Do I look OK, Nanny?' I asked, bending down to give her a kiss. 'I've redone my make-up.'

'Gilding the lily,' she said, reaching up and giving me a hug. 'But we were worried, Dottie.'

I straightened up and looked at Dad and Alistair. 'Sorry. I just needed to cool down.'

Alistair nodded but looked unconvinced.

'And you're feeling recovered enough to be up and about so soon, are you, Dot?' asked Dad with concern.

'Absolutely,' I smiled. 'So,' I said, addressing Nanny Flo, and anxious to move on from the topic of my health, 'how about we go and tear up the dance floor?'

She laughed loudly. 'No thank you, love. Your uncle Geoffrey has twirled me and my chair around quite enough for one evening. What was that song he had me dancing to, Don? The famous Beatles one.'

'*Twist and Shout.*'

I smiled. 'Oh, OK.' I turned to Dad and was just about to ask him if he'd like to dance when it struck me that he might be too tired and decline, which would then leave me drowning in the déjà vu of an offer from Alistair. So I said nothing and, choosing instead to play for time, crouched down and mumbled something about adjusting my heel strap.

'And besides,' continued Nanny Flo, placing a gentle hand on my back as I stooped down beside her. 'There's this handsome young man right here without a partner, ready and waiting to dance with you.'

I fiddled pointlessly for a little longer with my shoe, waiting for my stressed blushes to subside and preparing myself to stand up and graciously accept Alistair's kind offer.

'There, that's sorted,' I said after a moment.

I was aware of a hand being extended downwards to help me to my feet and, taking it, I stood up.

'OK?' asked Felix. He offered me a look of concern which somehow made the enquiry seem unanswerably enormous.

I gazed up at him, stretching my eyes to the max and tilting my head back slightly in an attempt to contain any tears.

I nodded.

'Good,' he said, 'because I've just talked the DJ into playing our song.'

'Yes, Felix went missing at the very same time you did,' chimed Nanny Flo. 'I said to your father, "They're making whoopee upstairs." Didn't I say that to you, Don?'

'Yes, yes you did, Flo,' said Dad awkwardly. 'More than once, in fact.'

'But Felix told me he went to the toilet, where there was a queue,' said my grandmother, a look of intense concentration on her face as she began to tick off Felix's movements on her fingers, 'and then he went to ask the DJ to play your special song, and then he went to look for you. Isn't that right, Felix?'

'It is,' he said, still looking at me.

Nanny Flo squeezed my arm. 'And now he's found you. Isn't that lovely, Dottie?'

I nodded again.

'She's overcome,' said Nanny Flo.

Felix smiled. 'Come on then,' he said, 'or we'll miss our song. It's on next.' And, still holding my hand, he led me across the bar and towards the doors to the disco.

As we reached them, I stopped short and pulled him back a little. 'Hang on a moment,' I said.

'Yes?'

'What *is* our song?'

'Who knows,' he shrugged. 'How about we decide when I open the door?'

I smiled. 'OK.'

He smiled back at me and, reaching out, pushed the door ajar. We were greeted by The Cure.

'*Friday I'm in Love!*' I exclaimed. 'Oh wow, I love this song.'

'Me too,' he replied as we went inside, 'so let's dance.'

Chapter 13

'And after that,' I yawned, leaning back in my swivel chair, 'we had a really nice time. We danced with all the wallflowers until the disco finished at midnight, and then we shared a taxi with a couple of Mark's mates back to Devizes.'

'Aw,' said Kate, smiling broadly as I finished my carefully edited account of the weekend. I had decided to omit any reference to my argument with Felix, saying only that we'd managed to catch up a bit during the day and that I had discovered that he'd split up with his girlfriend in April. 'And congratulations. You got away with it.' Kate raised her coffee mug to me in salute, before tipping it back, taking a final sip and replacing it on the desk in front of her.

I smiled a little uncertainly, the sense of guilt, which had happily faded as my relationship with Felix had improved, now resurfacing as Kate reminded me of the deception central to my weekend. 'Yes, but it was good to see Felix whatever the reason. And I'm going to text him later to invite him to Bristol for a weekend visit. I thought I might get us tickets for something. You know, to say thank you and to show him that I am genuinely interested in catching up and haven't just been using him.'

Kate's eyes narrowed. 'You had a row with him, didn't you?'

'What?' I laughed and shook my head dismissively. 'No. Not at all.'

'Yes you did,' she said. 'He said that you were just using him and you insisted you genuinely wanted to catch up. You're so transparent, Dot. You're walking talking cellophane.'

I thought about protesting, but knew from experience that denial would get me nowhere and wondered why I had tried to hide anything from her in the first place.

'OK, so my motives and approach might have been gently questioned by Felix at one point, but,' I continued defensively, 'we parted on good terms. And I always intended to offer him dinner or an evening out to say thank you. It's just that now that we've cleared the air and are more relaxed with each other, I think a weekend visit might actually be really good fun.'

'I'm sure it would,' agreed Kate. 'But as well as arranging *that*...' she paused and looked at me over the top of her glasses, 'you're going to have to think about that all-important chat with your mum and granny, aren't you?'

I nodded. 'I will, but I can't do it hot on the heels of Becca's wedding. Besides, I think it's the kind of thing I need to say in person, rather than over the phone, and I'm not sure when I'm next seeing Mum.'

'Hey,' said Kate sternly, picking up a pen and pointing it at me, 'no more fannying around. You don't have to phone her this minute and say *I've dumped him*, but you can start to lay the groundwork. Sort it out,' she concluded, tapping the desk with her pen for emphasis.

'I'm going to,' I insisted. 'I know I've got to. Especially now that Mum's got Felix's phone number. She'll be hassling him about birthdays and Christmas before too long.'

Kate looked appalled. 'She's got his phone number? How did that happen?'

I shrugged. 'She asked him for it and he gave it to her.'

'What?' She looked genuinely confused. 'You mean he gave your mother his *actual* number? The correct one?'

'He's not as instinctively evil as you, Kate,' I said.

'Or you,' she said. 'How many times did you give her the wrong number when you switched to O2?'

'That was a genuine mistake,' I protested, 'on each occasion.'

'Whatever,' she said. 'But you're right, your mum having direct access to him is definitely another reason not to faff about over clearing things up.'

'I won't, I promise.'

She smiled. 'Good. Well, I'm going to go and get us our Monday buns from next door,' she said purposefully, standing up before immediately sitting back down again. 'Ooh, but before I do, how did it go with, you know...' She concluded the sentence by mouthing the word *Alistair*.

'I hardly saw him,' I said. 'Although we did bump into him at dinner on Friday night, which wasn't great. I hadn't realised that he was staying at the Bear as well.'

'When you say *we* bumped into him – your mum wasn't there, was she?'

I nodded slowly and Kate's mouth stretched into an expression of dread. 'Eek,' was all she said.

I continued to nod and took a deep breath. 'It wasn't my favourite five minutes ever. But Mum behaved herself the next day, thank goodness, and I only had one brief chat with him in the bar before the disco. I was with Felix and barely sat down after that and didn't have time to think.'

'You mean you couldn't think because you were pissed?' asked Kate.

'A bit,' I admitted. 'And then I had breakfast in bed the next morning, because obviously I didn't want Alistair to see me eating breakfast without Felix.'

'Cunning,' she said, standing up again. 'And, like I said, you seem to have got away with everything. But I hope all this has been a lesson to you, Dot.'

'It certainly has,' I said, turning towards my screen. 'I shall never pretend to my grandmother that I have a boyfriend when she's dying of pneumonia ever again.'

'Ignoring the sarcasm,' said Kate, as she walked past me and towards the lobby, 'but just—' she began, only for the imminent advice fest to be interrupted by the ringing of the phone.

'Oh dear, what a shame, I'm going to have to get that,' I smiled, picking up the receiver gratefully as Kate's lips pursed in disapproval. 'Eat Fruit Design. Dot speaking. How can I help?'

'Hello, Dottie, Mum here. I know you're at work but I wanted a quick word.' My face fell as Kate's lit up.

'It's your mother, isn't it?' she whispered. 'That's karma.'

I glared at her before returning my attention to Mum. 'Well, it'll have to be *very* quick, Mum. We're busy here.'

'Yes, yes,' she said. 'I just wanted to catch you because I got no answer when I called you at home yesterday. Three times,' she added pointedly, pausing to allow me to explain my failure to pick up.

It was an opportunity I decided to ignore. 'OK,' I said.

'And I did just want to say again how much your father and I like Felix. He's as lovely a young man as he was a little boy.'

I massaged my left temple with my free hand and glanced up at Kate, who was eavesdropping intently and without shame. It was clear from her expression that she had heard if not the entire sentence, then at least the mention of Felix's name. 'Go on,' she urged in a whisper. 'Start the process. Drop some hints about things not being perfect.'

'Hang on a moment, Mum,' I said into the receiver before covering it with my hand. 'I will start the process,' I hissed at Kate. 'But not with you standing over me.'

'Calm down, calm down,' she said, reaching out to pat my shoulder before walking away.

I waited until I heard the main office door open and slam shut before removing my hand from the receiver.

'Sorry about that, Mum. Like I said, we're quite busy here.'

'Oh, but wasn't it a lovely weekend, Dot?' she gushed. 'Didn't Becca and Mark look gorgeous? And my goodness, how handsome is your Felix these days? Nobody I spoke to could believe how well you've done for yourself,' she said with obvious pride.

I frowned. 'You know, I'm not sure that's actually a compliment to me,' I said. 'But thank you on Felix's behalf, and yes, he's very nice.'

'Nice?' she laughed. 'Nice? I'd hope you think him a bit more than nice, Dottie.'

I heaved a sigh. 'Of course I think of him as more than nice.'

'You absolutely adore him, don't you?' she giggled.

'Yes, that's right, I absolutely adore him,' I replied hurriedly, now desperate to end the conversation. 'But Mum, I must go. I'll call you this evening, or tomorrow.'

'But I want to arrange popping to see you in Bristol while we're staying with Uncle Geoff and Auntie Dawn later this month.'

'That sounds great. Give me all the details when I talk to you later,' I said hurriedly.

'And hopefully we can see Felix too.'

I recommenced massaging my temple and closed my eyes in an added attempt to generate a state of well-being. 'Yes, I'll talk to Felix about coming. I'm sure he would love that,' I said quietly. 'But I must go now, or I'll be working through lunch, Mum. Bye.'

I waited until she had said goodbye before hanging up. On hearing a theatrical clearing of the throat, I turned my chair to see Kate standing in the lobby, looking at me disapprovingly, her arms folded. She clearly hadn't gone anywhere.

'What?' I asked, my chin jutting slightly as I attempted defiance.

'Nothing.' She shook her head despairingly, but laughed nevertheless. 'But if that's your idea of being direct, Dorothy Riley, God help us on your dithery days.'

I returned her grin with a sheepish smile of my own. 'It's not like cancelling the milk or a Sky subscription, Kate. It can't be sorted with a quick phone call. It's a complicated thing. There are a lot of feelings at stake.'

Kate shook her head a second time. 'Poor analogy. Trying to cancel my Sky subscription was impossible. I spent two hours talking to someone called Dafydd, whose final bundle was so attractive that I just couldn't turn him down.'

'OK,' I conceded with a sigh, now focusing determinedly on my screen. 'Scrub that. Let's just go with the milk analogy.'

'Yes, I haven't got a problem with that one,' she said. 'Oh, and you were right about another thing too,' she added after a moment, her voice fading as she finally opened the office door and exited. 'There are a lot of feelings at stake.'

Chapter 14

I relaxed back onto the cushioned wooden lounger, hand-crafted by Mark, and smiled. A visit to Becca's was always such great therapy, especially now, during the summer months, when she was free from the stresses and strains of school, and I was free from any sense of guilt associated with perhaps adding to her schedule.

Looking towards the end of the long, lawned garden, with its view of the church and green hillsides beyond, I momentarily envied my sister her village existence and lifestyle, and the increased sense of home and belonging which had come with her decision to live within just a few miles of her birthplace. But I knew it wasn't for me – not yet, anyway. While I was single, I still needed the easy-reach social and cultural distractions of the city: rurality and community could wait until I settled down and had a family. I closed my eyes and tilted my head back towards the early-evening sun. *If* I settled down and had a family.

I shrugged away the uncertainty, despite no one else being there to witness the gesture. And the absence of an audience was just as well, because even I wasn't fully convinced by it.

'Here.'

I opened an eye to discover Becca standing over me, smiling, a glass of Pimm's held in her outstretched hand.

She had arrived back from her Greek island honey-moon a week earlier and had wasted no time in calling to confirm my visit for a wedding day debrief and general catch-up. We had spent the afternoon walking the Kennet and Avon Canal and the Wansdyke with Mark, arriving home just in time for him to start preparations for the Saturday evening meal he always cooked on my weekend visits. He was a lovely man, whom I was happy to accept thoroughly deserved my sister, a feat I had always thought impossible until she had introduced me to him five years earlier.

They had met when he, then a locally-based police constable, had come to deliver the annual stranger-danger lecture to pupils at her school. As a favour to the head, he had additionally agreed to make brief mention of a string of pencil case thefts which were at that time occurring in Year 3. It was hoped that just a few words from a uniformed police officer would put an end to the crim-inality, and so it had proved, with the culprits dissolving into tears and fessing up at the first mention of Oliver Lewry's missing Transformers ruler.

Mark's fateful school visit was an anecdote recounted without fail by my mother on introducing him to anyone, with her emphasis always on his impressive law-enforcement presence, rather than on the fact that the event led to him dating her daughter. It was to Mark's credit that he always managed to maintain a smile during these introductions, although we all, with the exception of Mum, knew that this kindest of men did not count reducing two eight-year-olds to sobbing wrecks as the finest moment of his policing career.

I took the Pimm's from Becca with a smile. 'Thank you.'

She sat down on an adjacent lounger and sipped her own drink. 'Greece was great,' she said, 'but you can't beat a warm, still British summer evening, can you?'

'Agreed,' I nodded. 'If only we had more than three a year.' I ran a finger along the arm of the lounger, tracing the grain of the wood. 'Mind you, these would make any evening special. Mark is so clever.'

She smiled proudly. 'I know. He's making Mum and Dad a pair for Christmas. Not very seasonal, but I think they'll like them.'

'Of course they will!' I exclaimed. 'Mum will be beside herself.'

Becca sighed. 'Hopefully it'll ease her disappointment over the fact that we're spending Christmas with Mark's parents this year.'

'Let me be cruel to be kind and dash that hope for you right now,' I said, shaking my head. 'Because we both know that *nothing* will ease that disappointment. Ever. She's been bad enough about not getting to see Felix when he's in Bristol next weekend. And Christmas is in a whole different league.'

'Thanks for the reality check. I don't know what I was thinking,' sighed Becca. 'And I meant to ask you about that, actually. How on earth did you convince her to stay away while Felix is visiting?'

'It wasn't a problem,' I said. 'He and I are going to the Hippodrome on Saturday night, so we are genuinely not free for dinner, and Mum and Dad couldn't make lunch. So instead, they're coming to stay with me on Sunday evening on their way home from Avebury. By which time,

Felix will be long gone.' I raised my glass to Becca and she clinked hers against it.

'Serendipity,' she smiled. 'So what are you and Felix going to see?'

'*Dirty Dancing*,' I replied, pulling a slightly anxious face.

'What?' Becca choked on her drink.

'It was all I could get tickets for,' I explained, reaching out to pat her on the back. '*Girl from the North Country* was sold out at the Old Vic, there was nothing on at the Colston Hall, and I thought the cinema seemed a bit ordinary, in light of the humongous favour he did me.'

'But why not just take him out for dinner somewhere nice?' she asked, quite reasonably doubting Felix's desire to spend the evening surrounded by hundreds of women whooping at the sight of a young man with his shirt off.

'The thing is,' I sighed, 'he's arriving in Bristol in time for lunch, so we'll talk then. Then I thought we'd go for a walk around Ashton Court, so we'll talk then. Then I'm taking him on the open-top bus – love that.' I grinned like a child. 'And then I've told him we'll go for a drink before the show, so…'

Becca nodded. 'So you needed to cut down on the talk time.'

'Exactly. We were definitely more relaxed with each other by the end of the wedding, but I still have no clue how this is going to go. It might be that by seven thirty he'll be delighted to sit through two and a half hours of female fantasy if it means a break from me.'

She looked at me over the top of her glass. 'You do talk rubbish sometimes, Dot,' she said gently. 'I saw the pair of you at the disco. You had a whale of a time.'

'Whilst completely pissed,' I reminded her.

She tutted. 'It'll be fine. You'll have fun.'

'I hope so. But I still have quite a lot of ground to make up in the friendship stakes,' I added, smiling sadly. 'And that's quite aside from the whole pretend-boyfriend thing. He's asked me twice now whether I've straightened that out with Mum and Dad.'

'Is he worried?'

'He didn't sound worried, but I suppose he must be. Otherwise why mention it? Anyway, I told him yesterday that it was all sorted.'

Becca looked surprised. 'Is it?'

'Technically no,' I admitted. 'But it will be when I see Mum and Dad on Sunday evening. So when Felix asked about it again, I thought I might as well set his mind at rest there and then. He's got enough stress at the moment with work and the ex-girlfriend thing.'

'Well, if he's looking for a shoulder to cry on,' said Mark, emerging onto the patio carrying a tray laden with bowls of nibbles and a single open bottle of beer, 'I know a certain detective constable who would be happy to oblige.' He placed the tray on a low wooden table between Becca and me.

'Really?' I looked up at him, puzzled for a moment, until the penny dropped. 'Oh, you mean your friend Rosie.'

'She's the one,' he said, picking up a wrought-iron chair from the far side of the patio and setting it down next to us. 'She thought he was great. Everyone on his table at the wedding really liked him, actually. But she was particularly keen.' He winked and sat down, picking up the beer from the tray and lifting it to his lips.

I said nothing but felt my eyebrows raise involuntarily.

Mark lowered the bottle without taking a sip and looked between Becca and myself. 'What?'

I shook my head. 'Nothing.'

'Then why the forehead twitch?' he pressed.

I shrugged. 'Well, it's just that he was there as my boyfriend, wasn't he? It's a bit naughty of her to be eyeing up someone else's man,' I smiled, wagging a finger at him.

'But he's not your boyfriend. He's single,' said Mark, his expression now one of deepening confusion.

'Well, yes,' I said with a sigh. 'But she didn't *know* that. That's the thing. It's not a huge problem. It's just a principle of sisterhood, that's all.'

'I see,' he said uncertainly.

Becca reached out and put a hand on his arm, while addressing me. 'Rosie's lovely and Mark's playing detective. He's making a deduction based on body language.' She turned to look at him. 'Rosie didn't actually *say* she fancied Felix, did she, Sherlock?'

'Yes, she did,' he said. 'Loads of times.'

Becca groaned and I laughed.

Mark looked at me for a moment, and then at Becca. 'I don't really understand,' he said.

'That's not unusual,' said Becca.

'I just thought it might be nice for Dot to pass on that Rosie fancied him.' Mark sounded apologetic as he appealed to his wife. 'I thought it might make Felix feel better about being dumped, and if he did decide to get in touch with her, she'd be over the moon.'

I leaned towards him and gave him a hug, his kind-heartedness making me feel churlish for even hinting at disapproval. 'You're absolutely right, and I'll tell him next Saturday, when he comes to stay.'

'Great,' he said, patting my back and sounding relieved. 'And now I'll go and get on with dinner,' he added, standing up. 'I know where I am with Mediterranean chicken.'

Becca waited until he had disappeared back into the house before she spoke. 'Rosie is genuinely lovely,' she said. 'Not the kind of woman to steal someone else's man.'

I smiled. 'I'm sure. And to be fair to her, I didn't really speak to Felix for the first three quarters of the wedding, and neither of us was behaving as if we were attached.'

'I can understand you being protective of him, though,' said Becca. 'It sounds like the split from his girlfriend has been a difficult one.'

I nodded. 'And goodness knows, I was very vulnerable after Alistair left, and ours was a relatively smooth uncoupling. I'd have dated Nigel Farage if he'd said I had a nice smile and an OK personality.'

'Don't be so silly,' she tutted. 'You were never that low.'

I shrugged. 'It's irrelevant anyway. Because Nigel would never have got through the human firewall that is our mother. Remember how she kept telling everyone during the referendum campaign that he had a look of the underworld about him?'

Becca laughed. 'I do.'

'Plus Kate said he looked like his neck was eating his head, and she's another pretty formidable firewall.'

I heard Becca sigh. 'Felix would get through all firewalls,' she murmured.

I turned to look at her to find her now gazing straight ahead. 'Thinking out loud?' I asked.

She turned towards me and smiled. 'He seems to be just as lovely as he was when he was younger, Dot. And undeniably good-looking.'

'Way too good-looking for me, apparently.'

'Says who?'

'Says everybody Mum spoke to at the wedding. She said that no one could believe how well I'd done for myself. Oh, the irony.'

Becca rolled her eyes. 'What rubbish.'

'It's not. I'm not blind. Rosie wasn't the only one eyeing him up at the reception. But in any case,' I continued quickly, preventing Becca from chipping in with the confidence-boosting compliments I knew she would have at the ready, 'it doesn't matter. I would just like us to be how we used to be.'

'You're not planning to dig out your DMs, are you?' smiled Becca.

'No, and I don't want Felix to put on four stone and wear an Alice band to keep his hair out of his eyes when he watches TV,' I laughed. 'I just mean that I would like to understand him again up here,' I tapped my head, 'and in here, I guess,' I added quietly, placing a hand on my chest. 'And right now, I don't. I don't feel like I've quite found the Felix I used to know.'

Becca looked at me for a moment and then smiled and raised her glass. 'Well, here's to you finding your Felix, Dot,' she said quietly.

'To finding Felix,' I echoed. And leaning back in my lounger and sipping my Pimm's, I wondered if I would.

Chapter 15

I glanced down at my mobile on the desk in front of me and groaned out loud at the appearance of yet another missed call from my mother; the third within the past hour.

It had been a busy and difficult week, with Kate having to leave work early on Tuesday afternoon after suddenly throwing up. And although she had since been attempting to work from home, her absence from the office had left me with three additional client meetings and double the number of phone calls to field. Consequently, repeated calls from my mother, no doubt to remind me, yet again, of her 5.30 p.m. arrival time on Sunday, were the last thing I wanted on a Friday when I was already looking at a very late finish.

I reached for my phone and quickly texted Dad to say that I would call Mum when I got home from work, adding that this would not be before eight. I knew he would take the hint, and sure enough, Mum's 2 p.m. call proved to be her last of the working day.

However, it came as no surprise whatsoever, as I staggered through the door of my flat at 8.05 p.m., to hear the landline ringing. I sighed as I dropped my laptop bag, coat and handbag in a heap on the hallway floor and plodded into the kitchen to pour myself a glass of wine, having no intention whatsoever of attempting to make it into the lounge in time to answer the phone before it went to voicemail.

Five minutes later, I was slumped on the sofa, glass of red in hand, and just wondering whether I should tidy up the flat before bed, or attempt to do it in the morning before Felix arrived, when the phone began to ring again. Irritated and exhausted, but bowing to the inevitable, I picked it up.

'Hello,' I said with a sigh so heavy it bordered on asthmatic. 'Yes?' I added impatiently for good measure.

'Dot?'

I frowned. The voice was male and it wasn't Dad's.

'It's Felix. I'm calling the landline because your mobile's going straight to voicemail.'

'Oh.' I sat up and put down my drink, feeling slightly flustered. 'Sorry, my phone must need charging. Hope I haven't left it in the office,' I added, looking round. 'I thought you were my mother, hence the grumpiness. Plus, I've only just got home. Kate's off sick, so it's a bit crap at work.'

'Not what you want on a Friday,' he said, sounding sympathetic.

'No,' I agreed. 'I'm knackered. Oh, but I'm still looking forward to tomorrow,' I added hastily, in case he thought I was trying to cancel. Then I hesitated as it crossed my mind that he might have called to do just that. 'Are you still able to come? Or has something else cropped up?'

'I'm still around if you are,' he said. 'And I got your text about the theatre. That sounds great. What are we going to see? You didn't say.'

'Didn't I?' I hesitated and wrinkled my nose as I imagined his reaction to the planned Saturday-night entertainment. 'Well, how about I make it a surprise?' I suggested.

He laughed. 'OK,' he said. 'Although I should warn you that I've already seen *Puppetry of the Penis*.'

'You have?' I gasped.

There was a pause before he replied. 'No, I haven't, Dot.'

I picked up my drink, leaned back on the sofa and smiled. 'I knew that really.'

'I know,' he said. 'You were just pretending to be gullible.'

'Yep. Anyway, are you still planning to get here around midday?'

'I am. But I wanted to double-check whether you'd told your mother that we were no longer going out together.'

I frowned into the phone, surprised at the question. His tone was calm and matter-of-fact, but the issue was clearly preying on his mind. 'Yes, it's all sorted. I've told Mum *and* Dad that we're still friends but that we're not going out any more,' I said, sharing my planned Sunday-night script with him. 'They were obviously a little sad but very accepting. They're just pleased it's all amicable,' I added, concluding the happy scene in my head.

'That's great,' he said.

'Yes.' I smiled and sipped my drink. 'I hope you haven't been worrying about it.'

'Not at all,' he said. 'I only raised it because I've just had quite a long conversation with your mother...'

I spat my wine back into the glass.

'...during which she said several times how delighted she is that we're going out together.'

'No...' I breathed, placing my glass on the table and putting my hand to my mouth.

'And from that,' continued Felix, 'I inferred that maybe you *hadn't* actually told her that we were no longer going out together. Can you see how I might have jumped to that conclusion?'

He stopped talking and there was silence between us for a few moments, while speechless shock morphed into total, but articulate, shame.

'I'm so sorry,' I said, my voice hoarse. 'I'm seeing Mum and Dad on Sunday evening and planned to tell them then. I just didn't want you worrying about it all any longer, so I told you the truth in advance.'

'Advanced truth,' he said. 'Nice spin.'

It was impossible to guess his mood over the phone, but reminding myself that he had just moments earlier confirmed that he was still coming to Bristol for the weekend, I tried to remain hopeful that he was leaning more towards despair than rage.

'So... what did you say to Mum?' I asked hesitantly, fully aware that the question was heavy with self-interest, but feeling that it had to be asked nevertheless. If my hysterical mother, or worse still, my disappointed father, was about to phone and tell me that they now knew that I had spent several weeks, and my sister's wedding day, living a lie, then I needed to be prepared.

'I said thank you, and then let her move on to the next topic.'

'Oh, that's so amazing of you,' I said, flopping back onto the sofa with relief. 'Thank you so, so much. Sunday will be the end of it, I promise.'

'I haven't told you what the next topic was yet,' he said, sounding serious.

I began to feel sick, the alternate tension and relief of the conversation having a similar effect on my stomach as the lurching of the ferry on a storm-hit school trip to France in 1995. 'What,' I asked weakly, 'was the next topic?'

Felix cleared his throat. 'Well apparently she's been trying to get hold of you all day.'

'She has,' I murmured, immediately regretting not picking up the phone to her.

'Because she needed to tell you that they are no longer free to see you on Sunday evening.'

'Oh, OK,' I said in surprise. I had been expecting worse.

'But she said you mustn't be upset, because she's had a brilliant idea.'

'Oh dear.' Every muscle in my body now involuntarily tensed, as I braced myself for my mother's brilliant idea. She'd had a spate of them since Alistair had left, all intended to cheer me up and all complete fails. Examples of her genius had included a surprise pamper session with her seventy-year-old beautician friend, after which I had resembled a seventy-year-old beautician, and a blind date with her new neighbour, Andrew, who was, she said, forty, good-looking and single. She had told me that she believed the latter was due to the fact that he was *shy and selective*, whilst Andrew had explained to me over dinner that it was actually because he was still getting over splitting up with his boyfriend.

'It's an idea,' continued Felix, 'which will enable them to spend some time with me after all.'

'Oh no.'

'She wants to meet us for drinks at six thirty in the Colston Hall bar.'

I nodded and closed my eyes, now beyond verbal expressions of hopelessness.

'Before we move on to the Hippodrome to see *Dirty Dancing*,' he added casually.

This final lurch of the conversational ship – the revelation that Felix had all along known the identity of the show we were to see – was somehow the worst of all. 'I feel a bit sick,' I said.

He burst out laughing.

'You're not cross?' I asked.

'Despairing,' he said, still laughing. 'But not cross.'

I smiled and felt like crying, whilst reflecting that New Felix seemed to have that effect on me rather a lot. 'I meant well,' I said quietly.

'I know.'

'So…?'

'So we're meeting your parents in the Colston Hall bar at six thirty,' he said. 'It wasn't an invitation I felt I could turn down.'

'I'm so sorry.'

'Don't be,' he replied. 'They're nice people.'

'They are.' Both my smile and my voice wobbled. 'Oh but we don't have to see *Dirty Dancing* if you don't want to. It's just that I couldn't get tickets for anything else.'

'It's not a problem. I've always wanted to see it.'

'I'm not that gullible.'

'Well done,' he said, before adding, 'I'll let you go and call your mother.'

'Yes, I suppose I'd better,' I said with a sigh. 'And I'm sorry, yet again, for putting you in such a difficult position.'

'It's fine. I'm taking comfort in that advanced truth,' he said. 'And I'll see you tomorrow.'

'OK,' I smiled. 'Bye.'

I hung up and sat for a moment or two, staring into space and replaying the conversation with Felix in my head. And then, uncertain whether it was the wine or Felix that had made me feel better, I called my mother.

Chapter 16

Thanks to M5 roadworks, Felix was late; only by forty minutes, but it was long enough to leave me feeling panicked at the thought of my meticulously planned day going down the pan from the off.

The fact was that I felt I had screwed up with Felix far too many times already, and so this weekend, completely against type, I was determined to leave nothing to chance and play nothing by ear. With this in mind, I had booked us a table for lunch in Clifton at 1 p.m., following which we would walk across the suspension bridge and stroll around Ashton Court. We would then cross back over the bridge and pick up the open-top bus tour from Clifton village at 3.25 p.m. According to its online timetable, the circular tour would last approximately one hour, which would leave us just enough time to stop for a coffee and a snack on the way back to the flat, before changing and taking a taxi to the Colston Hall to meet my parents at six thirty. It was to be the kind of perfectly scheduled day so loved by Alistair, and it crossed my mind more than once how surprised and impressed he would have been to find me checking timetables and estimating eat times.

And my forward thinking wasn't restricted to physical activity only. My mission was to show Felix how genuinely interested I was in him, whilst at the same time not causing him any distress, or putting my foot in it regarding any aspects of his personal life – primarily his Gwyneth Paltrow ex. I had therefore drawn up a mental list of enquiries about his friends, family and work, and had determined to make no references to relationships of the romantic variety unless he himself raised the topic.

His late arrival, however, threatened to throw all my careful planning into disarray from the outset. So after buzzing him into the flat, grabbing his overnight case from him and flinging it into the spare room, I immediately pushed him back out of the front door and we headed on foot and at speed for Clifton, eventually arriving within ten minutes of our original booking.

'Oh my goodness,' I said, flopping down in a chair after being shown to our table by a waitress. I picked up a menu and fanned myself. 'I'm so unfit.'

I smiled up at Felix as he pulled out a chair and sat down. It was the first time I had really had a moment to examine him since his arrival, and I now took in the open-neck floral shirt, the blue cashmere sweater, which he casually threw over the back of his chair, and, of course, the body and complexion, which, in stark contrast to my own, showed absolutely no signs of even mild exertion after our dash to the restaurant. I stared at him, genuinely fascinated by his complete physical and sartorial trans-formation from the sloppy, rotund teenage friend I had regularly chased, and caught with ease, in order to retrieve the hat/book/cake which he had stolen from me.

'What?' he asked, picking up his own menu.

'Sorry?'

'You're staring,' he said. 'Have I cut myself shaving?'

'Oh, no.' I stopped fanning my menu and instead turned it over to look at the lunch options. 'I was just thinking that you're obviously so much fitter than me.'

'These days.'

I looked up to find him smiling.

'Kate says I'm cellophane transparent,' I sighed.

'I wouldn't go that far,' he said. 'But my weight loss is clearly a fascination for you.'

'You're right and I'm sorry,' I said guiltily. 'It's so shallow, isn't it? I'm trying not to think about it, but comparisons with the old you keep popping into my head.'

'It's OK,' he said. 'I've had seven or eight years to get used to it, but the photographs of the Pillsbury Doughboy dotted around my parents' house still sometimes take me by surprise. Besides, I can't throw stones,' he added. 'I keep comparing you to the old Dot.'

'Do you?' I asked uncertainly, far from confident that any comparisons he might be drawing would be favourable.

He nodded. 'The old you wouldn't have been worried about being a little late for lunch. Or for anything else, in fact. I'm not sure I can remember you ever being on time. The movie had always started, the bus had always left…'

I picked up my napkin and, unfolding it, placed it on my lap. 'That must have worn pretty thin,' I said, more to myself than to him, my shoulders sinking as I pictured Alistair tapping his watch whenever I was running late. 'Really thin, actually.'

Felix meanwhile was now studying the menu. 'I never minded,' he said absently. 'It was just a quirk to be factored in.'

I smiled, touched by his throwaway acceptance. 'Well, thank you for all those years of tolerance.'

He looked up. 'And thank *you* for all those years of funding my pastry habit whenever I ran out of cash.'

'Is that gratitude or blame?'

'Maybe a bit of both,' he said, twisting in his chair to look over his shoulder at the specials board. 'The two often go hand in hand, I think.'

'Yes.' I nodded and wondered what he might consider the overall blame: gratitude ratio of his relationship with me to be. Despite now feeling more relaxed in his company, I was still pretty sure the odds weren't hugely stacked in my favour.

I looked across the table at him as he sat with his back now to me, his thick dark hair neatly cut to the edge of a curl, and thought again about the genial, wild-haired boy who had never once expressed impatience or told me to hurry up.

He turned around suddenly, causing me to start slightly. 'If you're wondering about my hair, I had it cut short in 2003,' he said. 'The Louis XIV dragged-through-a-hedge-backwards look didn't sit well on a trainee accountant.'

'It hadn't even registered with me that your hair was shorter,' I said casually.

'Of course it hadn't.'

'But now that you mention it, I always thought your look was more Brian May than Sun King.'

He nodded thoughtfully. 'I can't deny it was a bleak day when Tony the barber talked me into having a fringe.'

'Oh my goodness, yes!' I exclaimed. 'And he cut quite a bit off the back too, didn't he? And then you were worried that you looked like Deidre from *Coronation Street*!'

'As I remember it, I was worried that I looked like Deidre from *Coronation Street* after you told me that I looked like Deidre from *Coronation Street*,' he said drily.

'Yes, but only when you put on those big purple joke glasses.'

'Which you bought for me.'

'So I did!' I laughed. 'But don't worry, your fringe was nowhere near as bleak as my Sporty Spice phase.'

'My fringe was way bleaker,' he said, shaking his head. 'More on a par with your Björk obsession.'

'The bindi eyebrows!' I gasped. 'I loved them but they kept falling into my food. Remember when I choked on that pasta at your house and then coughed up three of the things into a piece of kitchen roll?'

He nodded slowly. 'Yes, I do remember that. It was one of the few times I felt unable to finish a meal. Anyway, how about we just call my ill-judged fringe and your lethal eyebrows a very bleak draw?'

'Yes, let's,' I replied, looking down at the menu, 'particularly as I am now starving. Do you know what you'd like?'

'Well, I had been considering the pasta. But strangely enough, I've suddenly gone off that idea,' he murmured, looking once again at the menu. 'So I'll have the chicken.'

'That does look good. I'll have the same,' I said, hurriedly replacing the menu on the table and turning in my chair to look for our waiter. 'And actually we'd better get a move on and order, because we've got a bus to catch.'

–

Post lunch, the day went beautifully to plan. We completed our walk, didn't miss the bus and there was just enough time for a leisurely ciabatta, and for me to execute a quick change from jeans to floral frock, before we set off for the Colston Hall.

Conversationally things had gone well too, and I congratulated myself on being interested, but not intrusive, with my line of questioning as we talked about our respective routes to self-employment, agreeing that nothing had been more important to our professional happiness and success than being blessed with excellent business partners. And, reading between the lines, it seemed to me that Kevin was as significant a personal support to Felix as Kate was to me.

When it came to significant relationships *outside* work, I referred to Alistair obliquely a couple of times in connection with house-hunting and holiday destinations, but he never became a topic in his own right. And as for Gwyneth, well she never so much as raised her beautiful blonde head, obliquely or otherwise.

All in all, I felt the day was proving a success. I found myself genuinely enjoying Felix's company and dared to believe, from his relaxed body language and frequent laughter, that he was enjoying mine too. In fact, it was only as I clambered out of the taxi at the rear of the Colston Hall and Felix paid the fare, that my first real nerves of the day began to kick in.

I checked my watch, and after a slight dip in spirits upon discovering that we were running early and that it was only six twenty, I tried to calm myself by focusing on the fact that we would realistically still have just forty minutes at most with my parents. And so long as I could keep Mum chatting about Becca's wedding, or what she had planned for the rest of the weekend, we would, I told myself, be fine.

I followed Felix as he trotted down the steps a little way ahead of me, holding open the large glass door. And I was both relieved and a little envious to see no sign of anxiety on his face whatsoever.

'It's downstairs, isn't it?' he asked as we went inside.

I nodded, smiling as brightly as I could.

'It'll be fine,' he said reassuringly.

'I hope so,' I replied as we made our way towards the stairs. 'I still feel bad for making you do this.'

'For making me have a pre-show drink?' he asked, looking surprised. 'Hate to break it to you, but I was always going to need one of those. Obviously, I'm a huge fan of men in tight trousers and frenzied female audiences, but still...'

I sighed. 'Well the way I feel right now, I think I should have had a pre-pre-show-drink drink.'

He smiled and was about to reply but was cut short by my mother's highly delighted and very loud 'Hello, darlings!' as she caught sight of us from the far side of the bar, where she was standing with Dad. 'There they are, Don!' she exclaimed, waving frantically. 'Oh my goodness, we thought you'd never get here, Dorothy. Wherever have you been?' she added, extending her arms towards me as we reached them.

'We're actually five minutes early, Mum,' I said, as she squeezed me like an orange in a juicer.

'I did tell her that,' said Dad as she released me and he leaned in for a kiss on the cheek. 'But she wouldn't have it. You know how she operates to her own clock.'

He turned to Felix and held out his hand. 'There's Green-wich Mean Time, British Summer Time and Helen Riley Time. Good to see you again, Felix.'

'And you,' said Felix, smiling and shaking his hand.

'Oh Felix, let me look at you,' said my mother, taking a step back and gazing at him admiringly. 'Doesn't he look even more handsome than at the wedding, Don?'

My father sighed. 'I'm sure Felix doesn't need me reas-suring him regarding his attractiveness, Helen. What can I get you to drink, Felix?'

But Mum was already in full flow. 'You see, it takes a certain kind of masculinity to carry off a floral shirt, doesn't it, Dottie? I'd get your father one, but people would think he was wearing one of my blouses.'

'Thank you,' said Dad.

'But Felix here wears it beautifully,' concluded Mum.

'It's my escape-from-the-office shirt,' said Felix.

'Well I'm sure you look just as wonderful in your plain work shirts,' said my mother. 'You know, you always were such a lovely little boy and teenager, it's no wonder to me at all that you have grown into such a lovely young man.' She looked up at him, her eyes shining, and gave him a hug. 'Thank you for looking after our Dottie then and now,' she said, clinging to him. 'I'll never forget when you brought her safely home to us after that wild evening in The Lamb.'

'When on earth was that?' I frowned and turned to Dad, but he just rolled his eyes and shrugged.

Felix meanwhile, didn't query the reference but simply hugged her back, whilst I looked on, experiencing a whole new category of guilt; one associated with finally presenting my mother with a boyfriend whom she obviously adored, only for him to be both fleeting and fake. If only she wasn't so fond of him. Why couldn't her lip curl, as it had over Sean Dowse's tattoo? Why couldn't she display the wary reserve she had always exhibited in Alistair's company? But no, there was not a hint of disapproval or discomfort when it came to Felix. Just my luck.

How these musings played out on my face I don't know, but while Mum and Felix sat down at a nearby table, Dad tapped my arm and beckoned me to come and stand next to him at the bar.

'I know your mum is a little bit overenthusiastic with him,' he whispered, 'but she just likes him. We both do,' he added.

I nodded. 'I know. It's not that.'

He smiled. 'You don't have to explain. I understand that her approval can be just as tricky to take as her disapproval, but it's different with Felix. The whole family has history with him.' He looked over at my mother, whose hand was now on Felix's arm as she asked him about our day so far. I took a deep breath and also some comfort in what Dad had said. He was right: Mum's relationship with Felix wasn't all about me. I had no doubt she would be disappointed to discover that he and I weren't heading for a happily-ever-after, but she could continue to dote on him as my friend. And the same would go for Nanny Flo.

I looked at Dad. 'It's fine. But I just don't want her getting her hopes up too high,' I said quietly.

'Don't worry,' he said. 'She can keep being wildly romantic and I'll keep pouring cold water on her hopes and dreams. It's a relationship that's worked for almost forty years.'

I tutted but laughed nevertheless.

'What are you two whispering and giggling about over there?' asked my mother, smiling at us affectionately. 'They're such devils, Felix. Always plotting. But oh my goodness, we haven't asked you what you would like to drink.'

Felix stood up. 'Let me get them,' he said.

'No, no,' said Dad, gesturing for him to sit down. 'Thank you, Felix, but you're here at our invitation and I'm at the bar. Now, what can I get you?'

'Just a beer would be great, thanks,' he said, sitting back down. 'I'll let you choose.'

'Brave man. And what about you, Helen?' asked Dad.

'Well, *obviously* I would like a glass of something fizzy to celebrate being here with my wonderful daughter and her lovely boyfriend,' beamed Mum.

'Right you are,' said Dad, turning back to the bar and leaning towards me. 'Quick, Dottie, dial 999 and ask for the fire brigade,' he muttered out of the corner of his mouth. 'I'm going to need a steady supply of cold water this evening.'

Chapter 17

'So,' I said to Felix, as we slowly made our way down the staircase from the Grand Circle to the foyer, along with the rest of the Hippodrome's predominantly female Saturday-night audience, 'what was your favourite bit?'

'Other than when Wendy from Westbury Park offered me one of her Revels after I helped her to pick them up off the floor, you mean?' he asked. 'It's impossible to pick just one moment. It was all so great.'

I smiled up at him. 'Well it's over now. And you can come home and recover with a beer, or a cup of tea.'

'No recovery required,' he said, as we finally exited the theatre and joined the growing throng on the pavement outside. 'I had a great time. And, *of course*, the lift was my favourite bit.'

'Is the right answer!' I laughed. 'How about we get a taxi?'

'Dot?'

I turned at the sound of my name to see Alistair, his hand raised, weaving his way towards us through the crowd.

'Oh, hi!' I smiled, surprised but not unhappy to see him. 'Fancy seeing you here. We're just getting a taxi back to my flat. We could drop you off on the way, if you're heading home.'

'Thanks, but we're going for drinks.'

It was only as he said 'we' and negotiated his way past the final small gaggle of women standing between us that I realised he wasn't alone. Holding his hand was a slim, petite, dark-haired woman of around my age. My immediate thought, which was not an uplifting one, was that Alistair's new girlfriend was much prettier in person than in the single photo I had seen of her. I looked down at her. She couldn't have been much more than five feet tall, and at five-seven I towered over her.

'Hi, Alistair,' said Felix. 'How are you?'

Alistair smiled. 'Great, thanks. Naomi, this is Felix and Dorothy.' At the mention of my name, Naomi blinked slightly, but her smile remained in place.

'Felix and Dorothy? Hi there. Great to meet you. Are you two having a good evening?' she asked, in a high-pitched but soft southern Irish accent, her voice light and lilting.

I nodded dumbly, reluctant to speak, convinced that I would sound like Brian Blessed by comparison.

She looked up at me expectantly, clearly awaiting a verbal response.

I continued to nod.

'Well that's… grand,' she said, a little uncertainly, turning to look up at Alistair.

I felt Felix's elbow knock against mine as he put his hands in his pockets. I wasn't sure if it was deliberate or accidental, but either way it served as a prompt to pull myself together.

'Did you enjoy the show?' I asked Naomi, bending slightly and nodding my head towards the entrance to the theatre.

She put a hand to her cheek and burst out laughing in a way which brought to mind several generations of Disney princesses. 'Oh my goodness, we haven't been to see *that*!' she exclaimed, moving her hand to my arm as her expression transformed into one of mock horror. 'But thank you for not looking appalled when you asked. Ooh, but I guess I should keep my voice down,' she added, glancing guiltily over her shoulder at the group of women next to us. She turned back and leaned conspiratorially towards me. 'Personally, I can't think of anything worse, can you, Dorothy?' she asked breathily.

'Yes, I'm not sure exactly how insulted to be by your assumption that we would pay to see that, Dot,' added Alistair, now also laughing. 'We've actually just had dinner around the corner. What about you two?'

I looked up at him and considered my lose-lose options. Either I could lie about where we'd been, thus saving face but also making it obvious to Felix just how needy and pitifully desperate for approval I still was when it came to my ex. Or I could tell the truth, thereby not only creating a tricky social situation but also ensuring that I would be judged culturally undiscerning.

I took a deep breath.

'We've been to see *Dirty Dancing*,' I said with a shrug.

Naomi's smile froze and Alistair's eyes widened slightly, which I knew was indicative of mild panic, before he suddenly relaxed. 'You're joking,' he said, a slow smile spreading across his face.

I shook my head, and as his smile fell away, I imagined the word AWKWARD flashing above us in neon-blue, foot-high capitals.

'What Dot *isn't* telling you,' said Felix, smiling at Naomi, 'is that I bought the tickets as a surprise. I just had it in my head that it was a show every woman wanted to see. But don't worry,' he added, nudging me, 'I've got the message and will stick to Bernard Shaw and Brecht in future.'

Naomi looked relieved. 'Oh, but it's always a nice treat to go to the theatre, whatever you see, isn't it, Dorothy?'

'I really enjoyed *Dirty Dancing*, actually,' I said.

'She's so tactful, isn't she, Felix?' smiled Alistair, his tone affectionate, as if he was discussing the merits of a previously owned, much-loved car. I felt a sudden urge to be gone.

Naomi too now appeared keen to end the encounter. 'We should really let these lovely people get home, Alistair,' she said, tugging meekly at his sleeve like a very glamorous house elf and nodding at the taxi rank.

Alistair looked down at her as if confused for a moment before turning towards the dwindling number of taxis lining the edge of the road. 'Oh yes, I guess you'd better get one before they're all gone.'

'Come on then, Dot,' said Felix, placing a hand on my back and applying gentle pressure, easing me towards the taxi rank. 'Enjoy the rest of your evening, you two.'

'Thanks,' they said simultaneously, and, waving goodbye, they headed off in the direction of Harbourside.

Felix and I walked the few paces to the first available cab and, having given the driver my address, climbed inside. I leaned back into the seat and Felix wordlessly buckled himself in next to me as the cab pulled away. I gazed into the brightly lit foyer of the Colston Hall as we passed by, miserably fascinated by the way in which all my meticulous perfect-day planning had been scuppered by a single chance encounter. I had thought the rendezvous with my parents was going to be the most stressful part of my time with Felix, but in fact that had turned out to be an absolute breeze in comparison to the two minutes thirty seconds spent with my ex-partner and his cute Polly Pocket girlfriend. My heart sank at the thought and I wished I didn't care, but I did.

'All good?' asked Felix.

I turned to him and smiled. 'Sure,' I said. I wanted to add something light-hearted about bumping into Alistair, but didn't trust myself. And besides, the fact that Felix had assumed responsibility for the ticket purchase meant he had read both me and the situation perfectly. My mood sank a little further at the thought of his insightfulness, and I turned back towards the window. 'I really enjoyed the theatre,' I said, attempting positivity.

'So did I,' he said.

I nodded, believing him to be sincere, but at the same time unable to shake a rather ominous feeling that things were starting to unravel. And little did I know, as we headed back to my flat in somewhat subdued silence on my part, that the unexpected appearance of Alistair and Naomi was only the beginning of the eleventh hour disintegration of our day.

Chapter 18

I turned the key in the lock, leaned against the slightly stiff front door to open it and walked into the hallway of my flat, holding the door for Felix as he followed me inside.

'Oh look at that,' I tutted, pointing to a glow from the living room. 'I left the lamps on again.'

We walked into the living room and through into the kitchen. 'And the spotlights are on in here too,' I said despairingly.

'Have they been on since last night?' asked Felix. 'We didn't switch them on before we left, did we? It was still light.'

'God, you're right. My environmental footprint must be the size of an elephant's by now.' I opened the fridge door and scanned the contents. 'OK, so there's beer, white wine open, red wine in the rack, or,' I stood up, 'a cup of tea or coffee.'

'It's way too late for caffeine,' he said.

'Yay!' I said, grabbing the bottle of white. 'Now I don't feel so guilty about having a glass of this. 'Ooh, unless,' I said, turning to him questioningly, 'you meant you wanted a peppermint tea, or to hit the sack.'

'A beer would be great,' he smiled.

'Coming up,' I said, reaching into the fridge a second time, taking out a beer and handing it to him. 'Bottle opener is in the drawer behind you. Next to the sink.'

I poured myself a glass of wine while he opened his beer, and then we headed back into the living room, me flopping down onto the sofa and Felix settling himself into the blue armchair.

'It swivels,' I said.

'And why wouldn't it?' he smiled, raising his bottle. 'Cheers.'

I lifted my glass, wondering what to say next. Instinctively, I wanted to talk about Alistair, but the part of me which had worked so very hard to keep the day on track held me back. A conversation about my ex might well be cathartic for me, but it was hardly going to be a barrel of laughs for Felix, and this weekend was supposed to be a thank-you to him, I reminded myself.

'Do you think—' began Felix suddenly. But that was as far as he got before we heard the cough.

It was undoubtedly male and undoubtedly in the flat. We both sat up sharply.

Felix looked over his shoulder and then back at me.

'Did that come from the bedroom?' he asked quietly, calmly putting his beer down on the coffee table and standing up.

I nodded anxiously and stood up too. 'The spare room, I think,' I confirmed breathlessly, my hand shaking as I put down my glass.

'You stay here,' he said. 'And call the police,' he added, turning towards the door into the hallway.

I reached out and took hold of his arm. 'Felix, don't,' I whispered. 'Let's just go outside and wait for the police.'

He shook his head. 'You're on the ground floor. He could be long gone with all your stuff by then.'

'I don't care,' I said. 'Please don't go in there.'

'It's fine,' he reassured. 'It'll be an opportunist who just needs scaring off. But you still need to call the police.' And with that he walked out into the hallway.

Dashing into the kitchen, I grabbed my bag before hurrying after him, reaching him just as he leaned forward and pressed his ear against the spare room door. I tapped his shoulder, causing him to whirl round and then roll his eyes when he realised it was me.

'Take this. It's really heavy,' I whispered, handing him my Le Creuset griddle pan.

He looked down at the pan and then at his hand which was now covered in something brown and sticky.

'It was in the sink,' I added apologetically. 'I did sausages in it and they had apple in them.'

He heaved a sigh, then whispered, 'Police?' before pressing his ear to the door once again.

I nodded vigorously, fishing my phone from my bag and then swearing under my breath as I realised that I had switched it off in the theatre. But within a few seconds it was back on, and I was just about to dial 999 when Felix placed his hand across the screen.

I looked up to find him frowning and pointing with the griddle pan at his overnight bag, which, instead of being in the spare room where I had left it, was now at the far end of the hallway, outside my bedroom door. His blue jumper, which he had decided against taking to the theatre, had been placed on a hanger and hung up behind the bag on the handle of the door.

I was just wondering what kind of OCD burglar worried about creasing the jumper which he was about to steal, when two things happened in quick succession. Firstly, my phone began to bark and ping loudly and repeatedly, indicating the arrival of at least half a dozen texts and voicemail messages, all from my mother; and then immediately after that, I heard Mum's voice – her actual voice, not a recorded version – calling out to me from the spare room.

'Is that you, Dottie?'

Felix looked at me, his expression one of extreme surprise tinged, I thought, with a slight weariness. He took a step back from the bedroom door.

I opened my mouth to say something, but realising that I had nothing helpful or enlightening to contribute, I remained silent and instead closed my eyes, in the vague hope that when I opened them I would find myself in a less confusing time and place.

'Dottie?' My mother sounded anxious and I felt Felix pat my shoulder, as if in commiseration, as he brushed past me. I opened my eyes and turned my head in time to see him disappearing into the lounge.

'*Dorothy?*'

Feeling a little dazed, I opened the bedroom door to discover my mother sitting up in bed, wearing a pale green nightdress, her Kindle on her lap and her glasses perched on the end of her nose. 'Oh it *is* you,' she breathed, putting a relieved hand to her chest. 'Do you know, for a moment I thought you were being burgled. I tried to wake your father, but he's out for the count. He's starting with one of his chests and has taken a Night Nurse – on top of that beer at the Colston Hall,' she added, as Dad coughed loudly in his sleep and rolled over. She smiled and patted his arm, but her face quickly fell as she looked up at me. 'Why, whatever is the matter, Dot?' she asked, removing her glasses. 'You look as if you're in shock.'

'Do I?' I said distractedly, my brain scrambling for any facts which might make sense of the current situation. 'I suppose I am a bit.'

'Oh darling, what's happened?' she asked, patting the bed. 'Come here and tell me all about it. You haven't fallen out with Felix, have you?'

'What?' I screwed my face up in genuine confusion. 'No, Mum. I'm shocked because you and Dad are in my spare room.'

She blinked and looked slightly affronted. 'Well I phoned you several times and sent you three text messages, and your father watched the whole time to make sure I pressed all the right buttons.'

I looked down wearily at the phone in my hand. 'I switched it off during the show.'

'Oh well then,' she said briskly. 'That explains that then, doesn't it?'

'Not really, no. Because as I didn't get your messages until approximately one minute ago, I still don't know why you're here.'

She smiled mischievously. 'You'll laugh when I tell you.'

'Doubtful,' I murmured.

'You know how Uncle Geoffrey was re-boarding his loft?'

'No.'

'You do. I told you about it last week. I told you how he'd got a good deal on the timber at Wickes.'

I put a hand to my forehead. 'OK.'

'Well he was up there at teatime today, hammering away, and…' she paused and began to chuckle, 'he was just about to put the last few boards down when he…' She paused again and shook her head, still laughing. 'I'm so sorry, Dottie, but it really is very funny. You see, he stumbled over his toolbox, fell very heavily and crashed through the only bit of floor he hadn't boarded. He went straight through into the bedroom below. Auntie Dawn's brand-new Egyptian cotton quilt cover and pillowcases, the ones she went on and on about at the wedding, were completely ruined. Can you just imagine the scene?' she added delightedly.

'Yes,' I said, absolutely appalled, 'I can actually and it's not funny at all. Poor Uncle Geoffrey.'

She waved a hand dismissively. 'Oh, he's perfectly fine. He fell onto the double bed and only one little bit of plasterboard and a box of nails fell on top of him. He FaceTimed us an hour ago and he's got a tiny cut above his left eyebrow and that's it.' She giggled and dabbed at her eyes with the edge of the quilt cover. 'Daddy and I were in stitches, but, of course,' she continued, her smile suddenly fading, 'the sad thing is that we can't stay with them this evening.'

'That and the fact that Uncle Geoffrey could have broken his neck and he and Auntie Dawn have a huge hole in their bedroom ceiling,' I pointed out.

'Oh, it's only the guest room, darling. Why on earth are you being so sombre about it? That's not like you. Remember how you laughed when Daddy fell off the stepladder and into the pond when he was pruning the rowan last year?'

'That was quite funny,' I admitted grudgingly.

'There you go!' she said brightly. 'Think of this as being just the same, except without the water and the gnomes.'

'OK, I'll try,' I nodded, opting for exhausted acceptance. 'And I suppose I'd better let you get to sleep and explain to Felix...' My voice cracked at the thought and I cleared my throat. 'And explain to Felix what has happened.'

'Yes. And do assure him that we're heading off to Avebury bright and early tomorrow, so we won't spoil your morning. I know!' she said, clapping her hands. 'How about I bring the pair of you some breakfast in bed, as a thank-you for having us?'

'No!' I exclaimed.

'Eggs Benedict. Your favourite,' she beamed. 'Dad can pop out and get anything you haven't got.'

'No, really, Mum, don't. You mustn't,' I added emphatically.

She blinked. 'Why ever not?'

I hesitated before deciding to apply my favoured fighting-fires approach to the situation. 'Felix is allergic to eggs.'

She put a hand to her mouth. 'Oh, how sad. Is that a recent allergy?'

I nodded. 'Yes. Very recent.'

'I'll just bring him the buttered muffins and tea then.'

'And he's gluten intolerant.'

'So just the tea.'

'He doesn't drink tea. Or coffee,' I added quickly, as she raised a hopeful hand. 'And he's dairy and citrus intolerant too. So don't worry, he'll get anything he needs for himself. He never likes to be a bother.'

My mother frowned and put a thoughtful finger to her lips. 'But I thought I saw him eating cheese and biscuits at the wedding...'

'Must have been gluten free,' I said, backing out of the room and starting to close the door. 'And dairy free.'

'But there was a cream sauce on the chicken. You should have told us.'

'It was fine. He scraped it off.'

'But didn't he drink beer this evening? Can you drink beer if you have coeliac disease? I thought hops—'

'I'd really better be getting to bed, Mum.'

'But my goodness, Dottie. The poor boy. All those allergies. I expect that's why he's so slim these days.'

'Yes, it is. Good night.'

I clicked the door shut and then leaned my forehead against it while taking several deep breaths. After a moment, clueless as to what I was going to say to Felix, I miserably made my way back to the living room.

When I got there, I saw that he was once again seated in the swivel armchair, his back to me. And for one horrible moment, I experienced a flashback to the evening of Becca's wedding day, when I had discovered him sitting alone in the lounge.

I hesitated in the doorway, paralysed by the memory of that traumatic encounter, before eventually, like a badly miscast Bond villain, Felix swivelled slowly around to face me and offered me his second eye roll of the evening.

Managing at last to move, I stepped into the living room, closed the door quietly behind myself, and then went and sat back down on the sofa, reaching for the glass of wine I had placed on the table in such panic ten or so minutes earlier.

'My parents,' I began in a monotone while staring straight ahead of me, 'are here because—'

'Because Uncle Geoffrey has ruined the Egyptian cotton quilt cover,' interrupted Felix.

I turned my head and gazed at him impassively, lacking the energy for facial expression.

'I heard,' he said, leaning forward and picking up his beer.

'Right,' I said.

'I also heard that I'm basically allergic to life.'

I continued to look at him but said nothing.

'In fact, I should probably be living in a bubble,' he said. 'And by the sound of it, I'm looking at nothing but cooled boiled water for breakfast tomorrow.' He paused and took a sip of his beer. 'In a sterilised beaker.'

I transferred my gaze from him to my wine glass and heaved a sigh. 'I would say sorry,' I began quietly, feeling troublingly close to tears, 'but I'm afraid that word is becoming overused in our relationship. And always by me. So overused that you probably feel it doesn't really mean anything. I keep saying I'm going to sort things out and then I don't and you keep being put in awkward situations because I'm either too lazy, too stupid or too cowardly to fix things. I should have told Mum in the hospital, when Nanny Flo was ill, that I didn't really have a boyfriend – but I didn't. And after that, I had weeks to tell the truth – but I didn't. Kate told me to stop fannying around after Becca's wedding and set the record straight, but – ooh, what a surprise,' I laughed while actually still wanting to cry, 'I didn't.'

I looked up to find Felix staring at me and looking almost as miserable as I felt. I took two large gulps of my drink and then replaced my near-empty glass on the table. 'I'm going to sort it out,' I said, standing up.

'What? Wait. How?' asked Felix, looking shocked.

'I'm not going to fanny around any longer.'

'What does that mean?'

'It means that I'm going to tell them that we are not going out together and that we never were and that's why I'll be sleeping on the sofa in here tonight.'

'Hang on,' he said, leaning forward and gently pulling on my arm so that I sat back down. 'Don't make a panic-based decision you'll regret.'

'I'm not panicked,' I replied. 'I'm perfectly calm.'

'You're not calm,' he said, shaking his head. 'You're stunned. You're confusing serene with concussed.'

'It doesn't matter. I can't let this go on any longer, Felix. It's completely unfair to you.'

'I don't think you should tell them tonight.'

'That's very selfless of you, but you've done enough and put up with enough already.'

He shook his head. 'I'm not being noble,' he said. 'I just don't want to be here when you tell them. And in particular when you tell your mother. Ideally I'd like to be in a different country and time zone, with my mobile phone switched off. I certainly don't want to be sitting less than thirty feet away.' He shrugged. 'Not a hint of selflessness about it.'

I leaned back on the sofa and covered my face with my hands. 'I just don't know what to do.'

'How about not thinking too far ahead? You're good at that.'

I lowered my hands to find him smiling.

'That was a compliment,' he added.

I tried to smile. 'But we'd have to share a room,' I said.

'You haven't got a waterbed, have you?'

I shook my head.

'Then I'm OK with sharing a room,' He sighed and then standing up, beer in hand he picked up my wine glass from the table. 'Why don't you go and clean your teeth and I'll take these into the kitchen. And I can wash that griddle pan while I'm at it.'

Chapter 19

I cleansed, moisturised, and brushed my teeth on autopilot before vacating the bathroom for Felix and wandering, in something of a daze, down the hallway, only vaguely aware of the sound of my father snoring as I made my way to my bedroom. And I might have been able to maintain this relatively comfortable, zombie-like state into sleep had not opening my bedroom door and switching on the light had the same effect as a violent shake and a good slap.

The problem was that I had so exclusively focused my available time and energy on ensuring that the spare room, and all other parts of the flat in which Felix might set foot, were immaculate, that my own room had been completely ignored. And as I gazed around it now, I felt my mood changing from numbed despair to the panicked variety.

The top of my long chest of drawers was strewn with jewellery, a consequence of a last-minute, and ultimately fruitless, search for a specific bracelet and pair of earrings to wear to the theatre. The surface of the, unmade, bed was similarly littered, but this time with clothes, a lack of forward thinking having resulted in me removing a dozen or so dress/shirt/skirt options from the wardrobe before discounting and discarding them in turn. The dress which I had worn on Friday to work and the top and jeans that I had worn for most of Saturday meanwhile lay in a heap on the floor, along with some stray items of underwear and the contents of a basket of cardigans through which I had rifled just before heading off to meet Mum and Dad. And all of this recently created chaos was merely additional to the everyday level of clutter, including books, screens, make-up, sketchpads, brushes, pencils and pens, which habitually littered my bed, bedside tables and armchair.

After a moment of horrified, cartoon-like immobility, spent with my mouth hanging ajar and both hands in my hair, I pulled myself together and opened my wardrobe, scooping up and pushing all stray items of clothing inside, before leaning hard against the heavy wooden doors to jam them shut. I then opened the largest top drawer of my chest of drawers and, with a single sweep of my right arm, cascaded all the jewellery into it. Finally, I piled all remaining items of clutter into my large oak blanket box, a hand-me-down from Nanny Flo, and, congratulating myself on the fastest tidy-up in history, climbed into bed – before immediately climbing out again after realising that I was still fully clothed.

Hearing the loo flush, and aware that Felix could make an appearance at any moment, I rushed back to the chest of drawers in search of pyjamas and groaned upon seeing my nightwear buried under the newly created, sparkling slagheap of jewellery. Beginning to dig, I had just managed to excavate a modest floral pyjama top, and was unhooking multiple earrings and necklaces from it, when Felix tapped lightly on the door.

I hurried over. 'Just give me two minutes to put on my pyjamas,' I whispered, holding the door ajar and peering out.

'No problem,' he said, invisible in the darkened hallway. 'I'll wait here.'

'Great.' I pushed the door to and crossed the room, grabbing a pair of pyjama bottoms from the chest of drawers and scattering jewellery as I did so. I then took off my dress and underwear, consigned both to the blanket box, put on my pyjamas and made my way back to the bedroom door. Once there, I switched off the light, whispered, 'OK, all clear,' and then, somewhat breathlessly, scrambled across to the far side of the bed, lying down and pulling the covers up under my chin.

I turned my head towards the door as I heard Felix step inside and close it quietly behind him.

'Er, it's pitch black,' he said.

'I've got blackout linings in my curtains,' I explained. 'My bedroom is east-facing, so they're great in the mornings.'

'Not so great for navigating my way around a room I've never been in before,' he murmured.

'Sorry. I didn't think of that. The bed is just to the left of you.'

'OK,' he said, a statement closely followed by a minor crash and several expletives.

'Ooh, but be careful because there's a small table next to it,' I said.

'Yes, I just found it,' he whispered tensely, 'with my knee.'

'Sorry.'

'It's fine.' He sighed audibly, sitting down on the edge of the bed and leaning forward, I assumed to examine his knee. Then he pulled back the quilt and climbed in. 'Good night,' he said, lying down.

'Night.'

I lay on my back, staring up into the darkness, feeling a mixture of both relief and regret that Felix had decided to go to sleep right away. I didn't have the heart for happy chit-chat about lunch, or the bus tour, or the show; besides, any attempt at cheeriness on my part would have been so obviously forced and insincere as to make it more depressing than uplifting. But at the same time, I hated that the day was ending on such a low. I had hoped that this weekend would mark the rekindling of our friendship. Now I was pretty sure it would be its death knell.

I turned my head as I felt him roll over to face me, and through the darkness could just about make out the outline of his almost-curls and the firm jawline which had, years before, been hidden under a layer of podge which wobbled whenever he laughed. I smiled sadly as I continued to examine his silhouette, wondering if this would be the last time he and I would meet. The thought brought with it an unexpectedly sentimental urge to touch the friend to whom I might never be close again.

His breathing now slow and indicative of sleep, I turned my body towards him, lifting my hand from under the covers and moving it tentatively towards his arm. He shifted slightly in his sleep and then let out a sudden yell.

'I wasn't doing anything! I didn't touch you!' I exclaimed, quickly pulling away my hand.

'God,' he said. 'Something bit me.'

'Bit you?' I asked, sitting up. 'Are you sure?'

'Yes. Or stung me.'

I reached to my left and switched on the lamp. Felix, flushed and frowning, was sitting up with his right hand clasped over his left shoulder. I looked at him with concern, whilst at the same time trying not to notice how his twisted position, in conjunction with his clearly top-quality, semi-fitted grey T-shirt, emphasised his arm and chest muscles.

'Do you think it was a wasp? Or a bee?' I asked, dragging my eyes away and looking around the room. 'I don't hear anything.'

'I don't know what it was, but it hurt,' he said, still clutching his shoulder.

'Oh, you're bleeding,' I gasped, noticing a very small but growing patch of blood on his top.

'I think there's something stuck in my shoulder,' he said, lifting up the sleeve of his T-shirt and then wincing as he removed the something and held it between his thumb and forefinger.

'What is it? Is it dead?' I asked, shrinking back in horror and pulling the quilt up to just below my eyes.

He looked at me. 'It's been dead for quite some time,' he said, holding his hand out towards me. 'Several million years, in fact – if that's a real diamond.'

I slowly lowered the quilt and stared at the bloodstained jewelled stud in the palm of his hand.

'It's cubic zirconia,' I said quietly, not taking my eyes off the earring.

'That somehow makes the pain less worthwhile.'

'I think maybe I brought it to bed attached to my pyjamas.'

'Of course.'

'The butterfly back is missing, so the stem must have gone right into you.'

'That explains the agony.'

'I was trying to find it to wear to the theatre. I couldn't see it anywhere.'

'Well, I'm so glad to have been able to help you with that.'

I lifted my eyes and looked at him, lost for words but shaking my head in an attempt to convey at least some of the regret and general sense of hopelessness I was at that moment experiencing, and to which this latest minor catastrophe had merely added.

He turned and placed the earring wordlessly on the bedside table.

'Do you need a plaster?' I asked.

'Maybe,' he said, examining his arm. 'Although my T-shirt does seem to be soaking up the blood quite nicely.'

'I'll get you one.' I got out of bed and retrieved my handbag from the armchair. 'I'm sure there's one in here. Yes, here you go.' I climbed back into bed and handed him the plaster.

'Thanks,' he said. 'But can you stick it on? It's in a bit of an awkward place.'

'Sure.' I took the plaster from him and, as he lifted his sleeve, I stuck it over the small puncture wound, which was now beginning to bruise. Then we slid back down under the covers and I reached out and switched off the lamp, feeling a tear escape and roll down my cheek as I did so.

There was silence for a moment before he spoke.

'Thanks for today,' he said, 'and for going to so much trouble. You'll have to come to Cheltenham so I can return the favour – minus the parents and the bleeding.'

I nodded, uncertain whether or not he could see me, but afraid to say anything in case words turned into blubs.

'I should have said that earlier,' he said.

In lieu of a reply, I reached out and patted his shoulder.

'Ow,' he said.

I laughed, punctuating the sound with a bubbly snort as a sob escaped me, and I was aware of Felix turning his head towards me. 'Are you OK?' he asked gently.

I shook my head, and then, keeping my sentences short and my voice as steady as possible, said, 'I wanted today to go well. I tried to plan. But then Alistair. And the burglar. And Mum. And my room was chaos. And you're bleeding. It's like a stress dream.'

I heard him sigh, but it was a moment or two before he spoke. 'Look, not knowing what was going to happen next was always the best bit about hanging out with you. Of course lunch and the bus tour were great, and I even enjoyed you interviewing me like you were filling out a census form. But the burglar, the griddle pan and the bedtime conversation with your mother were in a whole different league.'

I smiled and felt relieved that he couldn't see my tears.

'And as for the way you've paired a flowery pyjama top with red tartan bottoms… Round of applause for vintage Dot,' he said.

My tears increased and I became aware that I could no longer breathe through my nose. 'You know that I'm crying, don't you?' I managed eventually.

'I do,' he said solemnly.

'That's good,' I said nasally, sitting up and switching on the lamp for a second time, 'because I need a hanky.' I picked up my bag from beside the bed and took out a small packet of tissues, propping myself up on a pillow while I opened it.

Felix meanwhile repositioned his own pillows and sat up.

I extracted a hanky and blew my nose. 'I'll be OK in a moment,' I hiccoughed. 'I just have to let my nose clear.'

He nodded but didn't say anything.

'I'm sorry for being so emotional. I just don't feel very...' I hesitated, searching for the right word, 'very successful right now. Because if today is me trying hard and doing my best and it's still all going wrong, then...' Unable to continue, I shrugged and blew my nose again.

Felix shook his head. 'It's about perspective, and from where I'm standing, I can't agree that everything went wrong. I meant it when I said I enjoyed the day. *Especially* when you freestyled,' he added.

I turned to him, pointed at the bloodstain on his T-shirt and rolled my eyes.

'It's just a flesh wound,' he said dismissively. 'The scarring will be minimal, and provided sepsis doesn't set in, everything will be fine.'

I smiled tearfully but gratefully and leaned my head against his shoulder.

'Ow,' he said, but I didn't move. Instead, I unfolded a second hanky and blew my nose for a third time, before resting my hands, and my two damp screwed-up tissues, on my lap and taking a deep breath.

'The Alistair bit was hard,' I said quietly.

'I know.'

I lifted my head and looked up at his profile as he stared impassively at the blackout curtains. After a moment, he turned his head towards me, offering me a rueful smile and a slight shrug. 'I can relate.'

'Yes.' I returned my head to his shoulder.

'Ow.'

'Hey, I know what I meant to ask you.'

'What?'

'Did you know what my mother was talking about when she mentioned a wild night at The Lamb?'

'Yes,' he said, sounding surprised. 'Didn't you?'

I looked up at him and shook my head. 'Not a clue. And neither did Dad.'

Felix smiled. 'She mustn't have told him.'

'Told him what?' I asked, intrigued to learn that Mum and Felix apparently shared a secret.

'It was the night before I left for university,' he said, looking at me and frowning. 'You don't remember any of it, do you?'

'Of course I do,' I said, tutting. 'We went to The Lamb with… Ian Watson and Chris Fry. Or did they just turn up?' I closed my eyes as I tried to remember the details. 'God, I didn't snog one of them, did I?' I asked, putting a hand to my mouth.

I opened my eyes to find Felix looking at me expressionlessly.

'Did I?' I asked again.

He shrugged. 'If you did, it must have been very quick and I didn't see it happen. Besides, I thought you and tattoo boy were exclusive.'

I laughed. 'We were. But I wasn't going out with him by then, was I?'

'It was hard to keep track.'

'Excuse me,' I said sternly, 'but I had just one more relationship in school than you did, Felix Davis. Making a grand total of one.'

'I was just biding my time,' he said.

'Saving yourself.'

He smiled. 'Something like that. Anyway, no, you didn't snog Chris or Ian that night – so far as I am aware.'

'Must have dreamt it,' I said. 'But I still don't know why my mother thinks the evening was a wild one.'

'You don't remember how you got home?' he asked.

'Didn't we walk together as usual?'

'*I* walked. *You*,' he raised his eyebrows disapprovingly, 'were incapable of walking.'

'Oh dear.' I pulled a face.

'And we didn't have any money for a taxi.'

'So…?'

'So I carried you across the road to Safeway…'

'Yes?'

'…popped you in a trolley…'

'You didn't!'

'… and pushed you home.'

'Half a mile in a trolley?' I laughed.

'In a trolley,' he grinned. 'And your mother was, quite rightly, appalled at you and very grateful to me. I even got a thank-you card.'

I laughed again. 'Oh Felix, why didn't you tell me?'

He looked thoughtful. 'I can't remember. I suppose it was just a very busy time. I left home the next day and you went the day after that, didn't you?'

'I did.' I smiled up at him. 'Funny times.'

He nodded. 'They were.'

'I'm really surprised that Mum didn't have a go at me about it.'

'Two days before you left home?' he said. 'She wouldn't have wanted to spoil things.'

'You're right,' I said, feeling guilty. 'She loves Becca and me to bits.'

I sat for a moment, smiling as I imagined my mother's expression when presented with me unconscious in a shopping trolley, before suddenly recalling that for the first time in just over a year I was not actually alone in bed and that Felix would probably quite like to go to sleep.

'Sorry,' I said. 'My nose is clear now and I'm keeping you awake. I'll turn off the light. Oh, and don't worry,' I added, reaching towards the lamp, 'I'll smuggle in a choccy croissant for you tomorrow morning.'

'Too kind,' he said, lying down. 'I'll try not to get crumbs in the bed.'

'Great.'

I lay down too and closed my eyes. But although exhausted, and now in possession of a much-improved perspective, I still felt that the air between us wasn't completely clear. After five minutes of indecision, and still nowhere nearer sleep, I rolled over and squeezed his arm.

'Felix?' I whispered.

'Ow and yes?'

'Are you asleep?'

'Guess.'

'I never got your letters.'

'My letters?' he asked, turning his head towards me.

'At Becca's wedding you said I'd ignored your letters.'

He didn't reply, and I stared into the darkness, trying and failing to see his expression.

'I wrote to you a couple of times after university, that's all,' he said after a moment. 'It's not a big deal. I mentioned the letters because I'd just had a crap text from my ex and you suddenly became another woman making me feel like

I wasn't trying hard enough. I lost my temper with you because you happened to be the woman in the room, not the one on the end of the phone. It wasn't fair to you and I'm sorry. I thought I'd apologised at the reception. I certainly meant to.'

'You probably did. The disco was loud and I was tipsy,' I murmured, whilst wondering in what context this kind, forgiving and remarkably well-toned man with nice pyjamas wasn't trying hard enough for his ex. I considered asking, or empathising and confiding in him the aspects of my own personality which fell short of Alistair's expectations. But increasing tiredness, together with a reluctance to think about Alistair any more than I had already that evening, stopped me. 'Anyway, I just wanted to tell you,' I said quietly, 'that I wouldn't have ignored your letters.'

'I know that.'

I smiled, reflecting on the fact that thanks to those three hugely reassuring words, the day felt like it was ending on a high after all.

'Good night, Dot,' said Felix, yawning and turning onto his uninjured shoulder, his back now to me.

'Night, Felix,' I replied, and then, still smiling, I pulled the covers back up under my chin and fell asleep almost immediately.

Chapter 20

'You're not ill as well, are you, Fred?' I asked with concern as Kate's husband opened their front door to me, his shoulders sagging and dark purple smudges under each eye magnified by his rimless specs. 'You don't look great.'

He smiled wearily and ran a hand through his short dark hair. 'Secondary fatigue,' he said softly, beckoning me inside and closing the door behind me. 'Come and have a cup of tea in the kitchen before you pop up. I'm pretty sure Kate's asleep at the moment anyway – thank goodness.'

'Is she being difficult?' I asked, following him down the hallway.

He smiled at me over his shoulder and pushed his glasses to the top of his head. 'I know you don't really even have to ask. But it's kind of you to imply the possibility of her being otherwise.'

I nodded. Kate wasn't ill very often, and when she was, she usually worked through it. But on the rare occasion she was forced to stay home, she found it difficult to keep a lid on any frustrations regarding an underperforming body and mind – behaviour which obviously impacted on Fred. But as I sat down on a tall stool at the kitchen island and watched him set about making a pot of tea, I still thought he looked unwell, even taking into account the undoubted strain of having an irritable Kate on his hands.

He was a gentle, implacable giant of a man, mild-mannered, thoughtful and chilled; the perfect foil for the high-energy, cut-to-the-chase immediacy of his wife. He would usually have tutted affectionately at her inability to accept illness and managed her anxieties with unfailing good humour. But this evening he looked genuinely burdened by it – depressed even. It was something I hadn't seen before and it added to the mild concern I had felt when he had called me at work that afternoon to ask if I was free to pop round and see Kate on my way home.

'Everything's OK, isn't it, Fred?' I asked now, trying to keep my voice light. 'Kate's not more poorly than she told me on the phone, is she?'

He didn't reply or turn around, instead keeping his back to me as he reached for the kettle and poured boiling water into the teapot. It was only as he carried the pot, together with two mugs, to the table that he answered the question. 'I'm not sure what's going on,' he said quietly, turning to the fridge and taking out a carton of milk, before sitting down opposite me. 'I was hoping you might be able to fill in some of the blanks for me,' he added, finally making eye contact.

'What do you mean?' I looked at him, aware of a rising sense of dread. 'Has a doctor been to see her?'

He shook his head and began to pour the tea. 'I don't think it's physical. Not primarily anyway.' He paused, replacing the teapot on the table without pouring a second mugful. 'The truth is, Dot, I'm worried it's something to do with me,' he said quietly, staring at the empty mug. 'She's been behaving strangely for a couple of weeks now, maybe longer. Impatient over silly stuff and crying about things she'd usually brush off. But over the weekend it's been much worse. It's as if she can't even bear the sight of me, let alone talk to me.'

I reached across the table and patted his hand. 'She's just feeling crap. When I had flu, I couldn't be bothered to talk to anyone and I remember getting really fed up when well-meaning people called and gave it a go.'

'No,' he said, shaking his head. 'She hasn't really looked or sounded ill at all today. In fact, she looks really well. I think it's up here,' he added, tapping the side of his head, 'and I'm ninety-nine per cent sure that I'm the problem – or at least a big part of it.' He sighed unhappily, picked up the teapot and poured a second mug of tea. 'So I was wondering if you could tell me if there's anything I'm missing, or have missed.'

He slid a mug towards me, along with the carton of milk, smiling whilst somehow managing to look utterly miserable. And while I genuinely had no information to share that would indicate anything other than that Kate was as besotted with him as ever, he clearly thought otherwise, and that shook me. Fred was not a man to jump to irrational conclusions and he knew Kate as well as anyone ever could. So if he now had concerns that their relationship was wobbly, or that her feelings towards him had somehow changed, I didn't feel able to dismiss them out of hand.

I took a deep breath, determined to weigh my words carefully. 'Fred, I promise you that Kate has said nothing negative to me about you or your relationship, other than the usual stuff about you being far too tolerant of people,'

I added jovially. 'In particular, that plumber who put the hot and cold taps on the wrong way round. Twice.'

I looked at him, waiting for him to laugh or smile, but he did neither. Instead he just gazed at me and nodded thoughtfully.

I took a deep breath and ploughed on. 'As for her behaviour changing, she might have been a little bit more clipped on the phone at work recently, I suppose,' I began thoughtfully. 'But we have been very busy, so actually that's stretching a point to its elastic limit. I think, on balance, I'd have to say she's been pretty much herself. Although she was certainly not happy when she threw up last Tuesday. And neither was I. She's not a great shot, you know. It was *everywhere*!' I laughed, but my smile froze on my face and then quickly faded as Fred once again showed zero acknowledgement of my attempt to lighten the mood.

'So if she's been fine with you and fine at work, then I guess that pretty much confirms that I'm the problem,' he said.

My shoulders drooped and I closed my eyes, saddened by just how unbelievably rubbish I was at this kind of thing. I should have stopped after the plumber reference and then encouraged him to talk. I knew now that that was what Becca would have done. But no, as usual I had said *way* too much and now had to attempt situation retrieval.

'No, no, no,' I said, smiling and waving a hand. 'I don't think it means that at all. It just means...' I hesitated, not actually having a clue what any of it meant. 'It just means that Kate's more willing to... to be super-unpleasant to you. And that's because she loves you so much. They say we're always most unpleasant to the person we love the most, don't they? I'm sure I've heard people say that,' I added. 'Expert people, like psychiatrists and relationship counsellors.'

Fred offered me an expression of deeply unimpressed gloom.

'Well anyway,' I continued, hugely daunted but unde-terred, 'I can put your mind at rest about one thing: there's absolutely no way in the world Kate's having an affair, because I'd definitely know if she was,' I said flatly, picking up my mug and swigging my tea in what I hoped was an unconcerned, no-nonsense manner. 'So you can just get that idea out of your head right now, Fred Morgan.'

'That idea hadn't even crossed my mind, Dot,' he said, sounding appalled.

I slowly lowered my mug. 'Oh, hadn't it?' I murmured uncertainly. 'Well, er, it was very good of you not to think that. It just shows, erm, what a very positive man you are – totally without cynicism. Kate's so lucky to have you, because a lot of men would have jumped to that conclusion immediately, wouldn't they?' I concluded, relatively pleased with the attempt at recovery,

'Would they?' Fred's voice wobbled slightly. 'I just thought that maybe she was bored of me and tired of our relationship.'

'And I'm sure you're right!' I said brightly. 'I'm sure that's absolutely what's going on and not that she's having an affair. I don't know why I even mentioned an affair. She's definitely just bored... and... tired... of...' My voice faded to a whisper and I took another sip of tea before clearing my throat and starting again. 'I'm so sorry, Fred. I'm hopeless at this. She loves you. That's all I know.'

He offered me another indescribably sad smile. 'I put you on the spot. That wasn't fair.'

'No, I just don't know when to keep quiet. But the flip side is that you can be sure I'm not hiding anything.'

He continued to smile and was just about to say something when Kate's voice rang out from upstairs. 'Fred? Fred? Who's there?'

I looked at him. 'She doesn't know that you called me?'

He shook his head.

'OK,' I said. 'I won't say you asked me to come round.'

'Thanks, Dot.'

'Just try not to worry,' I said, getting up from my stool. 'I know Kate – and I know that she adores you.'

He offered me an unconvinced nod and then rose to his feet. I shook my head. 'You stay here and enjoy some down time. I'll make my own way up.'

'Do you want to take your tea?' he asked, gesturing towards my mug.

'No, it's OK,' I said, heading out into the hallway. 'Maybe I'll have another one with you before I go.'

'Have you left the radio on?' Kate's voice, high-pitched and irritable, reached us again. 'I can hear it all the way up here!'

I looked back down the hallway at Fred as he stood forlornly in the kitchen doorway. 'What is she like?' I smiled, rolling my eyes at him.

He didn't reply but simply shrugged good-naturedly, disappearing back into the kitchen as I began to make my way up the stairs.

'Dot? Is that you?' called Kate, her tone now surprised and suddenly much lighter.

I took a deep breath and positioned a smile on my face. 'Yes, it's me. And I'm coming in, so you'd better not be smoking dope in the nude.'

'It's OK, I'm not in the nude,' she said, as I pushed open the bedroom door. She was laughing while sounding, I thought, a little emotional.

'So is that a yes to the spliff, then?' I asked, poking my head round the door and sniffing.

'Come in, come in, you idiot.' She held out her arms to me from where she sat on the bed, fully clothed, cross-legged and surrounded by papers.

I walked towards her, taking the opportunity to examine her appearance as I did so, and my immediate impression was that Fred was right: she didn't look at all unwell. In fact, make-up-free and presumably well rested, she looked fresh and positively glowing. But she did also look upset, and a genuinely bright smile couldn't disguise the fact that she had been crying.

'Hello!' I smiled, bending down and giving her a hug. 'Are you feeling better?'

'I am,' she said, kissing my cheek and patting my back maternally before releasing me. 'I'll definitely be in tomorrow.'

'If you feel up to it,' I said, sitting down on the edge of the bed.

'I do. Definitely.'

'Well, that's great,' I smiled. 'I know it's been less than a week, but the office seems very empty without you. I was even pleased when Mum called at lunchtime.'

Kate leaned forward and grabbed my arm excitedly. 'Ooh yes! How did the weekend with Felix go?'

I rolled my eyes. 'Oh God, Kate, there was a massive change of plan. Felix and I got back from the Hippodrome to find Mum and Dad in the spare room!'

Her jaw dropped. 'You… are… kidding.'

I shook my head. 'Nope. At the last minute they couldn't stay with Uncle Geoffrey, and so as they have a spare key to my flat…'

She burst out laughing. 'You and your family are the best. So what happened? What did Felix say?'

I smiled. 'He was just so lovely about it all. And in a funny way, I think it really helped things between us. We were two teens in a scrape again.'

Kate nodded, and then her eyes suddenly filled with tears.

'What on earth's the matter?' I asked, frowning.

She shook her head and put a hand to her mouth. 'Nothing,' she gasped. 'I just love the idea of you and Felix being such old friends and now new friends. You know, starting afresh but with that shared history. Just wonderful.'

She dabbed at her eyes with the sleeve of her cardigan, while I looked on in a mixture of confusion and horror. This was not the Kate I knew. For a start, just one week ago the mention of Felix's name would have immediately prompted questions as to whether I had had *the conversation* with Mum and Dad. And secondly, although she was both caring and loving, Kate was far from sentimental, and a friendship, especially one of which she wasn't even a part, was not something which would have previously reduced her to tears.

'Kate,' I said gently, leaning towards her and placing my hand on hers, 'why are you crying?'

She shook her head and continued to wipe away her tears.

'Seriously, what's wrong?' I asked. 'This isn't like you.'

She still didn't speak.

'If there's a problem, either at work or at home, you know you don't have to keep it to yourself, don't you?'

At that, she looked up abruptly. 'Did Fred ask you to come?' she snapped.

I threw my hands up despairingly. 'Do I have this kind of stuff written across my forehead?'

Her face softened briefly into a smile before crumpling again. 'Oh Dot,' she sobbed. 'I've been so horrible to him. I know I have.'

I moved some papers and shifted my position on the bed so that I was now sitting next to her and able to place an arm around her shoulders. Learning from my recent unfortunate experience with Fred, I remained determinedly silent and waited for her to explain.

'A thing has happened,' she said eventually.

I took a deep breath and tried to quell the same sense of dread I had felt when talking to Fred. 'OK.'

'And now everything feels like it's out of control.'

'Right.'

'And I don't like being out of control,' she said, leaning her head against my shoulder.

I tilted my head sideways, so that it was resting against the top of hers. 'I know you don't,' I said softly. 'Fortunately, I am an expert in being out of control. So why don't you just tell me all about it?'

She was silent for a moment and I felt her trembling as she continued to sob. And then, after a huge sniff, in a barely audible whisper she said, 'I'm pregnant, Dot.'

'What?' I sat up and turned towards her, placing my hands on her shoulders and giving her a slight shake. 'What did you say?'

She looked up at me, her mouth stretching wide so that she now resembled a suicidal frog as she dissolved into a fresh bout of sobs.

Lost for words, I stared at her for a moment before pulling her to me and letting her soak the left shoulder of my blouse with tears. After several moments of blind panic, during which all sorts of incredibly selfish business-related scenarios screeched at breakneck speed through my mind, I redirected my full attention and concern towards one of the best and most precious friends I had ever had.

'And why is this a bad thing?' I asked.

She sniffed and sat up, looking surprised. 'Well, because…'

'Yes?'

'Because I'm forty, it's not planned, I love my job, and Fred and I are very happy. Or at least we were,' she added, her forehead wrinkling and her mouth stretching in preparation for more tears.

I held up a hand. 'I know you're emotional, Kate. That'll be the hormones as well as the situation, but please try to hold it together for just a few minutes.'

She nodded rapidly. 'Sorry, yes,' she said, taking a deep breath and exhaling slowly in a rather hiccoughy manner. 'I must regain control.'

'So,' I began, determined to keep my own voice steady, 'the first thing is: are you absolutely sure?'

She continued to nod. 'Absolutely. I did a test on Friday. I did three actually. Just in case the first two were iffy. They can be, you know.'

I heaved a sigh. 'I've never heard that before but OK.'

'I did the tests because I had the coil removed last December and I remembered that after Sue Ross's birthday party in Kings Weston at the end of May, Fred and I hadn't used anything.' She spoke rapidly, staring directly ahead of her. 'Since then I've only had one really light period and skipped one and then the one that was due a week or so ago never came, but I thought that maybe...' She paused for breath and turned her head slowly towards me. 'Do you know what I thought?'

'What?'

'I thought that maybe it was the menopause.' She grinned at me in a dazed and slightly maniacal manner, which made me think it might be best to move things along.

'OK, but it wasn't the menopause, so let's not dwell.'

She stopped grinning and nodded. 'Then I threw up on Tuesday and again on Wednesday, Thursday and Friday, but it didn't feel like a bug and I suddenly remembered Sue's party and the missed periods and I...' She hesitated, and fearing the return of tears, I spoke again.

'You did a test...'

'Three tests.'

'Yes, three tests – very thorough – and now you know you're pregnant. Have you been to see the GP?'

She nodded. 'I got an emergency appointment on Friday afternoon.'

'Good. And...'

'And I'm very well and I'm pregnant. Fourteen weeks.' She looked down at her stomach and placed a hand on it. 'There's a baby in my body.'

'Kate…'

'In my body, right now,' she said absently, still staring at her stomach.

'Kate, look at me.'

She slowly lifted her face towards me. 'Yes?'

'What are you worried about?'

'I'm worried about Fred and about you and about the business and about my marriage and about my age and about having no plan.'

'Are you worried about the baby in your body?'

'I am,' she said quietly. 'I just want it to be OK.'

I smiled and put my hands to my face, now feeling on the verge of tears myself. 'Well thank goodness for that,' I said. 'Now just pull yourself together and tell Fred what's going on, because you and the baby are all that he's going to be worried about.'

'But aren't *you* worried, Dot?' she asked anxiously, reaching out and taking my hands in hers.

'Only for you and for the baby in your body.'

'But what about the business? What will we do?'

'We'll plan as much as we can, but we're also going to wing it,' I said.

'But—' began Kate, looked panicked.

'Shh,' I interrupted, putting a finger to my lips. 'I was told this weekend that I'm at my best when winging it. I'm good at it and you're going to have to get good at it too. You're going to have to accept lots of unknowns and variables and not look too far ahead.'

'But what about Fred? I'm so worried about him.'

'Yes, actually, I'm worried about Fred too,' I conceded. 'Because right now he's downstairs thinking you're having an affair.'

Her eyes widened. 'What? Why would he think that?' she asked, suddenly angry. 'The bastard.'

I shook my head. 'That was my fault,' I admitted.

'Oh, OK,' she said, relaxing. 'Did you try and say something helpful?'

'I did.'

'Fair enough.' She took a deep breath and gave me a hug. 'I'm just a bit afraid.'

'I can see how it might have all come as a bit of a shock.'

'It's not that. I just want Fred to be as happy as I am and I'm terrified he won't be. He just seems so low at the moment.'

'Well,' I said, releasing myself from her embrace and pushing her gently away from me, 'I think part of the problem for Fred right now is that this,' I pointed at her bright red tear-stained face, 'together with all the screeching and calling him a bastard, isn't coming across as happy.'

She nodded. 'You're right. I've been so stupid and muddled about everything, Dot. Thank you for helping me to focus,' she said emotionally, biting her lip.

'No problem, but please don't cry any more,' I said. 'It's unsettling. And buy a box of tissues on your way into the office tomorrow. I think you're going to need them.'

'I will,' she said. 'It's so weird you being the sensible, insightful one, isn't it?'

I sighed and stood up. 'And with that back-handed compliment ringing in my ears, I'm going to go and fetch Fred for you.'

She smiled and, after bending to give her a kiss on the cheek, I stood up and walked to the door.

'Ooh, hang on, I forgot to ask,' she said suddenly.

'What?' I asked, opening the door and looking at her over my shoulder.

'You did tell your mum that you're not going out with Felix, didn't you?'

'Nearly,' I said, and then, before she could say any more, I slid out of the room, closed the door behind me and, ignoring her irately insistent yells for me to come back immediately, I headed downstairs in search of Fred.

Chapter 21

One week later and things had calmed down considerably. Kate had returned to work the day after my home visit, telling me that Fred was at first speechless and then cautiously ecstatic about the pregnancy. His sole concern, as I had predicted, was for his wife and their unborn child.

Kate herself, meanwhile, was largely as ever, the only exception being that her matter-of-fact, unsentimental approach to life was now occasionally interrupted by brief out-of-the-blue bouts of inexplicable tears, rambling philosophising and, worst of all, high-profile vomiting. The latter occurred at least once a day, and as our loo was separated from the office only by a very thin partition wall, and as Kate's coping mechanism when vomiting was to give repeated and very loud assurances to herself, it was an event impossible to ignore.

But other than that, she was pretty much her old self. So much so that she hadn't even removed her raincoat on day one of her return to work before she was demanding to know why Mum and Dad still thought Felix and I were an item. However, my ready-and-waiting explanation – namely that that I hadn't spent any time alone with my parents during their Bristol stopover and that they were now on a three-week tour of France and Spain in their motorhome — was enough to set her mind temporarily at rest over the matter and let her focus instead on work – and, of course, on crying, philosophising and vomiting.

But despite the almost total return to day-to-day workplace normality, I still felt unsettled. Because although I had a natural disposition towards, and preference for, winging it, Kate's pregnancy and its implications for the future did still, at times, feel a little scary and overwhelming. What would it mean for our relationship? Would she find closer friends and greater commonality within ante- and post-natal groups? How would I feel working alone during her maternity leave, or, worse still, on a permanent basis if she decided to exit the business altogether?

She had assured me that the latter was not going to happen, and I believed that she meant it. But I also knew that parenthood was capable of radically transforming even the strongest of personalities and the firmest of priorities.

However, the most unsettling train of thought sparked by Kate's pregnancy was actually none of the above, but rather the realisation that for the first time in my life, I had no idea who to turn to for advice. Kate was obviously not an option, and although I had no doubt that Becca would be an excellent listener and counsellor regarding friendship issues, both she and my parents were too far removed from the realities of my business relationship with Kate to be able to provide holistic advice. And this being the case, I felt that bothering them with my concerns, certainly at this stage, would be needlessly worrying for them, and not particularly worthwhile for me.

This sense of lacking a confidante became all the more acute when it occurred to me that the person in whom

I would have confided in the past was Alistair. It was a realisation which, once made, I was unable to ignore, and from then on, in marked contrast to recent months, when he had crossed my mind infrequently and fleetingly, I found myself thinking about him, and poring over our failed relationship, on a daily basis. In this way, a focus on his absence – a barely related ripple emanating from Kate's pregnancy – actually affected my mood and dominated my thoughts to a much greater extent than the pregnancy itself.

And it was upon this darkly fascinating fact that I was yet again dwelling as I took off my cardigan and flopped down at my desk on the Tuesday morning seven days after Kate's return to work. Such miserable brooding would not usually have been an option, as Kate always beat me into the office and never failed to start talking rapidly at me before I'd even closed the outer door. But this morning she had a scan and was going to be late in, thus gifting me the agonising luxury of regretting, again and at length, the loss of Alistair as my partner in life.

I had just, for the thousandth time, begun to wonder exactly what Naomi had that I didn't, other than an elfin physique, a voice like a tinkling bell and a high-brow disdain for popular culture, when the phone rang. I picked it up with a sense of relief.

'Eat Fruit Design. How can I help?'

'Hi, Dot. It's Felix.'

'Felix!' I exclaimed smiling. 'How are you? It's so lovely to hear from you,' I added.

He laughed. 'I haven't told you what I'm calling about yet.'

'Oh God,' I groaned. 'My mother hasn't phoned you from the Vendée, has she?'

'Er, no,' he said. 'Why would she do that?'

'She wouldn't, she wouldn't,' I said quickly. 'I'm talking nonsense. Haven't had a coffee yet.'

'OK, well I won't keep you from that. But I have some dates to suggest for you coming to Cheltenham and thought I'd throw them at you while I've got my calendar onscreen.'

'Oh, that's so nice of you, Felix. It'd be great to get away.'

'From what?' he asked. 'Is work stressful?'

'Not work so much. Well, kind of work…' I hesitated, wanting to tell him all about Kate and the baby and my renewed glumness over Alistair, but very aware that eight forty-five on a Tuesday morning, when I had designs to work on and Felix no doubt had lots of numbers to add up, was not the best time to offload. 'Just some tricky stuff,' I said. 'So a distraction would be nice.'

There was a slight pause before he spoke again. 'Look, I was going to suggest next month, but you're welcome to come up this Saturday. I'm going to a fortieth and you could come with me.'

I smiled at his kindness. 'I couldn't crash that,' I said. 'Don't worry. I'm not suicidal or anything.'

'You wouldn't be crashing. There's no paper invitation. And you'd be doing me a favour. I hate turning up to that kind of thing on my own.'

'Shut up,' I laughed. 'I bet you'll know everyone there.'

'Hardly anyone,' he replied. 'I wouldn't be going, but it's an open bar.'

I hesitated, not for one second fooled by his protestations of social insecurity, but at the same time realising that his offer was one I desperately wanted to accept. At that moment, I was facing a Saturday night home alone, and in my current state of mind, that wasn't at all an uplifting prospect.

I tutted. 'Well why didn't you say it was an open bar right away? *Of course* I'll come, even if you are inviting me out of pity.'

'Which I definitely am.'

'Don't care. It's an open bar.'

'Great. It's in the diary. I'll text you my address. Or if you're getting the train, I'll pick you up from the station.'

'Thanks, Felix,' I smiled. 'Looking forward to it already. Ooh, but what kind of party is it? What shall I wear?'

'It's fancy dress,' he said. 'The theme is *Under the Sea*.'

I sighed. 'It's not.'

'No, it's not. But I was hoping you might make an aqualung out of lemonade bottles. Like you did for Ellie Bream's sixteenth birthday party.'

'Oh my goodness, so I did! You remember absolutely everything!'

'No I don't. I just remember more than you do. And that's because I was never quite as drunk as you were, Dorothy Riley.'

'Condescend all you like, but that aqualung was the biz.'

He laughed. 'Can't disagree. But only because I haven't got time. Linda has a client waiting for me. See you Saturday.'

'Hang on,' I said quickly. 'The dress code?'

'It's drinks and dancing at a posh pub. Smart casual, I guess, but I'll double-check and let you know. Bye.'

'Bye,' I said, and put down the phone, grateful for the call and for the invitation, but most of all, suddenly very grateful for Felix. I was cheered by the thought of seeing him and, I realised with mild surprise, had no problem with the idea of sharing my troubles, both personal and professional, with him.

I stared thoughtfully into space for a moment or two, and was just considering retrieving my phone from my bag and texting Becca a few lines on the subject of Felix, when my phone began to ring. I bent down, picked it out of my bag and, seeing Alistair's name on the screen, frowned and took the call.

'Hi, Alistair.'

'Hi, Dot. Have you got two minutes?'

'Sure. Fire away.'

I heard him take a deep breath. 'I've been thinking about you a lot since I bumped into you outside the Hippodrome,' he began. And as he told me how much he still cared for me and how he would very much like to meet me for a drink as soon as possible, I leaned back in my chair and, smiling and feeling a little dazed, I forgot all about texting Becca, and all about Felix.

Chapter 22

'Well, I think I've got a good idea of what you're after, Stephanie, and I'd be very excited to work on this for you.' I smiled winningly at the slim, greying woman sitting opposite me, a local bank manager who wanted to self-publish her novel and had come to discuss cover options.

'Oh my God, here it comes!' Kate's voice reached us from the toilet, quickly followed by the sound of violent retching.

Stephanie glanced uncertainly towards the partition wall.

'You're OK, Kate,' said Kate. 'It'll be over soon.'

'*Is* she OK?' asked Stephanie anxiously, nodding her head towards the wall.

'Pregnant,' I said, as Kate continued to gag. 'But best not to mention it. She's still a bit shy about it.'

'Oh, I see,' said Stephanie, still looking worried.

'She's fine,' I reassured her. 'She's had all the tests and has a consultant keeping an eye on her and everything's great.'

'You shouldn't have had that bun,' gasped Kate, clearly to herself, but still nevertheless completely audibly. 'Straight back up along with all the...'

Thankfully the remainder of the sentence was drowned out by the sound of the flush.

'So what I would propose,' I said, returning to business and determinedly maintaining eye contact with Stephanie in the hope of recapturing her full attention, 'is that if you decide to go ahead, I present you with four design options, based on our discussion this afternoon. You should allow two weeks for me to complete the designs and I would charge a flat fee, with a level of tweaking to your preferred design included in the price. I'll send you all the specifics in an email, along with a quote. How does that sound?'

'That sounds great,' she smiled.

'Fabulous,' I said. 'Do you have any other questions?'

'No, I don't think I do,' she replied, standing up and holding out her hand. I shook it just as Kate emerged from the toilet, her face pink and her eyes red and watery.

'Great meeting you, Stephanie – even briefly,' she said slightly breathlessly, walking quickly towards us, her hand extended.

Stephanie hesitated for a moment, staring doubtfully at Kate's hand, clearly with the recent vomiting on her mind, before reaching out and shaking it lightly for a nanosecond.

'And you couldn't have picked anyone more talented than Dorothy to work with,' added Kate.

I smiled at her before turning to Stephanie. 'I'll show you out,' I said.

'Thanks,' she replied. 'I'm heading back to the bank now.'

'But it's six o'clock,' I protested, 'on a Friday.'

'I know,' she sighed, 'but I have one or two things to sign off. It shouldn't take long.'

'Well, I hope you have something nice planned for the weekend,' I said, walking with her to the lobby.

'I'll be gardening tomorrow and then having dinner with friends. Terribly dull and middle-aged.'

I opened the outer door. 'Not at all. Sounds great.'

'It'll be relaxing rather than exciting,' she said, as she stepped outside, 'but that's fine by me.'

I smiled my agreement, watching as she walked away and then closing the outer door and returning to the office, where Kate was now packing up her laptop in readiness for going home.

'Is the job in the bag?' she asked as I went to my desk and sat down.

'Hope so,' I said. 'I'd genuinely like to do it. It'd be fun.'

'Well, it sounded like the pair of you were on the same page,' she said, picking up her satchel then coming over and sitting down opposite me. 'The same page! That's a pun, Dot,' she laughed.

I rolled my eyes. 'Yes, thank you, Kate. I got that.'

'Oh, right,' she said, still grinning. 'Only I thought you hadn't, because you're not laughing.'

'That's because I'm not pregnant.'

'Oh, you misery,' she teased, leaning across my desk and punching me lightly on the arm. 'Why don't you come home with me and cheer up with a Friday-night glass of wine? Or at least you and Fred can have a glass of wine and I'll have a mug of ginger tea.'

'A lovely offer,' I smiled, swivelling in my chair and turning my back on her while switching off my screen, 'but I'll pass if that's OK. I'm partying with Felix tomorrow night, don't forget.'

I kept my back to her and reached down, picking up my bag and rummaging through it, making a pretence of searching for something. Kate remained silent and I turned to find her looking at me through eyes narrowed in suspicion.

'Where are you going?' she asked.

'Tomorrow? Cheltenham, of course.'

'Not tomorrow – tonight,' she said.

I slumped back in my chair, knowing resistance was futile. 'I'm meeting Alistair for a drink,' I said quietly.

'Alistair?' Her eyes widened in surprise, an expression rapidly replaced by a frown. 'Why are you meeting *him*? Has something happened? When did you arrange that? Is there a reason you didn't mention it?'

'Why don't you just hand me a questionnaire and I'll fill it in over the weekend?' I asked.

'Is it a happy drink or a stressful one?' she persisted.

'I honestly don't know yet,' I began uncertainly, 'which is the reason I didn't mention it. Nothing bad has happened. He wants to see me because he cares deeply for me and I've been on his mind pretty constantly since Becca's wedding. I'm quoting him there, by the way,' I added, gazing down at the desk. 'He called on Tuesday, while you were at the hospital.'

'And does the fact that he's thinking about you and caring deeply for you make you happy?'

'It did while I was talking to him on Tuesday.' I looked up at her and sighed. 'You know much I missed him when he left, Kate.'

'I do.' She smiled sympathetically.

'And I've been thinking about him and noticing his absence a lot more again just recently. So yes, on Tuesday it made me happy to think that he has missed me too – that the feeling of loss wasn't completely one-sided.' I offered her a small smile and a shrug.

'And today?'

I placed my elbows on the desk and rested my head in my hands. 'A bit muddled, I guess. I've been thinking everything through since he called, and the thing is, I do feel *really* sad when I think about the relationship ending. But that doesn't feel quite the same as wanting him back. It's nearly the same, but not quite. I miss him – hugely at times – but I'm not unhappy day-to-day without him in my life and I'm not convinced I'd be happier if we were back together. Does that make any sense?'

'God, how many things about relationships ever make sense?' she asked, smiling and reaching across the desk again, this time to squeeze my hand. 'So why don't you stop overthinking it and just see how the drink goes? Call for a chat afterwards if you want to. Or come round,' she added. 'We'll only be watching *Gogglebox* under a tartan blanket, and there's always room for a third.'

'Thank you,' I said quietly. 'And I would have told you about it but I didn't really know what to say. I haven't mentioned it to Becca either.'

She shook her head. 'I understand. Sometimes trying to explain things to other people can just make a situation seem more complex, can't it?' she said gently, before adding briskly, 'So, what time are you meeting him?'

'Seven at the Cosy Club. But I'm going to try to be early.'

'Good for you, and in that case,' she said, checking her watch and standing up, 'I'd better let you go. Just try to enjoy the drink, whatever the circumstances. Let it happen and then think again. Take everything one step at a time and don't look too far ahead.'

I laughed. 'You know I don't think you have *ever* told me not to plan ahead before.'

'I'm merely batting your own excellent advice right back at you, Dorothy,' she said, smiling and beginning to walk towards the lobby. 'You recently told me that waiting and seeing has its place. And you know what? You were absolutely right.'

Chapter 23

I arrived at the Cosy Club at six forty-five. There being no sign as yet of Alistair, either upstairs or down, I bought a cocktail and sat at one of the high tables which ran the length of the bar, making sure that I was facing the door onto the street. Then, sipping my drink, I took a deep breath, gazed up admiringly at the ornately arched and coved ceiling high above me and tried to relax. I knew that Alistair wouldn't be late, but I was hoping for ten minutes alone to allow a little alcohol, and the Friday-night atmosphere of the bar, to work their magic on my nerves. Because despite Kate's advice, I was having great difficulty not overthinking the situation, and during the twenty-minute walk from the office I had managed to create four different hypothetical scenarios in some detail.

Each one began with Alistair reiterating that he cared deeply for me and that I was constantly on his mind. After that, direction and outcome depended upon my response to his declaration, namely either: (a) letting him down gently; (b) suggesting we go away and think about it; (c) verbally reciprocating his feelings in a modest manner; or (d) snogging his face off.

I was in no doubt that alcoholic intake would heavily influence which option I plumped for, and I had just decided to restrict myself to one drink and was replaying scenario (b) in my head as my much-preferred response to whatever Alistair might have to say, when he walked in.

He spotted me immediately and smiled, before gesturing that he was going to get a drink and then come over. I nodded, still a little anxious, but relieved to realise that I felt neither the heartache of our encounter in the Bear, nor the crushing sense of inadequacy I had experienced outside the Hippodrome. And as I watched him thank the barman for his beer and begin to make his way towards me, I realised something else too: that at this moment I didn't actually find him attractive. In fact, I found myself struggling to recall the last time I had. His smile, face, hair and physique were all unchanged, but they prompted no sense of physical longing in me – or emotional for that matter.

The realisation came as something of a surprise, and must have registered on my face, because Alistair's smile faded and he looked at me with concern as he sat down opposite me. 'Everything OK?' he asked.

'Yes,' I said, examining the mousy swept-back hair, slim face and blue eyes and digging deep for any sense of attraction.

'You sure?' he asked.

'Yes, definitely.' I waved a hand and smiled. 'My mind just flashed back to work for a moment.'

He nodded. 'I have three anxiety flashbacks every evening. As you know,' he added, picking up his beer. 'Cheers.'

'Cheers,' I said, tapping my glass against his. 'So how is work?' I asked, still feeling a little thrown and not exactly dreading the conversation becoming more personal, but not feeling quite ready for it either.

'It's OK. Esther's back from maternity leave, which makes everything a bit easier. But she opted for a two-day week in the end.' He shook his head and smiled. 'She told me she'd actually like to give up work altogether for a couple of years. It's weird, because I never had her down as someone who'd want to be at home full-time with a child.'

I nodded, whilst making the obvious comparison between Esther and Kate and feeling my mood selfishly dip at the potential loss of my business partner to motherhood.

'Are you sure you're OK?' asked Alistair.

I looked at him and wondered whether I should tell him about Kate. 'God, yes,' I smiled. 'I'm just not quite out of work mode. I probably needed another ten minutes with my cocktail.'

He laughed. 'I couldn't quite believe it when I saw you here, actually. I was sure you wouldn't make an appearance until quarter past at the earliest.'

'Hmm, well I've decided to work on my timekeeping.' I looked up at him and smiled ruefully. 'I think my attitude to it has been a little too casual up until now, and I have realised, shamefully late in the day – appropriately enough – how frustrating that might be for other people. I know it drove you mad,' I added.

He shook his head. 'It wouldn't have been great for us both to be time-obsessed,' he said affably. 'One of us needed to stay relaxed, and we never missed a flight, did we?'

I frowned slightly, remembering all the watch-tapping of the past and surprised by his retrospectively magnanimous acceptance of my inability to keep track of the time.

He shrugged and smiled. 'We were yin-yang.'

Yin-yang? My frown deepened at this ongoingly positive take on our contrasting personalities. And I couldn't help wondering whether it was an attitude which Alistair would be able to maintain in a rekindled relationship – or whether he would discover that he could put up with my quirks, as Felix called them, only when he didn't actually have to.

'So why the change of approach?' asked Alistair.

'Change of approach?'

'What made you want to improve your timekeeping?' He smiled encouragingly at me.

'Oh, it was just something Felix said.'

It hadn't been a conscious decision to introduce my pretend boyfriend into the conversation, and I immediately regretted mentioning him. I really didn't want to have to lie to Alistair about the relationship, but I was even less keen to tell him the truth.

At the mention of Felix's name, Alistair's smile faltered and he looked down at his pint. 'And how is he?' he asked, his tone predominantly bright but with a definite edge to it.

'He's well,' I said, and then, eager to change the subject, added, 'But tell me more about Esther. She had a little boy, didn't she?'

'She did. They've named him Benedict.' He didn't look up. 'Had you and Felix had a good day when we bumped into you outside the Hippodrome? The weather was great, wasn't it?'

I picked up my glass, kicking myself for not anticipating this. If Alistair wanted to revisit our relationship then of course he would want to talk about my current one. The two issues were inextricably linked.

I sipped my cocktail and then replaced the glass on the table. 'We were so lucky with the weather. We managed to spend practically the whole time outside in the sunshine. How about you and Naomi? Did you make the most of it?'

He hesitated for a moment. 'The restaurant was good,' he said, now looking up. 'I'd recommend it. And it was such a surprise to run into you. *Dirty Dancing*?' He laughed incredulously. 'You were good to sit through that.'

'I loved every minute of it,' I said, trying to remain relaxed but experiencing a creeping tension in my spine. 'Genuinely.'

He laughed. 'OK.'

'Alistair,' I said, determinedly keeping my tone light, 'just because you never took me to see a musical doesn't mean I can't enjoy one.'

He continued to smile. 'I said OK. I'm sure you already have your tickets booked for *Hairspray*.'

'I didn't know it was coming to Bristol.'

'Next March, I believe.'

'Well thank you for drawing it to my attention.'

'Pleasure.'

We looked at each other for a moment, neither of us speaking, and as our smiles faded in sync, I decided to cut to the chase.

'I was quite surprised when you suggested a drink tonight,' I said quietly. 'It's been a long time.'

'Too long.' He paused and took a deep breath. 'I actually thought about calling you the week after Becca's wedding.'

'Really?' I said, surprised by the admission. 'Any particular reason?'

'More than one,' he said hesitantly. 'But amongst other things, you didn't seem quite yourself – just not very happy at times. So I wanted to make sure everything was OK.' He concluded the sentence with a smile, which bordered on apologetic, and a small shrug.

I felt my throat tighten as it suddenly dawned on me that this evening wasn't about rekindling relationships or revisiting feelings; it was about Alistair checking up on my emotional welfare. I stared at him, unsure whether to feel grateful for his legendary sensitivity or patronised by his belief that he could and should intervene in my personal life. I opted for the latter.

'I'm not sure you're in the best position to claim to be worried about what makes me happy, Alistair,' I said stiffly.

He nodded. 'I appreciate that,' he said. 'But I can't help caring about you, Dot, whether you think I've forfeited that right or not. And after I saw you and Felix outside the Hippodrome, I—'

'You've got a problem with my relationship with Felix?'

'Have you?' He looked at me questioningly. 'Were you OK with the way he behaved towards you at the reception?'

I stared at him, taking a deep breath in an attempt to steady myself before answering. His objective assessment of Felix's behaviour at the wedding was not unreasonable, and in different circumstances I might have viewed such concern as insightful and well meant. But at this moment, on an evening when I had thought he had invited me here to express his regret that he had ended our relationship, I felt nothing but huge resentment at his attempt to pry into my relationship with Felix and, more significantly, at his implied criticism of Felix himself.

I lowered my drink. 'Yes, I was OK with it,' was all I said.

'I still care about you, Dot.'

'So you've said.'

'I'm repeating the fact because I'm not sure you believe it,' he sighed. 'I thought a lot about whether I should ask you to come out with me tonight, and in the end I had to because I needed to know—'

'If I was capable of making my own decisions and managing my own relationships post you?'

'Not at all. I'm only mentioning Felix because he seemed—'

'Seemed what, Alistair?' I interrupted a second time, losing patience and unwilling to hear any further criticism, implied or otherwise, of Felix. 'Hurt? Used? Wronged? Because that's how he was feeling at Becca's wedding. I had treated him really badly that day and a less forgiving man might actually have simply buggered off home. But he didn't. Because he is kind, selfless, cares about me and about my family, and demonstrates all those qualities in a practical way. You would not believe how he has helped and supported me over the past few months, and throughout ten years of growing up for that matter – including, you should know, pretending to have bought those bloody tickets for *Dirty Dancing* so that I didn't feel small in front of your small girlfriend. Felix knows me and understands me and he doesn't want to change me. Things about me which you saw as failings, he values. He makes me feel better and want to be better and I love him very much.'

I stopped talking abruptly, aware that my voice had risen above an acceptable conversational level and that heads were now turning in our direction. Alistair meanwhile was looking shell-shocked.

I picked up my drink and took a gulp. 'I'm sorry,' I said, keeping my voice low. 'But Felix isn't at fault here.'

Alistair nodded. 'I see,' he said quietly. 'I apologise.'

'I'm sorry I lost my temper,' I continued. 'But I can't help resenting the fact that you, of all people, have invited me here to offer relationship advice; to tell me who, in your opinion, is right or wrong for me. What on earth do you think qualifies you to do that?'

'Nothing,' he said. 'And I'm sorry that's how it seemed to you.'

'I don't see how else it could have seemed, Alistair.'

'Dot, I didn't come here to offer you advice. I came here to find out if you were happy.' He paused and shook his head. 'I'm pleased for you that you are. I misread the situation.'

I stared at the table as we sat in miserable and uncomfortable silence. I had no clue what was going through Alistair's head, but my own thoughts remained a whirl of anger and resentment that the man sitting opposite me – a man who had dumped me – honestly thought he was best placed to tell me who should or shouldn't replace him in my life. And his rush to judge Felix was just the icing on the cake. I was desperate to spell out for him exactly how wonderful a friend Felix had been to me, saving me from my own idiocy for over twenty years. Whether it was persuading me against a Sean Dowse tattoo, pushing me home in a shopping trolley or sharing my bed and pretending to be lactose intolerant to save me from an awkward conversation with my mother, Felix had always been, and was again, there for me.

I looked up. 'I think I should probably go home.'

Alistair nodded but didn't speak as I climbed off the bar stool and bent down to pick up my bag. 'Have a good weekend,' I said, straightening up.

'You too. Enjoy the party.'

'Thanks,' I replied, making to leave before turning and asking, 'What party?'

'The party you're going to tomorrow. You mentioned it earlier,' he said, staring at his beer.

I frowned. 'No I didn't.'

'Or you mentioned it on the phone,' he said. 'Is it a problem?'

'Of course not. I just don't remember telling you.'

'OK. Well enjoy it anyway,' he said, now turning to look at me. 'And I'm sorry again,' he added, 'if you thought I was interfering.'

'I know your intentions were good,' I said quietly, trying to calm down.

He smiled sadly. 'Debatable.'

'What do you mean?'

'I'm not sure,' he said, shrugging. 'I'm still thinking it through myself, which isn't like me, is it? Acting first, thinking later?'

I stared at him, waiting for some further explanation. When he offered none, I hesitated, considering pressing him on the matter and waiting to hear what else he might have to say. But in the end I decided that there was nothing either of us could say which would make the other feel better at that moment. Besides, like Alistair, I had some things to think through, and I couldn't do that with him sitting opposite me. So after leaning forward to kiss him lightly on the cheek, I slung my bag over my shoulder, turned away and left.

Chapter 24

I considered asking the taxi driver to detour to Kate's house on the way home from the Cosy Club. It was still early and I felt in desperate need of cheering up. But deciding that in my current mood it would be unfair to crash her sofa evening with Fred, I didn't bother and instead headed straight home. I would, I decided, microwave a chocolate pudding, pack an overnight bag to take to Cheltenham and then get into my pyjamas and watch something mindless on telly in bed until I fell asleep. The alternative, I knew, would be several pointless hours of late-night angst spent running and rerunning the pub conversation with Alistair in my head.

However, as I stepped into the hallway of my flat, wearily closing the front door behind me, my pudding-pack-telly plan was delayed by the arrival of a text from Becca asking if I could call her for a chat when I got home – if I wasn't too tired. Delighted to hear from her and eager to grasp the opportunity to offload about Alistair, I waited only as long as it took me to dump my bag, kick off my shoes and flop down on the sofa before dialling her number.

'Hi, Dot! Where are you?' She sounded immediately upbeat, answering the phone before the second ring.

'I'm at home – just,' I replied. 'You sound excited about something.'

She laughed. 'I have news.'

'Ooh! What?' I asked. 'A promotion?'

She didn't reply, and instead I heard Mark saying something in the background and Becca's muffled reply. A moment later, she was back.

'Sorry, Dot,' she said, now sounding subdued. 'Can I call you in two minutes? Mark has something to tell me and he has to go back to work in a moment.'

'Poor guy. No problem,' I said. 'I'll go and shove something in the microwave. Call whenever you're ready.'

'Great. And sorry again. I'll call ring you straight back.'

In fact, I had microwaved my pudding, eaten it and was staring into my wardrobe trying to decide what to wear to the party the next evening by the time Becca called back. And when she did, she sounded quietly anxious, in marked contrast to the excitement of her first call.

'Hi, Dot,' she began. 'How are you?'

'I'm fine,' I replied, 'but what's happened there? You sounded so happy half an hour ago.'

There was a pause before she spoke. 'Mark's been incredibly stupid. We've had quite a big row.'

'You and Mark?' I blinked in confusion. Neither my sister nor my brother-in-law were confrontational types, and to imagine them having a row with anyone was difficult. To imagine them having a row with each other was impossible. My stomach lurched at the level of misdemeanour Mark would have had to commit for Becca to be angry with him.

'Oh Becca, what's he done?' I asked anxiously. 'Are you OK?'

'I'm sorry, Dot, but he's been talking to Alistair. I didn't know until just now.'

'I don't understand,' I said, frowning. 'He talks to Alistair a lot, doesn't he?'

'He's been talking to Alistair about you,' she explained.

'Oh, I see,' I murmured, sitting down on the bed. 'I've just seen Alistair tonight actually.'

'I know,' she said quietly. 'Mark got a text from him about it just as you phoned. That's why he wanted to talk to me before he went out.'

'Look, Becca,' I said, feeling horrible at the thought of my ex updating my brother-in-law on his failed attempt to manage my love life, but at the same time trying to see the situation from Mark's point of view, 'Mark can't help it if Alistair confides in him, can he? Obviously I'd rather he didn't. But I don't think it's something to get cross with Mark about.'

'I'm cross because Alistair told Mark almost a week ago that he was thinking of calling you and arranging a drink,' she replied, sounding increasingly strained.

'And you're upset that Mark didn't mention the conversation to you?'

'I am, yes,' she replied. 'Very.'

'Well please don't be,' I sighed. 'Maybe it slipped his mind. Anyway, it's not like he knew what Alistair was going to say to me, is it?'

There was silence at the other end of the line.

'Becca?'

'Yes, I'm still here.'

I frowned into the phone. 'Mark *didn't* know what Alistair was going to say to me this evening, did he?'

There was a further pause before she spoke again. 'Alistair told Mark exactly why he wanted to see you, Dot,' she said eventually. 'And then he asked Mark whether he thought talking to you was a good idea.'

'But Mark told him it was a really *bad* idea, didn't he?' I asked, desperate for Mark not to be the complete and utter idiot of the piece. 'I'm assuming he did but that Alistair just went ahead anyway.'

'I'm afraid, Dot,' said Becca hesitantly, 'that Mark encouraged Alistair to talk to you.'

'He *what*?' I exploded. 'Why on earth would he do that? Mark knows I'm not going out with Felix! Why would he encourage Alistair to lecture me about a relationship which doesn't even exist?'

'I don't think Alistair—'

'Oh my God. Mark didn't tell him the whole Felix thing was a sham, did he?' I asked, my mind racing through the possibilities in a state of enraged panic. 'Was this evening some sort of lads' joke?'

'Of course it—'

'I cannot believe I sat through such a shitty conversation, with Alistair in full patronising-agony-uncle mode, giving me advice about a non-existent relationship, only to discover that it was Mark who told him to do it! Mark – who knew that I didn't even have a bloody boyfriend in the first place! And who *also* knew that the man Alistair was slagging off was actually doing me a huge favour by pretending to be my boyfriend and...' I stopped shouting and flopped back on the bed, placing my hand across my eyes. 'I'm so pissed off, Rebecca,' I seethed. 'I never thought I could ever be pissed off with Mark, but I am now. What on earth did he think he was doing?'

'Dot, I think that maybe—'

'I tell you, it's a good job he's gone to work, because otherwise I'd make you hand over the phone. I'd love to talk to him, I really would.'

My sister now remained silent, not unreasonably having given up trying to get a word in edgeways.

I lay on the bed, eyes closed, phone to my ear, trying to make sense of what Becca was telling me. But I could find no explanation for Mark telling Alistair to go ahead and share his thoughts on Felix which would make it possible for me to forgive my brother-in-law any time soon.

'I don't know why he would put me through that,' I said quietly. 'Unless he thought it was funny,' I added.

'Of course he didn't think it was funny, Dot,' said Becca gently. 'Mark loves you to bits. You know that. Can I just explain what happened?'

'This has to be my crappiest evening in a long time,' I said miserably.

'I can appreciate that, but will you just listen for a moment?'

'Go on,' I said sulkily.

She hesitated briefly, but when she did speak, her words were clear and rapid. 'Alistair and Mark met up last Saturday for a drink. While they were out, Alistair told Mark that he'd split up with Naomi. Apparently he was never that sure about her, which was one of the reasons he came alone to the wedding. He said he missed you a lot and had realised that although you were two very different people, he needed a counterbalance to his own personality. Then he asked Mark whether he thought things were serious with Felix, to which Mark obviously said no. Alistair also asked whether he thought you ever missed him, to which Mark, rightly or wrongly, said yes, he thought that you did. Mark then encouraged Alistair to tell you how he felt – to talk things through with you – which he has done, or has tried to do. Disastrously. I was furious with Mark for not telling me all this earlier, but, Dot, he thought he was helping.'

I remained motionless, my eyebrows knitted and my mouth slightly ajar, as I tried to absorb what Becca had said, and to reconsider my conversation with Alistair in the light of the new information she had just provided.

What I actually achieved was a period of intellectual chaos, followed by an inability to feel or think anything at all. I preferred the latter.

'Dot?' said Becca. 'Are you still there?'

'My head hurts and I can't think about it,' I murmured.

'Well I'd rather not hang up till you do.'

'It's all a mess. A confusing mess.'

'Just try to break it down and focus on one aspect of it at a time,' she suggested, suddenly in teacher mode. 'For example, would it have changed the evening if you'd known that what Alistair *actually* wanted to discuss was getting back together?'

'I don't know.'

'It's an important question, Dot,' she said, sounding as close to stern as she ever could.

I sighed and, with my hand still covering my eyes, tried to think. 'If I'd known Alistair had wanted to get back together, I still would have defended Felix,' I said quietly. 'I still would have got cross.'

There was a pause before Becca spoke again. 'And would you still have told Alistair that you loved Felix?'

I removed my hand and opened my eyes. 'Did I tell him that?'

'That's what he told Mark.'

I thought back to the conversation. 'Maybe he's right. Maybe I did.'

'Well, from what Alistair said to Mark, it's clear that he thinks that you're very committed to a relationship with Felix.'

I reclosed my eyes, feeling no less confused for all Becca's attempts to help me clarify things. 'Right.'

'Dot, I think the important thing is whether, now that you know Alistair's feelings, you regret that he thinks you're happily dating Felix and that there is no future for the two of you. If that is the case, then it's something to sort out.'

I thought about it for a moment. 'Right now, I do not want a relationship with Alistair,' I said firmly. 'And I can't think of anything short of a time machine that would change that.'

'OK.'

She didn't say anything more, and after a moment I spoke again. 'You should call Mark, Becca. And I'm sorry for ranting. I wish he'd told you about speaking to Alistair, but I don't think he really did anything wrong.'

'He said he had no idea Alistair planned to see you so soon,' said Becca with a sigh. 'Apparently he spoke to Mark yesterday about a golf day and asked after you in passing, but he didn't mention anything about going out for a drink tonight. Mark said he told Alistair about the birthday party in Cheltenham tomorrow, but he also said that he thought things between you and Felix were very low-key. He was trying to be as honest with Alistair as he possibly could be without dropping you in it. He didn't mean to mess things up for you; he thought he was doing a good thing. He'd intended to tell me about it, but…' She hesitated before continuing. 'Well, there's just been a lot going on here and other things took over.'

'Tell him it's fine,' I said wearily, sitting up. 'Honestly. I don't think it changed anything.'

'You feel as if you're over Alistair?'

'You don't sound surprised about that.'

'I'm not really,' she said, now sounding as exhausted as I felt. 'I had thought recently that maybe you were moving on. That's part of the reason I wished Mark had talked to me before offering Alistair any advice.'

'I felt very differently about him tonight, Becca,' I said sadly. 'I know it's superficial of me, but when he walked into the pub, the first thing I thought was that I didn't fancy him. And that was even before he had a pop at Felix. God, the whole thing was just awful,' I added with a groan.

'It must have been.'

'But I suppose I should really try to sort things out with him.'

'With who? With Alistair?' She sounded both anxious and surprised at the thought. 'Not tonight, Dot.'

'No, don't worry, not tonight,' I reassured. 'And I'll do it in writing so that I can think it all through and not make anything worse. I'll email him when I get back from Cheltenham, if he hasn't got in touch first. I was still pretty angry when I left the pub tonight and I don't want to leave things that way between us. What did he say to Mark?'

'Just that things hadn't gone too well.'

'Master of understatement.'

'I'm so sorry.'

'Don't be,' I said, smiling sadly. 'If we track this back, the situation is no one's fault but my own. And,' I added, 'there was an upside to it all.'

'Really?'

'Yes, it made me appreciate Felix even more.'

'That's good.'

'I know. It brought home to me again just how supportive he was about the wedding – and since. He was so lovely the night everything went pear-shaped with Mum and Dad.'

'Yes,' she said quietly. 'He's been very... resilient throughout.'

I smiled at her careful choice of words. 'Did you know, by the way, about him pushing me home drunk and totally out of it in a shopping trolley?' I asked, attempting to lighten the conversation a little.

'What? Recently?'

'No,' I tutted. 'When we were teenagers. I didn't remember it because, obviously, I was drunk and totally out of it in a shopping trolley at the time. But Mum knew.'

'I don't recall hearing any screams.'

'She's never mentioned it.'

'Wow.'

'I know. Astonishing, isn't it?' I sighed. 'Anyway, you go and call your husband and I'll tell you the full shopping trolley story another time.'

'And what are you going to do?' she asked.

'I'm going to pack for tomorrow and then watch telly in bed.'

'Sounds good. Are you looking forward to seeing Felix?'

'I really am,' I said. 'It'll be nice to have a relaxing and uncomplicated weekend. It's just what I need.'

'You should make a point of telling him how much you appreciate him, Dot,' said Becca gently, but with just a hint of deputy head. 'Friends like Felix don't come along every day.'

'You're right,' I said, standing up and beginning once again to study the contents of my wardrobe.

'Have a lovely weekend. Tell me all about it next week.'

'I will. Hey, but hang on,' I added quickly, sitting back down, 'you haven't told me your news yet.'

'Oh… yes…' she said hesitantly. 'It's OK, I'll save that for next week too. You've had quite an evening and need to get on with packing.'

'Tell me!' I insisted. 'I could do with hearing some happy news.'

'Well, OK then…' She paused, and I imagined her taking a deep breath.

'Yes?' I laughed. 'Oh for goodness' sake, Becca, spit it out!'

'I'm pregnant,' she said simply.

And after a moment which saw me put a hand to my mouth and gasp in astonishment and delight, the conversation began anew.

Chapter 25

To my mild surprise, I discovered that Felix didn't actually live in Cheltenham itself, but in a small rural hamlet about four miles to the south. And I was surprised again, as I turned off a winding B road and through aged iron double gates, to find myself on a narrow gravel driveway and heading towards a quirky Victorian cottage with small churchlike mullioned windows, two tall chimneys and an ornately gabled roof.

I climbed out of the car, retrieved my suitcase from the boot and stared up at the house as I began to walk around it in search of an entrance. I took my time, distracted by the flowers and trees crowding the large garden which encircled the property. And as I ambled and paused along a pathway running close to the house, I spotted Felix himself before I found a door.

He was wearing a dark checked shirt, jeans and black wellies and was crouching with his back to me at the far end of the garden. A spade stuck up from the ground next to him.

'Felix!' I called, waving in anticipation of him turning around, but he didn't move. 'Felix!' I repeated more loudly, cupping my hands around my mouth for increased projection, but still without result. Abandoning my suitcase, I left the path and began to make my way across the lawn towards him. As I drew near, I realised that he was wearing earbuds connected to a phone which protruded from his back pocket. I smiled and was just about to tap him on the shoulder when he stood up and turned towards me, grinning in surprise.

'Dot,' he said loudly, pulling the buds from his ears and stuffing them into his pocket along with the phone. He moved towards me as if for a hug before stepping back and holding up hands covered in mud. 'Better not actually,' he smiled. 'I thought I'd have this done and be cleaned up before you got here, but I've lost track of time.'

'I'm half an hour early. It's only just two,' I said, looking down at the border. 'Weeding?'

He shook his head. 'Planting. I thought if I didn't do it today I wouldn't get a chance till next weekend.'

'Well finish what you're doing,' I smiled. 'I'm quite happy to sit and watch. Or assist, if you trust me.'

'It's all done. I just need to clean up a bit.'

I looked him up and down. 'You're looking so rural,' I said. 'This is all,' I turned towards the house, 'just so rural, Felix.'

He laughed. 'Is that a surprise?'

'It is actually,' I said, still gazing at the house. 'I suppose I just had you down as a townie. You're so corporate and controlled these days, I thought you'd opt for something modern and minimalist.'

When I turned back towards him, I saw that his smile was now accompanied by a slight frown. 'That wasn't a criticism,' I added hastily. 'It's just that because you're a serious accountant and usually dress like a House of Fraser menswear ad, I hadn't pictured you living in a quirky cottage, wearing wellies and getting your hands dirty at the weekend. It's like when we found out that Mr Moorland at school was a Druid. Remember that?'

Felix nodded but the frown remained in place. 'I'm not sure gardening is on a par with dressing like Gandalf and hailing the points of the compass, but I sort of see where you're coming from,' he said.

'Oh, you know what I mean,' I replied, waving a hand. 'But it doesn't matter anyway because I love the house, I love the garden, I like your hair a bit wilder and you look great in your wellies.'

'That's all hugely reassuring,' he smiled. 'Cup of tea?'

'Yes please,' I said, and as his grin broadened and he beckoned me to follow, we made our way back across the lawn towards the house.

'This is fab,' I said, running my eye around the kitchen as Felix lifted the boiling kettle from the top of an elderly-looking Aga and set about making a cup of tea for me and coffee for himself. 'How long have you been here?'

'I rented in Cheltenham for about a year after we set up the business and then bought this place. So that's two years ago now,' he said, turning to look at me over his shoulder.

'And have you made lots of changes?' I pointed to the Shaker cabinets and heavy wooden work surfaces. 'Did you put all this in?'

He walked to the table, handed me a mug and then sat down opposite me. 'The kitchen and heating system are new and so is the roof, but there's still loads to do. Lots of the plasterwork needs replacing because there are damp patches everywhere. Upstairs is nowhere near finished.

I've spent far too much time in the garden this summer. Plus I've lost a little bit of heart for the refurb.' He looked as if he was about to say more, but instead picked up his mug and took a sip.

Wondering if his loss of enthusiasm for interior design might be related to the break-up of his relationship, I decided to sidestep the comment. 'I think I'd be the same – focusing on the garden, I mean – especially in this weather. Whenever I go to Becca's, I envy her the garden and the views. And it's the same at Mum and Dad's. I love my flat, but I definitely hanker after some outdoor space. This place seems perfect: privacy, character and just a stone's throw from Cheltenham. You're so lucky.'

He looked up from his mug and smiled. 'I am.'

'And,' I continued, keen to keep things upbeat, 'you're about to get a whole lot luckier, because I have, as every good guest should, come bearing gifts.'

'You're just so well brought up,' he called after me as I hurried out into the hallway, returning with a bottle of wine and a small square package, which I had that morning wrapped in pink tissue paper and tied with a silver ribbon. I placed the bottle on the table and handed the package to Felix, who looked up at me quizzically. 'What's this?' he asked.

'Only one way to find out,' I said, sitting back down and folding my arms.

He smiled and pulled at the ribbon, undoing the bow and carefully unfolding the paper. When the gift was revealed, he looked down at it, frowning for a moment before laughing loudly. 'Where on earth did you get this?' he exclaimed, holding up the framed photograph of the two of us standing side by side in the school Christmas play.

Delighted by his reaction, I stood up and walked around the table, sitting down beside him. 'My mother,' I said simply.

He nodded, gazing at the picture in his hands. 'I was such a great pudding,' he said.

'And not just at Christmas.'

'Low blow.'

'And I don't think I'm a bad candle either,' I said, pointing at my thirteen-year-old self. 'But was I really that much taller than you?'

'I know. I'm having trouble with that too, but you're clearly not standing on a box.'

'So when did that change?'

Felix lifted his head and looked thoughtful. 'I remember arguing with you in a school corridor about Sean Dowse wanting to give you that scone tattoo...'

'It was a leopard.'

'I saw the proposed design. It was a scone,' he said, unmoved. 'And I remember us arguing about it and suddenly realising that I was looking you in the eye.'

I thought back. 'We must have been about fifteen then. And after that, you shot up, because I remember sitting next to you in The Lamb that night with Chris and Ian and realising how much...' I looked up at him and frowned.

'How much what?' he asked.

I shook my head. 'Sorry, I just had a weird flashback moment to the pub. Do you ever get that? We were sitting just like this and...' I frowned again.

'This had better be good,' he sighed.

'I just remember realising that you were a good three or four inches taller than Ian.'

Felix stared at me impassively. '*Not* an anecdote worth waiting for.'

'Oh, shut up.' I laughed and nudged him. 'I love this,' I said, tapping the photo again.

He looked at it and smiled. 'One of the best gifts I've had in a long time.'

'My copy is in my living room,' I said, as he stood up and placed the photo on the shelf above the large fireplace.

He stood for a moment, his back to me, hands in pockets, contemplating the picture, before returning to his seat.

'So what's going on with you?' he asked, picking up his mug of tea. 'Why so keen to escape Bristol?'

'Oh, it's nothing,' I said, trying to sound casual. 'I'm just panicking over work things that haven't even happened. Actually, some things have happened, but mostly I'm obsessing about things that might happen and worrying about what I'm going to do if they do.'

He raised his eyebrows in surprise. 'That doesn't sound like you.'

'I know,' I sighed. 'It sounds like the opposite of me, doesn't it? It's all a bit weird. There's a complete role reversal in the office.'

'So Kate's not worried about the situation?'

I shook my head. 'Not any more.'

Felix stretched across the table, retrieving my cup of tea and handing it to me. I smiled and took it from him. 'Thanks.'

'So, are you going to tell me what the problem is or not?'

'I don't want to burden you.'

'You won't be. I'm genuinely desperate to know. It sounds like it might be juicy.'

I rolled my eyes. 'You're terrible.'

'You know I'm joking,' he said. 'Tell me. I might be able to help.'

'Kate's pregnant,' I said, looking up at him.

He nodded. 'Keep going.'

I took a deep breath. 'It was an accident, or at least very unexpected, and she went a bit loopy for a week, but now she's fine about it and very happy.'

'OK, and you're worried about a change in your relationship and because she may or may not come back to work. And you're reluctant to pressurise her on the subject, and even if she gives you what she thinks is a definite answer, you're aware that the situation and her take on things could change.'

I looked at him for a moment. 'Gosh, you're good.'

'I can relate,' he smiled. 'I also work with a friend and I can imagine how I'd feel if Kevin announced a significant change in his personal circumstances. Would you like me to help you with some business contingency planning? We could think about the possible scenarios, and take a look at how and where you could continue to operate if Kate is away for a while, or decides not to return. I could tell you the information I need you to send me and then we could go over it next time I'm in Bristol.'

'Felix... I don't know what to say. That would be great, if you wouldn't mind.'

'My usual rate is a hundred and twenty pounds an hour, but I'd do this for a hundred and eighteen, seeing as we go way back.'

'*Or* we could we offset it against all the pastries I bought you between 1992 and 2002?'

'Quits then,' he said.

'Thanks, Felix.' I smiled up at him, and then, remembering my recent conversation with Becca about being more vocal in my appreciation of him, I lowered my eyes to my mug and added, 'Thanks for everything – then and now – even when I don't deserve it.'

I paused, feeling as if I had more to say but clueless as to what that might be. And I briefly wondered whether putting my arms around his middle and gently resting my head against his chest, as I had so often done as a teenager, might be the most effective way of communicating the feelings I couldn't currently quite put into words.

However, not one hundred per cent convinced of the appropriateness of a hug and chest nuzzle at that particular moment, I instead placed my hands out of harm's way around my mug and, aware of a new and slightly artificial brightness to my tone, said, 'Oh, and while I think of it, I keep forgetting to tell you that Rosie – the policewoman you sat next to at Becca's wedding – really liked you. She'd be keen to see you again if, you know, you ever...' I continued to focus on my tea. 'There's no pressure, but I promised Mark I'd pass that on and give you her number.' I pulled my phone from the pocket of my jeans.

Felix didn't reply, and when I finally stopped tapping at my phone and forced myself to look at him, I found him to be as equally fixated on his hot drink as I had been on mine.

'That's a nice compliment and I'll bear the offer in mind,' he said.

'Well, you've got her number now,' I replied. 'I mean, I know the timing might not be great, but…'

He smiled and turned towards me. 'Not at all. She was very nice. Thanks for letting me know. Now drink up,' he said, standing up. 'It's time for you to get rural.'

Chapter 26

Felix route-marched me around a seven-mile circular country walk which somehow achieved the impossible feat of being uphill all the way – or at least that was how it felt to me. He, as usual, showed no sign of even mild fatigue, and while I sat down at the kitchen table with a second cup of tea and a magazine on our return to the house, he went outside to *quickly mow the top lawn*.

A couple of hours later, both showered and changed, and having shared a small jug of Pimm's on the newly mown lawn, we set off for the fortieth birthday party, which, Felix told me, was taking place not in Cheltenham but in a marquee in the garden of the White Hart, a gastropub just a short stroll away.

'Now, is it *really* just a short stroll?' I asked as we crunched down the cottage's gravel driveway towards the gates at just after eight o'clock. 'Only I don't want to be climbing over any stiles in these.' I looked down with early misgiving at the white cigarette pants I had teamed with a pale blue shirt and light brown jacket.

'It's about a ten-minute walk over flat terrain,' he said.

'And right away I'm feeling nervous about your use of the word *terrain*,' I sighed. 'I associate *terrain* with adjectives like *rough* and *difficult*. It conjures up images of mud and rock. I prefer words like *path* and *pavement* and *taxi*.'

'Well you're in luck then, because there is a pavement – most of the way. Here, let me take those,' he said, relieving me of the pair of beige strappy heels I was carrying, having decided to wear my walking boots to get to the pub.

'Thanks. And can I link your arm?' I asked as we reached the end of the drive and turned left onto the aforementioned pavement, which ran along one side of the road. 'That Pimm's hit me pretty hard. You make it really strong.'

'It was ninety-nine per cent lemonade, Dot,' said Felix despairingly, as he held out his hand to me. 'Have you ever considered the possibility that you might be allergic to alcohol?'

'It's only certain drinks that seem to knock me for six,' I argued, taking his hand.

'Just the liquid ones.'

'Shush, and are you sure that what I'm wearing is OK for the party?' I asked, glancing uncertainly at his jeans and the kind of floral shirt so admired by my mother. With his hair now curling and his skin increasingly tanned, Felix exuded effortless summer cool, and I couldn't help feeling as if I might appear to be trying to hard by comparison. 'I'm not sure that I look as—'

'You look fine,' he said.

'Hmm… I don't know,' I murmured, looking down at my trousers. 'I always struggle with what to wear. Some women just seem to know what to put with what, don't they? I'm so hopeless at layering. I might as well roll around in a pile of laundry and go out in whatever has enough static to stick. It doesn't help that I'm really self-conscious in heels, or that whenever I make an effort with make-up I end up looking like that meme of the monkey with the lipstick. You know, the one with—'

Up until then we had been walking quite quickly, but now Felix stopped so suddenly that I was jerked backwards. 'Careful,' I said, letting go of his hand and rubbing my right shoulder, 'I nearly fell over. 'What's the matter? Why did you stop?'

'Do you genuinely think you're unattractive?' he asked. His expression was benign but his tone was mildly frustrated.

'What do you mean?' I asked, a little taken aback.

'Ever since I've known you, you've gone on about how plain you are. Didn't that idiot Sean Dowse ever tell you that you were pretty? Surely Alistair must have reassured you from time to time. And what about all the ones in between?'

I said nothing, mentally picking apart the short, unexpected interrogation whilst staring up at him, aware of my face beginning to burn.

'All the ones in between?' I frowned. 'There hasn't exactly been a football team, you know, Felix. Not even a five-a-side.'

He closed his eyes and heaved a sigh. 'OK, I'm sorry,' he said quietly. 'I didn't phrase that brilliantly. All I mean is that you look great and you've always looked great, even in your Björk phase. That seems so obvious to me that I can't believe it's not obvious to you. You've got nothing to worry about.'

We stood in silence for a moment, Felix with his hands in his pockets, now staring into the hedgerow, and me feeling hurt by the compliment in a way that was inexplicable even to myself.

'I'm sorry. I didn't realise I banged on about it so much,' I said sullenly.

'You don't,' he said, still apparently fascinated by the hawthorn. 'It's me.' He now looked and sounded so subdued that I forgot about feeling wounded and became concerned.

'Is something wrong?' I asked. 'Because we don't have to go to the party if you're not in the mood for it. Or if you'd rather go on your own,' I added, as it crossed my mind that I might somehow be the problem. 'I'm fine to stay at home with the owls.'

He turned towards me. 'The owls?'

'And the badgers and the bats and...' I waved a hand, 'and all the other rural night-time creatures.'

He shook his head. 'I want to go to the party. And I want to go with you,' he said.

I studied his face for a moment and then, deciding that he was telling the truth, nodded.

'I guess I should check whether *you* still want to go,' he said.

'Of course I do,' I replied, taking a deep breath. 'To tell the truth, now that I've listed all the rural night-time creatures, I've realised that I'm actually quite afraid of most of them.'

'Me too,' he said. 'Especially the bats. So thanks for that.' He looked over his shoulder at the cottage for a moment and then turned back towards me. 'We'd better go, Dot,' he said, holding out his arm for me to link, 'or the free booze will have run out before we get there.'

'What?' I exclaimed. 'Why didn't you tell me that earlier? I thought it was an all-nighter.'

'It might be. I'm not sure,' he said, as we started to walk. 'Only do go easy, won't you? There aren't a lot of shopping trolleys around here.'

In the end, the walk to the party took around half an hour rather than ten minutes, due to a rerouting to avoid two stiles. I didn't mind the additional mile, being grateful not only for the preservation of my white trousers, but also for the extra time the detour put between us and the odd exchange with which the journey had started. It meant that by the time we approached the door of the White Hart, I had stopped worrying about whether Felix thought I had been obsessed with my appearance for the past two decades, and he seemed to have recovered from the bout of seriousness which had so taken me by surprise.

'You meant well,' he said with a grin as I finished an account of my attempts to set Fred's mind at rest over Kate's pregnancy behaviour.

'That's exactly what Fred said to Kate,' I sighed. 'But come on, tell me something horrendous you've said or done recently. Or do you never put your foot in it these days, Mr Smooth?'

'Only with you,' he said, reaching out to open the pub door for me. 'We have to go through the bar to get to the garden.'

'OK, but can you wait a moment while I slip those on?' I pointed at the strappy shoes still dangling from his right hand.

'Sure.' He let go of the door and handed over the shoes as I sat down at a nearby picnic table and bent to untie my boots.

'Why don't you tell me a little bit about the birthday boy while I change into my heels?' I suggested.

'Good idea,' Felix nodded. 'He's Martin McGarry and he's married to Gemma and they live next door to Kevin. That's how I met them. Martin's a keen footballer and cyclist and I occasionally join him for a bike ride. He also enjoys cooking and I've been to their house a few times for dinner. Is that enough to be going on with?'

'Yep,' I said, picking up my boots and standing up. 'Now, is there anything else vital we need to go over before we go in?'

'Other than whether you'd prefer to be my friend or my girlfriend?' he asked, turning and walking back to the door of the pub and once again holding it open for me.

I looked at him, utterly thrown by the question. Whether I was still suffering the mild after-effects of the Pimm's, I wasn't sure, but the sights and sounds of a summer evening seemed to melt into a haze as I lost awareness of everything but Felix. His head turned towards me and as the edges of his mouth curled upwards into a mischievous smile, I experienced a sort of blurred, top-speed rerun of the history of our relationship to date, including choir practices, cake runs, play rehearsals, pub visits, office encounters and, of course, Becca's wedding.

On that occasion, Felix's vastly changed appearance had simply increased my sense of loss and longing for the return of my nowhere-to-be-seen childhood best friend. This evening, however, his appearance was not a problem. He might be four stone and several inches of hair lighter, but he was, nevertheless, completely back *in situ* and fully recognisable as the funny, kind, supportive friend with whom I had grown up – a friend who now wanted our relationship to move to a new level; a closer, deeper one. And in that moment, as a final hazy recollection of a teenage evening at The Lamb floated through my brain, I knew absolutely that that was what I wanted too. Perhaps it was what I had always wanted.

I gazed up at him and, smiling in anticipation of being swept into his wonderfully toned arms, took the few short steps necessary to reach him.

Fortunately, that distance was just far enough for me to register the slightly confused expression on his face and, more importantly, to bring me to my senses.

'You're asking whether I'd like to pretend to be your girlfriend at Martin's birthday party,' I said, coming to an abrupt halt just a few inches from him. 'Like you pretended to be my boyfriend at Becca's wedding.'

Felix shrugged and continued to smile. 'I just thought you might like to return the favour. That way, I wouldn't evoke any local pity as a sad singleton and we could continue a tradition of lying through our teeth to friends and family at significant social events.'

'OK,' I said, taking a deep breath and desperately trying to ignore the fact that within the space of approximately ten seconds Felix had helpfully clarified my feelings and then crushed them like meringues under a steamroller, 'but as I remember it, we weren't particularly brilliant at faking it last time.'

He placed a hand on his chin, feigning thoughtfulness, and then nodded acceptingly. 'Good point. Friends it is then.'

'Friends it is,' I echoed, and, attempting to hide my agonising disappointment and aching stupidity behind a broad grin, I stepped past him into the pub.

Chapter 27

The marquee was already crowded and buzzing with the mingling sounds of laughter and music when we arrived. And our entrance immediately gave the lie to Felix's claim that he needed me on his arm for company and moral support.

Our progress to the bar, which was housed in a smaller, quieter annexe at the rear of the main marquee, was impeded several times by friends who were clearly delight to see him and eager to talk to him. And once we did finally reach the bar, he was gently but physically accosted three times within the space of five minutes by means of a hand on his arm. On each occasion, the attention was female, and I reflected on the fact that whilst just three hours earlier I would have found these slightly drunken flirtatious approaches entertaining and something with which to tease Felix, I now found them just a tiny bit annoying.

I managed to escape introduction to the first two ladies, one of whom was gone after the arm squeeze, a brazenly lingering kiss to the cheek and a tipsy explanation that she needed the loo, and the second of whom left after delivering a pouty demand for a dance later in the evening. But when it became clear that Admirer #3 was up for a lengthier exchange with him, Felix turned to introduce me.

'Carla, this is Dot. Dot, Carla,' he said, smiling at a tallish redhead whose sheer shirt, palazzo pants, silky cardigan and multi-string necklace revealed an enviable flair for layering. 'Carla is an accountant with a rival firm in Cheltenham.'

'Ooh,' I said, smiling my thanks to the barman as he handed me the pint of beer and glass of Prosecco I had just requested. 'Is it all calculators and spreadsheets at dawn?'

Felix took his pint from me. 'No,' he laughed, 'it's all very amicable.'

'That's a relief,' I said, smiling at Carla. 'Lovely to meet you.'

'Dot is one of my oldest friends,' explained Felix. 'We've known each other since we were eleven.'

At the mention of the word *friend*, I bravely maintained a smile while Carla's expression transformed from something remarkably like suspicion to obvious relief. 'Ah, how lovely is that?' she said, sounding as if she genuinely meant it. 'So what was this one like at school then, Dot?' she asked, looking up at Felix and playfully prodding his arm.

I took a sip of Prosecco, teetering on the brink of an honest but emotional declaration that Felix had been as patient, selfless, kind and fun at school as he was now, and that I hoped his friends in Cheltenham loved and appreciated him as much as I always had and always would. But at the last moment, I got a grip.

'Wider.'

Felix laughed and Carla frowned. 'Wider?'

'Yes,' I said. 'But no less handsome for it,' I added, unable to rein in my emotions entirely.

'I had a fondness for pastries and pies,' said Felix, smiling at me, 'which Dot would occasionally fund.'

'You're making me sound like a feeder,' I protested.

'Hmm... well now I think about it...' he said.

'I can't imagine you as anything other than fighting fit, Felix.' Carla ran her eyes up and down him appreciatively and placed her hand, *yet again*, on his arm. I clenched my jaw into a broader smile and wished my mother was there to tell Carla to keep her mitts to herself.

'Hello, Felix! Oh, and hello, Dorothy!' Recognising the voice, I turned to see Kevin a little way down the bar, leaning backwards in order to make eye contact behind the row of four or five drinkers between us.

'Hi, Kevin!' I called, pleased both to see him and of the excuse to move on from Carla who, although completely inoffensive, clearly had designs on Felix and I didn't want to witness the progression of the process. I nudged Felix. 'I'm just going to go and say a quick hello to Kevin.'

'I'll come with you,' he said.

'No, no,' I replied, waving a hand and looking at a crestfallen Carla, who was unable to hide her disappointment at the possible departure of her prey. 'You stay and talk to Carla. I'm fine. I'll come and find you if I get lonely.'

Felix's eyes narrowed slightly, but he smiled and raised a hand in greeting to Kevin as I headed off in the direction of the latter.

'Hello,' I said, reaching him just as he picked up his drink and took a few steps back from the bar.

'Hello, Dorothy Riley,' he said jovially.

'Permission to hug?' I asked.

'Permission to hug,' he confirmed, laughing and opening his arms. 'And how are you?' he asked on releasing me. 'I was so pleased when Felix said he was bringing you along tonight.'

'Thank you for saying so,' I smiled. 'I was pleased too. He's rescued me from a weekend of work worries. Oh, but nothing major,' I added hastily as Kevin's face fell slightly. 'And Felix has already calmed me down enormously about everything.'

'He's good at that, isn't he?' said Kevin, his smile returning.

'He is.'

'Mind you,' he continued, pointing at me, 'you do the same for him, so fair's fair.'

'Do I really?' I said with surprise. 'I don't think I've ever been labelled a calming influence before.'

'Well,' said Kevin, lowering his voice and looking round before leaning towards me conspiratorially, 'as you know, he hasn't had the best of years this year, but I can honestly say that you've turned that around. Linda thinks so too.'

I bit my lip, feeling genuinely touched. 'Really?' I said. 'That is so lovely to hear, because Felix has done so much for *me* recently. And not so recently actually,' I added.

'When *it* happened,' continued Kevin in a near whisper, with the air of a man who enjoyed confiding, 'he didn't let it impact on his professionalism or the business at all. He's far too thoughtful about Linda and me to let it do that. But in terms of his personality, we noticed a change. There was no anger, of course, but he was definitely more withdrawn, and, just occasionally, I saw something bordering on – dare I say – bitterness, which was fair enough in the circumstances, but not something I had seen in him ever before, even in the most testing of times. But then you came along and invited him to your sister's wedding,' he said, raising his pint to me, 'and boom, welcome back, Felix.'

'I really don't know what to say, Kevin,' I said, moved by the compliment, 'other than it's made me very happy to think that I might have helped Felix in some way – even if I didn't know it. But you know what's interesting?' I continued, lowering the level of my voice to match his.

'What?' he asked, his eyes dancing at the possibility of being party to a personal insight.

'When I visited Felix that day at your offices, I didn't recognise him. I mean, obviously I didn't recognise him physically, as you know. But I also didn't recognise him as a person. He seemed to have lost… his sense of fun, really. There was just no hint of it and I was quite thrown by that.'

Kevin nodded solemnly. 'We all were, Dorothy, we all were. Linda had her own ideas for sorting the situation, of course. She wanted to steal his phone so she could block texts from…' He paused and looked around once again before mouthing a name, employing the kind of exaggerated lip movements my mother used whenever Nanny Flo refused to wear her hearing aids.

'Sorry, Kevin, I didn't quite catch that,' I said, staring intently at his mouth.

'Beattie,' he repeated in a whisper. 'Felix's girlfriend.'

'OK,' I said, nodding but distracted for a moment by the discovery that Gwyneth's *actual* name was one that I had up until then only ever associated with the rather portly form of Nanny Flo's elderly friend

Beattie Blackwell. And in that context, the name was always preceded, quite justifiably, by the adjective 'Big'. The upshot was that the ex-formerly-known-as-Gwyneth immediately lost a little of her A-list gloss for me.

'Beattie,' I murmured thoughtfully, adjusting to the name change.

'Yes, yes.' Kevin nodded rapidly, holding a finger to his lips in a request for me to lower my voice even further. 'Linda wanted to block Beattie's calls but I talked her down. That's Linda all over, you see. Very protective of both Felix and me, which is wonderful, but also a little bit *too* protective at times. I think some clients are actually rather afraid of her, you know. But underneath all that surface rage and menace, she's actually a bit of a softy.'

He laughed and I nodded, recalling my foiled early attempt to obtain Felix's phone number from Linda, and making a mental note to tread carefully should I ever encounter her. 'The thing is, Kevin, I haven't really discussed Gwyn... I mean Beattie with Felix, so I don't know any of the details, other than that they split five or six months ago and that he was clearly unhappy about it.'

He looked thoughtful. 'Well I'm sure he will tell you all about it in due course,' he said. 'But while we're on the subject, I'm assuming you know that Beattie's—' He stopped abruptly before adding, 'Well that's just so interesting.'

I frowned at him. 'I know that Beattie's what?'

His eyes widened slightly as he nodded his head barely perceptibly to indicate something over my left shoulder and sipped his drink.

I turned just as Felix reached us. 'Oh, I see. Hi,' I said, trying not to look guilty.

'What are you two talking about?' he asked. 'It all looked very intense from over there.' He glanced questioningly between Kevin and me.

'Becca's wedding,' I said, just a little too quickly and a little too squeakily.

Felix raised his eyebrows sceptically before turning to Kevin. At which point I discovered that Kevin was about as adept at hiding things from Felix as I was from Kate – worse, in fact.

'We were discussing *you*, Felix,' he said, with the air of a puppy who had just been caught pooing on the carpet. 'More specifically, your...' He then soundlessly mouthed the words *recent personal difficulties*, his lips moving like a sink plunger seeing some serious action, while I stared at him, wondering if he had perhaps been hypnotised in the past and Felix now only had to look at him in a certain way to get him to tell the absolute truth – or eat an onion.

Felix shook his head. 'You two are so alike,' he said, smiling.

Kevin laughed. 'He wangles it out of me every single time, Dorothy. He's quite ruthless with his interrogation,' he added jovially, turning and picking up a couple more drinks from the bar. 'Anyway, I was getting these for Michael Conlon and Richard Webster, Felix, and they're going to be wondering where I am. We're sitting next door. Do you two want to come through and join us?'

'I'll introduce Dot to them in a little while,' said Felix.

Kevin smiled. 'Lovely. Well, I'll go and deliver these drinks and catch you two later.'

'Later,' smiled Felix, as Kevin raised his clutch of three glasses in farewell and headed off towards a group sitting at a table next to the, as yet deserted, dance floor in the main marquee.

'And Kate calls me transparent,' I said, looking after him.

Felix laughed and I turned towards him.

'Shall we sit?' he asked.

'You don't want to mingle?'

'Maybe later. Right now, I'd just like to enjoy my beer after that walk. We could stay in here for a while,' he said, gesturing towards a couple of stools at the far end of the bar. 'It's a bit quieter.'

'Sounds good,' I said, as we walked to the stools and sat down. 'Where did Carla go?'

'To get some food. I explained that you didn't know anyone here apart from Kevin and that I didn't want to abandon you.'

'You didn't have to do that,' I tutted. 'I was more than OK.'

Felix shook his head. 'I was happy to end the conversation.'

'Gotcha,' I replied, winking and tapping the side of my nose. 'And happy to be an excuse whenever required.'

'Thank you,' he smiled. 'And I'll reciprocate, obviously. Although you clearly didn't need rescuing from Kevin.'

I picked up my drink. 'He didn't tell me anything very personal, by the way,' I said, a little guiltily. 'He just said that things hadn't been great for you this year, but that you seemed happier recently.'

Felix shrugged. 'And both of those things are true.'

'Good. About things improving, I mean.'

'How about you?'

'Me?' I looked up from my drink.

'Yes, you,' he said, smiling. 'I know Kate's pregnancy has been a shock, but how is everything else?'

I put a hand to my forehead. 'Oh God, I haven't told you about last night yet, have I?'

'No, you haven't, but I'm already interested,' he said, pointing to my raised hand. 'It's looking stressy.'

'Well,' I began, putting down my drink, 'one bit wasn't stressy at all. Becca's pregnant.'

His eyes widened in surprise and then he laughed. 'Is pregnancy contagious?'

'Seems like it, doesn't it? She told me on the phone last night but she hasn't told Mum yet, so I'm bracing myself for that one hitting the fan. Oh, but in a nice way, of course. I just mean that Mum is going to...' I waved a hand and shook my head. 'Actually, I don't want to think too much about how my mother is going to react. But I think it's safe to say the reaction will be full-on.'

'I can imagine,' he said. 'And how are you feeling about being Aunt Dorothy?'

'God, that sounds aged, doesn't it?' I laughed. 'I'll be listening to *Gardeners' Question Time* and knitting blanket squares before you know it.' I looked at him and smiled, deciding not to add that Becca's pregnancy – hot on the heels of Kate's and the realisation that my relationship with Alistair was well and truly in the past – had only added to a growing sense that my life seemed somewhat directionless in comparison to everyone else's right now. Nor did I tell him that for the first time ever, I had last night found myself just a little envious of Alistair's penchant for forward planning, when it had occurred to me that being able to refer to a five-year plan – with built-in contingencies for any eventuality – might actually be of enormous comfort at a time when I didn't have a clue what was in store for me professionally or personally.

'And is Becca due around the same time as Kate?' asked Felix.

I frowned slightly at the question. 'Ooh, I don't know,' I said, uncertainly. 'Due dates are something you should definitely ask about, aren't they? She did say it was very early days and that that was why she wasn't going to tell Mum and Dad until they got home from touring, but she didn't tell me how many weeks she is and I didn't ask. The news was just one half of a rather weird conversation I had with her last night,' I added in my defence.

'Weird because of the stressy stuff?'

'Because of the stressy stuff,' I confirmed, nodding slowly.

'Go on then,' he said, smiling. 'Lay it on me.'

'So,' I took a deep breath, 'it turns out that Alistair…'

Felix's smile immediately dropped and he nodded. 'I'm stressed already.'

'Exactly,' I said. 'Anyway, Alistair had, unbeknownst to either Becca or myself, been discussing me with Mark.'

'OK, so now I'm stressed for Mark,' said Felix, pulling a face.

'You should be. Becca was not happy.'

'And you found out about this last night?'

'Yes, but only *after* I had met Alistair for a drink – at his suggestion.'

Felix had just picked up his beer, but now returned it to the bar untouched. 'He asked you out? What did he want to talk about?'

'Us,' I said with a sigh. 'He and Naomi are no more and, to cut an extremely long story short, he wanted us to get back together.'

Felix looked thoughtful for a moment and then said, 'I think I'd like to hear the extremely long story.'

'That's very brave of you, but I'm not sure you do.' I smiled up at him, but his expression remained serious. 'Don't worry, it's actually all fine.'

'So the story has a happy ending?'

I picked up my drink, taking a sip as a delaying tactic as I considered the question. Was I happy that Alistair finally seemed to have accepted me as me? Yes, of course I was. Was I happy that he had made an attempt, albeit a confused one, to tell me that? Well... yes again. Was I happy that I no longer yearned for him? OK, so there was an inevitable sense of regret that our relationship hadn't worked out – and also that the realisation that it was at an absolute end had been so abrupt for both of us – but clarity, no matter how it was achieved, was a positive thing.

But a happy ending?

I looked at Felix, wondering if now was a good time to tell him that he was suddenly, once again, very much a part of the story. I was acutely aware that we were in public, that I was staying over, and that if he was horrified by my growing feelings for him then we could be in for a very uncomfortable and awkward twelve hours. But I really didn't think that would happen. I was certain that however he felt, he would understand my feelings and respect them.

I took another gulp of Prosecco and cleared my throat. 'It's good that Alistair and I know how we feel about each other. I like that kind of clarity.'

Felix looked at me and nodded. 'Yes. I think that's a good thing.'

'And he and I, to quote Taylor Swift, are nev—'

'Hello, Felix.'

He turned towards the voice before I did. In fact, by the time I had stopped looking at him and realised that the woman who had spoken his name was the woman in the nightclub photograph – Beattie – he had already put down his drink and was on his feet. For some reason, I felt that I should do the same and slid hurriedly, and a little awkwardly, from my bar stool to stand next to him.

Neither of them looked at me.

'Hi,' said Felix, looking surprised and not entirely comfortable. 'I didn't think you were coming tonight.'

She smiled but was also obviously far from relaxed. 'It was a last-minute thing. I told Gemma and Martin I wouldn't be able to make it, but I'm here with Izzy Noble. She stopped by and dragged me along because...' She hesitated and shrugged. 'Well, she just did.'

Felix made no response, but, I noted, seemed to have regained his composure. The silence between them dragged on as he returned her gaze, and I started to feel like the very dictionary definition of a third wheel.

'It's good to see you,' she offered eventually.

He lifted his chin slightly in a sort of half-nod, but didn't reply, and she at last turned towards me. We looked at each other and, with no one speaking, I took the opportunity to examine her.

Her look this evening was somewhere in between the nightclub photo and the one Felix had shown me at Becca's wedding reception. She was wearing just enough neutral eyeshadow, brown mascara and subtle highlighter to enhance her green eyes and high cheekbones, and a smear of nude gloss drew attention to a pair of full lips. Her blonde hair fell in natural-looking waves to her shoulders and she wore a flowing pale-green dress. Her only accessory was a simple, heart-shaped silver pendant.

It didn't matter one bit that her name was Beattie and not Gwyneth, I reflected despondently. She could have been called Barry, Brian or Baldrick and would still have been indisputably glossy and gorgeous. And Felix's earlier lecture regarding my prettiness notwithstanding, I felt plain, plain, plain.

After looking at me blankly for a moment, Beattie turned back to Felix, whose eyes had remained fixed on her face. I was clearly as superfluous to the current situation as the bar stools we weren't sitting on, and it felt like the most complete, if unconscious, of dismissals.

'I just wanted to say hello,' she said quietly. 'I was worried when you didn't reply to my texts.'

At that, I recalled my earlier conversation with Kevin and wondered whether he might not have been *entirely* successful in dissuading Linda from purloining Felix's phone and blocking Beattie's messages after all. But when I glanced up at Felix, he didn't seem surprised at the mention of the texts, and all I saw in his face was a quiet sadness. My heart went out to him and moving closer, under cover of turning to retrieve my drink from the bar behind me, I gave his hand a quick squeeze.

He turned towards me and smiled. 'This is Dot,' he said.

I nodded and smiled as broadly as I could manage, waiting for him to tell me that her name was Beattie. When he didn't, I widened my eyes and, still grinning, inclined my head slightly towards her as a prompt. But he simply turned to look at her again, and as the incomplete introduction didn't seem to bother either of them, I just sighed and let it go.

'I didn't mean… to interrupt. I just… I wanted…' she began haltingly, before lowering her eyes and shaking her head. 'It doesn't matter. It's my fault. I shouldn't have come really. I'm not in the mood for this but Izzy didn't want me spending any more time alone.'

As she said the word 'alone', I felt Felix's arm tense against mine and I wondered if he sensed hope for the future – for *their* future.

'Listen, Felix,' I said briskly, womanfully feigning ignorance of the drama playing out under my nose, 'I think I'm going to go and find Kevin. I didn't really have a chance to talk to him earlier.' I patted his arm and turned to leave.

'OK,' he said. 'Let's go.'

'Great. Wait. What?' I said, stopping abruptly and turning around. 'No.' I frowned up at him and then looked uncertainly at his ex.

'Yes,' he said calmly.

I closed my eyes, heaved a sigh and began to despair a little. 'OK… well then perhaps er…' I hesitated, reluctant to acknowledge that I already knew Beattie's name, lest I appear like a stalker to Felix, and like someone who had been discussing her behind her back to Beattie. 'Perhaps your friend,' I continued, gesturing towards her, 'would like to come too. How about I get you a drink to bring along?' I added, smiling at her.

She said nothing, her eyes remaining fixed on Felix, and it was at that point that I threw in the conversational towel. Sitting back down heavily on the bar stool and downing the rest of my Prosecco, I raised my hand and smiled at the barman with a view to ordering a second glass, or possibly a bottle. I suddenly felt a need to start lining them up.

'Well, enjoy the rest of your evening,' said Felix to Beattie, which I couldn't help feeling was a bit like wishing Sir Bradley Wiggins good luck in the Tour de France as you slashed away at his bicycle tyres.

'I'm so sorry, Felix,' she replied, her voice breaking. And then, looking like a beautiful poster child for the wronged and misunderstood, she walked away, disappearing through the rear exit of the marquee and into the pub garden.

Felix sat down and swivelled on his stool to face the bar, just as a second glass of Prosecco was placed in front of me.

'Sorry about that,' he said quietly.

'No, no. It was really fun,' I said breezily. 'I'm just sorry she left. But fingers crossed we'll bump into her again later.'

He didn't look at me, instead focusing on his drink.

I sighed and turned slightly, placing my hand gently on his arm. 'I know you're probably not in the mood for sarcasm. But I do have some idea how all that must have felt, Felix, and if I was you, sitting in the middle of my friend's birthday party, I wouldn't want the person next to me offering pity and platitudes, or asking soul-searching questions. Not right now.' I turned back towards the bar and picked up my drink.

He was silent for a moment and then said, 'I told you I needed you here.'

I smiled and, feeling tearful for both of us, leaned towards him and gave him a hug. 'Talk about it later if you want to,' I said, my chin resting on his shoulder. 'Or not. It's up to you.'

'I don't want you to spend your Saturday night feeling sorry for me,' he said, as I released him.

'Not gonna happen,' I said. 'I always favour empathy over pity because it lets me focus at least fifty per cent on me too.'

He shook his head and smiled. 'And are you OK to stay after all that?'

'Am *I* OK to stay?' I laughed. 'What about *you*?'

'I'm feeling a bit numb, to be honest,' he replied, running a hand through his hair, 'and not quite sure what to do.'

'Well, how about I give you some choices?'

'Go on then.'

'Well, assuming you don't want to go and find her...'

'Which I don't,' he said firmly.

'... we could go and say happy birthday to Martin, then wrap some food up in napkins and leave,' I began, counting off our options on my fingers. 'Or we could say happy birthday to Martin, put some food on plates, eat it and then leave. Or we could say happy birthday, put some food on plates, eat it, mingle, put some more food on plates, eat it, dance, pick at leftovers, and then leave.'

'Hmm...' said Felix, frowning. 'I can't help noticing a heavy emphasis on food there.'

'Well, I'm *starving*. And did you see those prawn things and posh little pies on the way in? And the cakes? There was a whole separate area sectioned off for cakes, Felix. Oh, and for you,' I added, 'there were some slim things.'

'Slim things?' His frown deepened.

'Yes, salads, quinoa and couscous. That kind of thing. But,' I warned, 'I'm not sure how you'd manage to get that home in a napkin. I'd be fine with my cakes, but you might not have a whole lot of couscous left by the time we got back to the cottage, especially if we take the shortcut over the stiles.'

He nodded. 'In that case, why don't we go and say hi to Martin and then put some food on plates, join Kevin and take it from there?'

'Sounds good,' I said, smiling. 'If you're sure?'

'I'm sure,' he said, getting up and holding out his hand to me as I picked up my drink. 'Let's go.'

Chapter 28

At 11.45 p.m., there being no shopping trolleys available, Felix and I called a cab. On the way home, he chatted to the driver about some football match or other which was on Sky the next day, whilst I spent the journey happily slumped against him, silently, and somewhat tipsily, reflecting on the fact that the evening, after a rocky start, had, for me at least, been good fun.

Following the encounter with Beattie, we had, as planned, chatted to Martin and then gone to sit with Kevin, who told me in a murmur that Beattie had gone home, citing a headache. No one else at the table, nor anyone else at the party so far as I knew, mentioned her after that, so the remainder of the evening passed off without further emotional upset for Felix – or at least without *visible* emotional upset. I knew how a similar encounter with Alistair would have affected me, and more than once found myself scrutinising Felix as he chatted with Kevin and his other friends for any indication that he would rather be elsewhere. But he genuinely seemed fine, and this being the case, I decided that the most helpful thing I could do at that moment was to relax, enjoy the party and try not to worry. And that was exactly what I had done.

It was just before midnight by the time I slipped off my heels and threw down my walking boots in Felix's hallway, and made my wobbly way into the lounge, while he disappeared into the kitchen to fetch some drinks. Switching on a couple of lamps and feeling a mixture of happily tired and pleasantly woozy, I flopped down onto the soft, cream sofa next to the fireplace and small wood-burning stove.

Glancing around the room, I could see what Felix had meant about the house still needing work. At least one of the two ornately arched window frames needed attention or replacement, and there was a largish damp patch in one corner of the ceiling. But overall, the quirkiness, cosiness and peaceful location of Felix's home could, I decided, convert me to country living.

Or maybe it was the company.

The thought proved to be an unexpectedly painful one and I did my best to shrug it off, smiling at Felix as he entered the room and handed me a mug of peppermint tea. 'Thanks,' I said, as he sat down on an elderly and busily patterned armchair set at right angles to the sofa. 'I was just admiring the house again. What a find, Felix.'

He nodded towards one of the windows, the curtains of which were still open. 'If only it wasn't for all the terrifying night-time creatures,' he said, staring out into the blackness. 'Still, I suppose you could poison the little hedgehogs, set traps for the velvety voles and shoot the endangered owls.'

'Problem solved,' I said, raising my mug.

He smiled, taking a sip from his own mug before stretching out in the armchair and leaning back to gaze at the ceiling. After a moment of apparent thought, he raised his head and looked at me. 'I am sorry about the start to the party, Dot.'

'Oh shush, shush, shush,' I said, flapping my hand. 'It was no worse than the Hippodrome thing with Alistair.'

He raised his eyebrows sceptically. 'I think we both know that it was much worse than the Hippodrome thing with Alistair.'

'Well, maybe a tiny bit worse,' I conceded, narrowing my eyes in a completely unnecessary physical attempt to convey the concept of *small*. 'But then everything is so much more recent and raw for you two. Even so, it wasn't *that* much worse, and Alistair and I had had much longer to get over things.'

He nodded thoughtfully. 'You didn't get a chance to finish telling me about your drink with him last night.'

'Oh, that's right. Now, where was I...?' I murmured, sipping my peppermint tea whilst trying to remember how far I had got with the tale. My recollection of our earlier conversation on the subject was now decidedly hazy, but I seemed to recall that I had just told Felix that Alistair and I were, to quote Taylor Swift, *never ever getting back together*, when Beautiful Beattie had appeared out of nowhere, like the shopkeeper in *Mr Benn*.

Yes, that was definitely as far as I had got and, I decided, that was definitely as far as I was going to go. Because even with alcohol-impaired judgement, I knew that describing the angst of my brief drink with Alistair in any greater detail would be far from uplifting, and I didn't want to spoil an evening which was now so nicely back on track – or to depress Felix by droning on about my ex when he had just had such a miserable run-in with his own.

I smiled at him as he looked at me enquiringly. 'There's not a lot to add. Becca had a bit of a barney with Mark for not keeping her up to date, but he certainly didn't spoil anything for me and she quickly forgave him,' I said, determinedly keeping the details positive and peripheral. 'So no harm done.'

Felix frowned. 'So you and Alistair are good?'

I shrugged. 'We've always been good really. Things have been a little awkward sometimes, obviously, but there's been no blame, or bitterness, or burning bridges,' I concluded with a smile, congratulating myself on keeping things upbeat. 'We've been very lucky.'

'I'm happy for you.' Felix sighed and stretched out once again in his armchair. 'I wasn't surprised when you told me that he'd split up with Naomi, you know.'

'Really?'

He smiled at me, and despite my reluctance to crash a carefree evening with intense conversations about relationships, I realised that I was, emboldened no doubt by several glasses of Prosecco, once again teetering on the brink of telling him exactly how I felt about him.

I imagined myself putting down my tea and matter-of-factly declaring that I not only loved him as a friend but also fancied him. And that actually, while I had been spouting positive stuff about not burning bridges and not blaming exes, what I really wanted was for him to set fire to all remaining bridges between himself and Beattie, and for any kindly feelings he might still be harbouring towards her to disappear faster than the mini beef and ale pies at Martin McGarry's birthday party.

'Yes,' Felix continued. 'I was pretty sure Alistair still had feelings for you when we bumped into him in Bristol. He seemed pretty focused on you.'

'Did he?' I shook my head. 'I didn't spot that at all.'

'No,' he said quietly, looking thoroughly unsurprised.

I frowned a little, and was tempted to add that while I might not have noticed Alistair's apparent focus on me outside the Hippodrome, I had *certainly* noticed Beattie's *extreme* focus on Felix as she had stood before him earlier that evening: beautiful, alone and available. And I had also noticed that the focus had been entirely mutual – Felix on her as much as she on him – to the complete exclusion of everyone and everything else around them, including myself.

My frown deepened at the painful and semi-sobering thought and, Prosecco or no Prosecco, a sense of self-preservation told me that now was not the moment to lay my emotional cards on the table. I wasn't sure exactly what Felix felt for Beattie, but it was obvious that he still felt something. And call it cowardice or common sense, I was in no hurry to test those feelings and risk rejection. Not tonight.

'Are you OK?' asked Felix, now leaning forward in his armchair and placing his mug on the floor. 'You're frowning.'

'I think I may have had too much to drink,' I said, massaging my left temple. 'My mind keeps wandering.'

'To where?' he asked.

After a brief hesitation, during which I pressed my lips tightly together in order to avoid saying something I knew I would regret, I pointed towards the window. 'I was just thinking about the garden and wondering if you ever go out with a torch looking for…' I hiccoughed quietly, 'you know, for night-time stuff.'

'For fun, you mean?' he asked, looking confused. 'Because I do own a TV and lots of books, you know. And I'm only four miles from a large town with three cinemas, the same number of theatres and countless pubs. This isn't crofting, Dot.'

Despite my recent rather subdued train of thought, I found myself laughing. 'I know, I know,' I said. 'But don't you think it would be fun? One of Becca's friends tracked a fox to the bottom of her garden one night and fell into a hedge. And there were lots of people on the other side of the hedge at the time who all laughed at her. Apparently it was really funny.'

'Sounds like a riot,' he said. 'And don't worry, I'll be sure to schedule some night-time tracking into your next visit.' He smiled, leaning his head back against the top of the chair once again and this time closing his eyes.

'Great. And I'll be sure to bring my own torch. A really big, super-powerful one. Maybe we could get those ones you wear on your head,' I added, buoyed by the mention of another visit, until it occurred to me that if he did get back together with Beattie, overnight visits might not be something he was in quite such a hurry to offer, nor, for that matter, something I would be that keen to accept.

'What's the matter?'

I started slightly at the question and turned to find him looking at me quizzically. 'Nothing, why?' I asked. 'I thought you were falling asleep.'

'You looked very serious again all of a sudden.'

'I was just thinking – and it takes an awful lot of effort to do that.' I hiccoughed a second time. 'Especially after fizz. That must have been a look of intense concentration on my face.' I screwed my features into a ball and tapped a finger against the side of my head to emphasise the point.

He laughed and rose to his feet. 'Are you off to bed?' I asked, yawning.

'No,' he replied, walking into the hallway. 'I've just got to fetch something from the kitchen. I'll be back in a moment.'

'OK,' I called after him. 'I'll stay here and look after the sofa,' I added, adjusting the cushions and adopting a semi-reclining position. It really was a very comfortable sofa, and I wondered if I would even still be awake by the time Felix got back.

I don't know how long he was gone, probably just a matter of minutes, but I had definitely been on the edge of sleep when I opened my eyes at the sound of my name to find him standing over me carrying two large, heavy-knit jumpers, one of which he held out to me.

I took it, sleepily examining the huge item of clothing. 'Is this one of your old jumpers? Cos I think we could both fit in it, you know. Maybe a couple of other people too,' I murmured, standing up and gazing at it blearily. 'I mean, thank you. But I'm not cold.'

'Not in here maybe,' he said, jerking a thumb over his shoulder towards the window, 'but you will be out there.'

I frowned for a moment, looking between him, the enormous jumper and the window, before my tired and tipsy brain saw the plan. 'We're going looking for night-time stuff!' I exclaimed delightedly.

'We are,' he smiled, holding up the second jumper to reveal two torches.

'You are so prepared!' I laughed, pulling the jumper he had given me over my head and looking down as it hung almost to my knees. 'Wow, it's like wearing a knitted yurt, I love it. Hey, I wonder what we'll see in the garden.'

'Well I didn't like to mention it earlier, but there are a couple of bat boxes.'

'Ooh,' I said, a little anxiously.

'And a pond, so toads are a possibility.'

'Yay… toads…' I said weakly.

'But personally, I'm holding out for a woman falling head first into a hedge,' he continued, beckoning me to follow as he went out in the hallway and stepped into his wellies, 'and after that, I don't really mind.'

Chapter 29

It was a little over a week later, as I was on my way home from work, that I received the text for which I had been bracing myself. It was from Becca and was comprised of just two words:

She knows.

If I had been in any doubt – which of course I wasn't – as to who *she* was and what she knew, the matter would have been settled for me approximately twenty minutes later when I walked through my front door, removed my phone from my jacket pocket and discovered two missed call notifications, plus voicemail messages and two texts, all from my mother.

Opting for texts over voicemail, I began to read.

> Dear Dottie, we are now back at hint after our trip. I have just spoken to Rebecca and am trying to cake you on your mobile telephone and I have called your home telephone also but there is no and were. Please can you call me? It is urgent. Love from Mum xx

I smiled and moved on to the second text, which, I noted, had been sent just one minute later.

> Dear Dottie, your father is insisting that I
> store to say that the matter is not urgent. But
> please call me anyway. Love from Mum xx

Seeing no point in delaying the inevitable, I kicked off my shoes and, leaving my bags in the hallway, walked into the lounge, settled myself into the swivelly armchair and called her.

She answered within a single ring, sounding rather breathless. 'Hello? Is that you, Dawn?'

'No, it's—'

'Anne?'

'Mum, it's Dot.'

'Oh, Dottie, I'm so sorry, darling, it's just that I'm waiting for several people to return my calls. Hang on a moment and let me sit down.'

There was a clatter, followed by a pause, during which I heard Dad offering to bring her a cup of tea. I swivelled a full three-sixty in the chair and wished I'd thought to make myself a cup before calling her.

'There now,' she said, at last returning to the phone. 'Well, isn't it wonderful news about your sister?'

'It is,' I said, smiling. 'Lovely news.'

'The baby is just eleven weeks old.'

'That's right.'

'Mark emailed us a picture of the scan. He or she is the size of a peapod,' she added, her voice breaking with emotion. 'And I wanted to go and see Rebecca this weekend but your father won't let me.'

'Oh Mum, now don't cry. This is supposed to be a happy time.'

'It is, it is,' she managed, clearing her throat. 'But I wanted to go and help and make sure everything is all right.'

I closed my eyes, knowing that the last thing Becca needed right now was my mother 'helping'.

'The thing is, Mum, that Becca is so tired at the moment. I know for a fact that she spent most of last weekend asleep. And if you're there, she'll want to chat and do things with you and then she'll be exhausted going into school on Monday.'

'That's what your father said.'

'I think he's right. Why don't you save your visit for half-term? Actually, we're all coming to you for Nanny Flo's birthday in half-term, aren't we? You'll see Becca then.'

'Yes,' she said quietly.

'So that all works perfectly. You can look after Becca when she visits and make sure she has plenty of rest.'

'I suppose so, Dottie,' she said, punctuating the reluctant surrender with a quiet sniff. 'But really I wanted to see her right away to reassure myself that she's well.'

'You'll see her in less than two weeks' time,' I said. 'And you can FaceTime her before then,' I added.

'You're right,' she said, sounding a little brighter at the thought. 'We can keep in touch daily like that.'

'Maybe not daily, Mum,' I began uncertainly, but she had moved on.

'So what is your news, darling?' she asked. 'Becca was very vague and seemed to be suffering from memory loss when I asked her about you and Felix.'

'Did she?' I asked, disappointed that the conversation had turned to Felix at a time when I was actually trying very hard not to think about him.

The feelings-beyond-friendship I had experienced on the Saturday night of Martin McGarry's party had persisted into Sunday-morning sobriety, and I had found saying goodbye to Felix ridiculously difficult. But having managed to keep a lid on my emotions on his doorstep, I had returned home very relieved that I hadn't given in to my drunken urge to confess my feelings for him – and not just because any attempt to do so would undoubtedly have proved embarrassingly rambling and inarticulate. My main reservations actually revolved around his relationship – past and present – with Beattie. Without knowing how he felt about her, I was acutely aware that I risked either ending up in a relationship with a man I had caught at his most vulnerable and on the rebound, or experiencing the heartbreak and humiliation of an undoubtedly kind but outright rejection. If at all possible, I wanted to avoid both of those outcomes, and my plan therefore – and this was one of those rare situations which, I had decided, definitely called for a plan – was first of all to establish and maintain regular contact with Felix and then, crucially, to try and determine his feelings for his ex. Then, and only then, would I decide whether or not to talk to him about my own feelings.

With all this in mind, I had texted him several times since my visit, but after receiving a *Thank you so much, but I can't* response to my invitation for him to visit Bristol, and jovial but short replies to all my other enquiries, self-respect told me to back off and let him get in touch if he wanted to. The upshot of that decision had been six days with no communication of any kind between us. It was a situation which I had found hard at times, but which I was managing to accept, as far as was possible, by refusing to think about him. This approach was aided by the fact that my relationship with him seemed to have largely dropped off Kate's radar, supplanted during the past week by her concerns over a hormonal rash and acid reflux. Unfortunately, however, it seemed that my mother's radar was of a far higher spec than Kate's.

'Yes, Becca was *so* vague about Felix,' she said, with undisguised frustration. 'Your father claims that I was very forgetful during both my pregnancies, but I don't remember that.'

'My point exactly!' I heard Dad shout in the background, but Mum didn't miss a beat.

'Becca did say that she thought you and Felix went to a birthday party. Is that right?' she asked. 'That sounds like fun.'

'Yes, that is right. Felix's friend, Martin, was forty. But tell me about your holiday,' I said, now quite desperate to change the subject.

'It was perfect,' she replied. 'No rain, but not too hot. When will you and Felix go away, darling? The pair of you haven't had a holiday all summer, have you? I suppose it was difficult with the wedding in the middle of it and, of course, if you go later, you avoid the school holidays...'

'Hmm.'

'... air fares are so much cheaper...'

'Hmm.'

'... and there are still plenty of options.'

'That's true,' I said absently, not really listening as she talked about city breaks and autumnal warmth, but instead

258

closing my eyes and, resigned to the fact that I now had to think about Felix whether I wanted to or not, wondering if this might be the moment to tell my mother that he and I were not actually a couple. After all, she and Nanny Flo had Becca's baby news to buoy them up and, on top of that, she and Dad had been away and, with the exception of a couple of postcards, completely out of touch for several weeks. I could simply explain that during that time, Felix and I had realised that we worked better as friends; neither of us wanted to relocate and commute, our respective businesses were very demanding on our time and so we were taking a break. A break which could then, of course, drift into permanency. There was, I realised, really never going to be a better time to tell her than now. Right now.

I took a deep breath.

'Yes, a city break is an interesting idea,' I heard myself saying. 'I'll mention it to Felix and see what he thinks. Although, you know, he's very fit and outdoorsy these days, so maybe he'd prefer to go hiking in the Lakes.'

My mother laughed. 'Just like when you and Becca were little!'

'That's right. And we could take a boat out,' I said, smiling into the phone whilst picturing Felix rowing me across Coniston Water in the driving rain, wearing only a high-quality, form-fitting grey T-shirt and dark-blue pyjama bottoms, his hair plastered to his head in dripping ringlets.

'Well I think that's a marvellous idea,' said Mum. 'Now apparently I must let you go, Dot, because your father says people will be trying to call me. But I hate rushing away, so I'll ring you tomorrow and we can talk about your holiday plans some more then.'

'OK,' I said brightly, but with an underlying sense that something quite disturbing had just happened. 'Bye then.'

'Bye-bye, darling.'

She hung up and, still smiling inanely, I slowly lowered the phone, placing it carefully on the arm of the chair whilst replaying the conversation in my head. After a moment, I reached the conclusion that in essence two things had just occurred. Firstly, I had missed *the* perfect opportunity to put an end to the web of lies and deceit surrounding my relationship with Felix Davis once and for all; and, secondly, I had lost my mind.

Groaning, I leaned forward, placed my head in my hands and left it there until distracted some minutes later by the buzz of my phone. Sitting up, I stared at the screen for a moment and then picked it up.

'Hello, Becca,' I said quietly.

'Hi, Dot. You sound a bit subdued. What's happened?' she asked. 'Mum hasn't upset you, has she?'

'No, no,' I sighed, shaking my head as the full extent of just how pitiful I was hit home. 'Not at all. This is all my own work.'

Chapter 30

'Dot!' beamed Fred, holding the front door open wide. 'Great to see you. Welcome to the weekend. Come in and let me relieve you of that bottle of wine and your jacket, in that order,' he said, taking the wine from me whilst bestowing a kiss on each cheek. 'Priorities, priorities.'

I smiled up at him, contrasting his appearance and mood this evening with a month earlier, when his wife's out-of-character behaviour had been weighing so heavily upon him. 'I wasn't sure whether or not to bring that,' I said, pointing at the Malbec. 'It's a bit like rubbing her nose in it, isn't it?'

'Not at all,' he said brightly. 'You know how into her Ribena she has been this week, and I've just bought her a new six-pack.'

'God, it's been making my teeth ache just watching her guzzle those things,' I said, as I followed him into the kitchen, where Kate was checking something on the hob, pan lid in one hand, carton of Ribena in the other. She had taken to wearing flowing tops into the office, or shirts invariably untucked, but this evening she had on a long grey jumper dress and her eighteen-week bump was very obvious.

'Look at you!' I exclaimed, walking over and giving her a hug. 'And look at you too, whoever you are,' I added, smiling and placing a hand on her tummy. 'Oh my goodness, Kate, you're actually, *actually* pregnant!'

She laughed and took a noisy slurp of Ribena, clearly nearing the bottom of the carton. 'And don't I know it. We didn't sleep a wink last night, did we, Fred?' she said, turning to her husband.

'No we didn't,' he said, taking the lid from her and replacing it on the pan. 'We were very uncomfortable and we had to talk about just how uncomfortable we were throughout the night.'

'That's right, *and*,' continued Kate, raising the hem of her dress slightly and kicking off a pair of fluffy cream slippers, 'just look what's happened to my feet, Dot. They were fine this morning, but look at them now. It's like someone's set to with a bloody bicycle pump!'

'Ooh,' I said, gazing down at her undeniably swollen feet and keeping a comment about balloon animals to myself. 'Perhaps you should get some support tights, Kate. And definitely keep your feet up. That's what my Auntie Marge did when she was…' I hesitated, ending the sentence with a cough.

Kate looked at me. 'When she was what?'

'Ninety,' I said quietly.

Fred laughed and Kate sighed. 'Top tip from me, Dorothy. Never try to make anyone feel better. About anything. Ever.'

I nodded. 'OK.'

'Actually, that was very good advice from Dot,' said Fred, hurriedly handing me an unrequested glass of wine. 'So why don't you two go into the living room, where you can put your enormous feet up, Kate. I've got everything under control in here.'

Kate smiled and popped the straw back into her mouth, sucking hard. 'Maybe I'll take another one of these with me,' she said, moving towards the fridge, the straw still between her teeth.

'Why not pace yourself?' Fred placed a gentle hand on her back, steering her away from the fridge and towards the kitchen door. 'There's a bowl of blueberries on the table next door. Snack on a few of those. Dinner won't be long.'

'OK,' she said, turning her head and kissing his cheek before taking my hand and leading me out of the kitchen and into the lounge. 'We're just in the way in there, and I do need to sit down actually, Dot,' she said, flopping down as we reached the sofa and placing a cushion on the coffee table in front of her. 'I'll just pop my feet up on this,' she murmured, hoisting her feet onto the cushion and emitting a long, contented sigh as she did so. 'Ooh, that's better.'

I settled myself down next to her and she immediately took hold of my free hand. 'And how are things generally?' she asked, a little earnestly I thought. 'With you, I mean.'

'Things are generally fine,' I smiled, 'with me. You know they are. We were at work together just twenty-four hours ago.'

She nodded, and we sat in easy silence for a moment or two until she placed her other hand on top of mine so that it was now encased between hers. Frowning, I turned towards her, to find her smiling up at me. She squeezed and then patted my hand.

'What?' I asked.

'What do you mean?' she asked, still smiling.

'You're being weird,' I said. 'I mean weirder. What's going on?'

'Nothing,' she insisted, her eyes misting. 'I just wondered if there was anything that, you know…' she paused and patted my hand again, 'you wanted to talk about.'

Her lower lip trembled with emotion and I heaved a sigh. I had thought that I had become used to her erratic bouts of sentimentality and actually rather good at predicting them, but she was still clearly capable of taking me by surprise. 'Please don't cry, Kate,' I said gently.

She nodded rapidly. 'I think it's the Ribena.'

'And I think that's unlikely,' I said, raising my glass to my lips.

'I just thought you might want to talk about Felix.'

Taken by surprise for the second time in a matter of moments, I paused mid sip and slowly lowered my glass. She hadn't mentioned him for ages, other than to ask how my visit to Cheltenham had gone. In response to that enquiry, I had given her a very brief account of Martin's party, including a passing reference to Beattie, and she had asked nothing more. I hadn't been bothered by her disinterest, and hadn't really even thought of it as disinterest, but had instead welcomed the break from being pressed over how and when I was going to tell my family the truth about Felix. So for her to mention him now, and in such emotional terms, was odd and unexpected to say the least.

'Why on earth are you getting upset about Felix?' I leaned forward, placing my glass on the coffee table. 'Things are fine.'

'Have you been in touch much since your visit?'

I shrugged. 'The odd text last week.'

'That's nice.'

'Anyway,' I said, 'when is your next scan? That must be coming up.' I reached towards the large bowl of blueberries on the table, with the intention of passing it to her.

'Yes, it's next week. I was telling your mum about it—'

I sat back up, my head whipping round. 'My mum? When did you speak to her?'

'This morning, on the phone,' she said, smiling but still looking a little tearful. 'Becca had told her that I was pregnant and she called to congratulate me. Wasn't that lovely of her?'

'Yes, it was,' I agreed, feeling immediately guilty that I hadn't thought to pass on Kate's news myself.

'I think maybe she knows that I don't have that kind of interest from my own mum,' continued Kate. 'And she said that if I needed anything, or ever wanted a chat, just to call and she would always listen...' She stopped talking as a tear trickled down her cheek, '...and I could tell she meant it, Dot,' she concluded in a whisper.

I prised my hand free from hers and put my arm around her as she leaned her head against my shoulder. 'I have no doubt she did mean it,' I said. 'Although you do realise that you're going to have to block her calls now, or you'll never get any work done.'

'You're very lucky to have her, you know.'

'I know I am,' I said, smiling. 'But you're still going to have to block her calls.'

She laughed and sat up, slapping my arm and then dabbing at her eyes with the sleeve of her dress. 'So yes,' she began again, clearing her throat, 'we had a lovely long chat, which included...' She paused and lowered her head, looking up at me sternly as if over a pair of imaginary spectacles. She was now in no-nonsense mode, and I marvelled, not for the first time, at the current breakneck speed of her mood swings.

'Go on,' I sighed, retrieving my wine.

'... which included an account of the holiday to the Lake District which you and Felix are planning.'

'Oh.' I drank my wine.

'Except I don't think you and Felix *are* planning a holiday to the Lake District, are you, Dorothy?'

I shook my head and looked at her. 'No, we are not, Katherine.'

For a moment, her brow furrowed in frustration and her mouth hardened into a horizontal line of complete disapproval, before her features suddenly softened into a smile. 'Look,' said the one-woman good-cop-bad-cop, 'I haven't asked you about Felix lately because, well, it seemed pretty obvious to me that you really liked him. And I suspected that the real reason you hadn't told your family you weren't going out with him was because you actually wished that you were.'

Kate, I decided, might currently be as bonkers as a box of highly hormonal frogs, but she had lost none of her insight. It was my turn to feel tearful.

'So my question to you, Dot, is...' she continued softly.

'Why, at the age of thirty-six, I am fantasising about going on holiday with a pretend boyfriend and sharing that fantasy with my mother?' I suggested miserably.

She shook her head. 'God, no. Let's save that one for a trained therapist.'

'Er... OK,' I said, blinking a little.

'The question I was actually going to ask is why you haven't done anything about it.'

'About what?'

'About Felix. Why haven't you told him how you feel?'

I closed my eyes and took a deep breath. 'I came very close to it. I was going to tell him when we were on our own at the party, but then Beattie turned up and the moment was lost. And from the way he behaved, I'm pretty sure he's still besotted with her – or, at the very least, far from over her. And if that's the case, then I don't think it'd be a great time for me to throw my hat into the ring.'

She shook her head. 'Don't hide behind ifs and maybes, Dorothy.'

'I'm not,' I said simply, trying not to be distracted by the fact that, at this moment, she was sounding worryingly like my mother during my teenage years. 'I thought it all through very carefully when I got home and realised that I have to find out where he is at re Beattie. But I don't want to do that over the phone.'

'Fair enough.'

'So I decided I would invite him to Bristol. In fact, I invited him to come down this weekend, but he said he was busy.'

'Oh, OK,' said Kate, looking and sounding a little crestfallen.

'Yes. So he's not exactly champing at the bit, is he?'

'What reason did he give for not coming?'

'He just said that he couldn't make it. And then, after that, I sent a few texts about this and that and trying to fish about Beattie a little bit.'

'Good, good.' Kate nodded approvingly.

267

'And he replied quite quickly each time but gave nothing away. So as things stand, and reading between the lines, I think he's either back together with Beattie, or wants to be.'

'If this is what you want, Dot, then forget about reading between the lines. We need to know for sure.'

I raised my eyebrows. 'We?'

'You and me,' she said, looking puzzled. 'Who else would I mean? There's no one else in the room, is there?'

'Sorry, I just got confused because I thought we were discussing *my* life.' I placed a hand on my chest.

'You're veering off the point,' she said, sounding mildly exasperated. 'Do try not to get sidetracked. The important thing here is that you do not let this one drift. If ever there was a thing to pull your head out of the sand about, this is it. All you have to do is call Felix and tell him there's something you need to discuss and that either he can come to Bristol or you can go to Cheltenham.'

I nodded. 'I'll give it a couple of weeks and then make the call.'

'Oh for goodness' sake, why wait?' she exclaimed impatiently, bad cop once more in the ascendancy. 'What are you going to do in the meantime? Continue in a frustrated friendship? Or maybe lose contact altogether while you dither? Because time does have a tendency to march on, doesn't it, Dorothy? Especially in your world. Oh, but maybe you're OK with letting it all just bumble along while you continue to pretend to your parents and grandmother that he's your boyfriend. I mean, why not go the whole hog and claim that you're cohabiting? It's no biggie. He can just be down the allotment or in prison whenever they visit.'

'OK, OK, you've made your point.'

'You can do this,' she said, suddenly smiling, her eyes shining. 'And it would be a real shame not to. Becca and your mother *both* say how lovely he is.'

'Becca?' I frowned. 'You've spoken to Becca too?'

'Of course,' she said. 'And the general consensus is that you and Felix are perfect for each other. Your dad is just surprised…'

'My dad?' I exclaimed. 'Is there anyone you haven't discussed this with, Kate?'

'… that you didn't get together years ago,' she continued brightly, apparently oblivious to either the interruption or my annoyance, 'and he's so happy that you're together now – except, of course, that you're not,' she added, her tone momentarily disapproving again. 'And, although I don't know really know Felix, it's so obvious to me that you get on brilliantly. And I know what he's done for you lately – and I don't only mean the wedding. He's definitely helped you to move on from Alistair. And to be honest, he's so good-looking that he'd have to have a pretty shitty personality for this not to be worth a shot.'

'Ah, so the language of romance is not dead after all,' said Fred, entering from the kitchen. 'Is that what she used to say about me, Dot? A bit of a shit but worth a shot?'

I looked up at him and then across at Kate, wondering just how much of the conversation he had overheard.

'It's OK, Dot,' she said, in a tone which I assumed was meant to be reassuring, 'I've already told Fred absolutely everything.' She leaned forward, grabbing an enormous handful of blueberries and stuffing them into her mouth, whilst patting my knee.

'Marvellous,' I said wearily.

'Don't worry,' smiled Fred. 'I screen out approximately ninety per cent of everything Kate says at the moment. It's the only way to stay sane. But I do register her telling me every single day how lucky she is to have you as a friend.'

'Nice catch, Frederick,' I tutted, and then smiled. 'Fortunately, I feel the same way about her,' I said. 'She keeps me on track – whether I like it or not.'

'We keep *each other* on track,' said Kate, spitting blueberries and squeezing my arm. 'You are the sister I never had, Dorothy Riley. I don't know what I'd do without you. You are family to me, and you will be to this little one too,' she added in an emotional whisper, placing a hand on her stomach.

'And while I'm sure Dot is very touched by that, Kate,' said Fred quickly, with a nod in my direction, 'let's try not to cry before dinner. It's just about ready, and your Ribena is on the table.'

'OK,' she said quietly. 'And I'm sorry I keep welling up all the time. It's just hard when I'm surrounded by so much love and am feeling things so much more deeply than usual. I keep being overwhelmed by waves of emotion. I think it might be the Ribena, Fred.'

Fred sighed, offering me the tiniest of eye rolls as he extended a hand towards his wife and helped her to her feet. 'You know I think you're probably right, Kate. It's got to be the Ribena. Maybe you should give Fruit Shoots a whirl tomorrow.'

Chapter 31

Sadly, the weekend switch to Fruit Shoots did absolutely nothing to quell the emotional waves by which Kate was being overwhelmed; a fact I discovered upon arriving at the office two days later and being greeted by the sound of raucous laughter, immediately followed by low-volume seriousness.

I smiled to myself, hung up my coat in the lobby and headed for my desk, waving to her as I did so.

'I'll definitely do that, and yes, they're absolutely beautiful,' she said into the phone whilst smiling at me and pointing at a large bouquet of flowers on the conference table.

'Wow,' I mouthed, walking over to the flowers and picking them up in search of a card. Unable to find one, I turned back to Kate. 'Who?' I whispered, but she had chosen that moment to bend down and extract a Fruit Shoot from her bag.

'Thank you,' she said, straightening up and smiling broadly. 'And you and Don must come for dinner next time you're visiting Dot.'

I had just sat down at my desk and now swivelled in my chair to face her. 'My mother?' I whispered, frowning questioningly.

She nodded briefly, covering the mouthpiece of the phone. 'Bless her,' she said quietly.

I smiled and shook my head. 'Be careful,' I murmured. 'She's trying to adopt you.'

'Oh, OK,' said Kate, the conversation clearly drawing to a close. 'Yes, yes, I will. And thanks so much again, Helen. You and Don really have made my day. Bye now.' She replaced the handset on the desk and looked up at me. 'They were delivered about ten minutes ago,' she said. 'How thoughtful is your mum?'

'Very,' I agreed.

'Such a lovely surprise,' said Kate, getting up and walking over to the flowers.

'And, of course, the other surprise is that you got off the phone to her in under ten minutes.'

'You're awful,' she tutted. 'I think she would have chatted for longer, but your dad was calling her.'

'Yes, he's good like that. He rescues me regularly,' I smiled. 'Where are you going to put those?' I asked, as she picked up the bouquet.

'The sink, for now,' she said, walking towards the loo. 'I don't think we've got a vase in the office, have we?'

'No, I don't think—' I began before being cut short by the ringing of the telephone on my desk. I hesitated before picking it up. 'Three guesses who this is,' I called to Kate. 'Did you tell her I wasn't in yet?'

The only reply was the sound of a tap running, and after another brief hesitation, I resigned myself to my fate and picked up the phone.

'Eat Fruit Design. How can I help?' I asked, resisting an urge to add the word 'Mum' to the enquiry and desperately trying to sound like someone extremely pushed for time.

'Hi, Dot. It's Felix. Are you free to talk? You sound like you might be busy.'

Feeling as if I'd been caught on the hop, I didn't reply immediately. I had spent Sunday intermittently thinking through what I would say when I called him, whilst not once factoring in the possibility that he might call me first.

'Dot?'

'Yes, hi. Sorry, I'm just not quite with it yet. Monday morning and all that.' I tried to sound casual, whilst wondering whether I would be able to bend the conversation round to the fact that I wanted to see him.

'Is now not a good time?'

'No. I mean yes, it's fine. I haven't got into anything yet, so yes...' I paused, holding the phone at arm's length and taking a deep breath, 'it's a good time,' I concluded, returning it to my ear. 'How are you? How was your weekend? I've forgotten what you said you were up to.' I congratulated myself on managing a sneaky enquiry, despite feeling flustered.

'Oh, nothing much,' he said brightly. 'I caught up on some gardening and house stuff and went out last-minute for dinner on Saturday night.'

'Lovely,' I said, immediately crushed to discover that he had turned down my invitation to visit for *nothing much* and a *last-minute* thing. My own fault, I decided, for being sneaky.

'How about you?' he asked.

'Dinner at Kate's,' I said. 'She's hitting the Ribena pretty hard and it's playing havoc with her emotional well-being.'

'It used to do the same thing to me in primary school. But look, I'm phoning because I'm in Bristol on Friday and—'

'Yes!' I said, before clamping my hand over my mouth.

'Yes what? Are you talking to me?'

'Er… no. Kate was just asking if I wanted her to make me a coffee. Sorry, you carry on. You're in Bristol on Friday?'

'Yes, and I wondered if you were free for a drink after work.'

'I'll just check,' I said, delighted not only by the prospect of seeing him but also by the fact that it was at his own suggestion. 'Yes, I can do that. And if you're free, why not come round for dinner?' I added, my eyes screwed shut and my fingers crossed.

'Thanks, but I'm having dinner with a client. That's why I'm in Bristol. I thought it might be a good time to explain what I need from you.'

'What you need from me?'

'Yes, the information I need so that I can help you with your forward planning. I'm going to put everything on a memory stick and thought I could give it to you on Friday, rather than emailing it. It'll be quite a large file.'

'Will it? Oh, right. Thanks. That's really kind of you.'

'No problem.'

'So, what time do you get here?'

'I'm going to catch the train after work, so I should be able to meet you around seven. My meeting is at eight.'

'Great,' I said, and then, unable to help myself, added, 'You know you're welcome to stay over.'

There followed an unexpected and excruciating pause, during which it occurred to me that he was probably wondering how to turn down yet another invitation from Dot without hurting her feelings.

'But I expect you'll be tired after your meeting and just want to get home,' I said, offering him a helping hand out of the hole which I had dug for him.

'Yes, and I have plans for Saturday, so really need to get back,' he replied.

'That's fine,' I said, trying not to sound deflated. 'Hope your Saturday plans are pleasure and not business,' I added, whilst actually hoping that Saturday was part of the least pleasurable business trip ever.

'Yes, it's pleasure.'

'Lovely,' I said, feeling increasingly miserable. 'Well you'll have to tell me all about it when I see you. But I'd better go now as I've got a client meeting at nine,' I lied, reflecting sadly on the fact that, against all expectations, I couldn't wait to get off the phone.

'See you Friday, and let's text details.'

'Will do. Bye.'

I hastily replaced the phone in its cradle and then rested my head in my hands, only looking up when Kate placed a mug of coffee in front of me.

'Apparently I asked if you wanted one,' she smiled.

'Thanks,' I said.

'Want to talk about it?' she asked lightly, returning to her desk.

I shook my head. 'No. But thank you.'

'OK, but I just hope you're not reading between the lines,' she said, swigging her Fruit Shoot.

'I'm reading the writing on the wall.'

'Dot...'

I held up a hand to stymie the lecture. 'I will go and meet him on Friday, Kate, but I meant it when I said that I don't want to talk about it. I've got loads to do today and just want to get on with it. Is that OK?'

She looked at me for a moment and then smiled benignly and shrugged. 'Of course it is.'

'Really?' I said in surprise. 'You're not going to push it? Even slightly?'

'Don't be silly,' she said, still smiling. 'I'm going to leave it entirely up to you.'

'Wow,' I murmured, turning towards my computer and preparing to get on with the day, 'I don't know what they put in Fruit Shoots, but they definitely get my vote over Ribena.'

Chapter 32

Astonishingly, Kate was as good as her word, and did leave the matter entirely up to me, making no mention of Felix whatsoever for the rest of the working week. In fact, I might have assumed that he had been erased from her hormonally overloaded brain altogether, had it not been for her screeched advice to *avoid reading between the lines*, which she delivered as she exited the office on Friday evening. It was counselling hastily followed by the determined slamming of the outer door, thus depriving me of any opportunity to retort.

Not that I would have argued. I had spent much of Friday reminding myself not to prejudge either the situation or Felix's feelings. True, he had now turned down two invitations to stay with me in Bristol, but, on the other hand, drinks had been his suggestion, not mine. He could have posted the memory stick to me if he'd wanted to, and although we wouldn't have long together, he was still making time to see me. More importantly, he hadn't directly told me that he still had feelings for his ex, or that he was seeing her again, and I was determined not to infer either to be the case. So as I left the office at 6 p.m. to meet Felix that Friday evening, I did so in good spirits, having done a pretty good job of convincing myself that the situation was a hopeful one.

We had agreed to meet in the Port of Call, a small side-street pub just off Whiteladies Road, and half an hour's bus ride from the Eat Fruit office. I had, however, decided to allow myself double that travel time because, as when meeting Alistair for drinks, I was determined to be early. This time, however, it was not so that I could steady my nerves with alcohol – far from it; I wanted to be stone-cold sober for this particular conversation. No, this time I was keen to be early because Felix had uncomplainingly tolerated me being late for every single social occasion during the first ten years of our relationship and it was something I didn't feel he should have to put up with ever again if it could possibly be helped.

So it was with mild frustration at good intentions foiled that I stepped out of the October rain and into the warm and welcomingly lit Port of Call, only to discover Felix already there, sitting at a corner table with a serious look on his face and gazing fixedly at his phone. However, determined to be positive from the off, I reminded myself that I was still running early – he just happened to be earlier – and I refused to entertain even the vague possibility that he was texting Beattie, opting instead for focusing upon the undeniable thrill I experienced at seeing him again. Whatever did or didn't happen this evening, I would enjoy his company.

He looked up while I was in the middle of this internal pep talk and, after the most minute of hesitations, smiled and raised a hand. I smiled and waved back and then walked towards him, watching him rise to his feet as I approached.

'Hello,' he said, his hands in his pockets as he leaned forward for a kiss.

'Hi.' I pecked him on the cheek, aware of a strong sense of having missed his company.

'I got you a drink,' he said, pointing to a glass of red wine on the table.

'That's great, thank you,' I replied, sitting down and waving an early goodbye to my plan of absolute sobriety.

He sat down too and for a moment we looked at each other in silence across the table. I had no idea what he was thinking, but my own thoughts were fully focused upon the young friend whose company and affection I had enjoyed, and perhaps taken too much for granted, for ten years, and the man whose company and affection I enjoyed now and would never take for granted again.

'I know it's a bit dull, but as we haven't got long, can we just get business out of the way?' he asked suddenly. 'My meeting start time has been brought forward to seven thirty.'

'Oh.' I couldn't prevent my face from falling. 'You should have texted, Felix. I could have left the office earlier.'

He shook his head. 'The change was last-minute and I didn't want to put you under any pressure. Anyway,' he leaned forward, picking up and opening a briefcase, 'I've got this for you.' He took out a memory stick and placed it on the table in front of me. 'It sets everything out.'

'Right,' I said, staring fixedly at the small red and black oblong of plastic and metal.

'It'd be great if you could check it's readable on your Mac tonight or tomorrow,' he said. 'And then, if there's a problem, I can sort it out on Sunday before I'm back in the office.'

'Do you want to talk about any of it now?' I asked, looking up.

He shook his head. 'No, it's self-explanatory provided it's readable.'

'OK. Well, it's really kind of you to help me when you're so busy,' I said quietly, picking up my drink. 'I'll definitely look at it tonight when I get home and text you if there's a problem.'

'It'll literally be a question of opening it up,' he said. 'But how are you? What's the latest from the world of Dot?'

'Well the office is bursting with hormones and my mother is bursting with anticipation of babies.'

'Plural?' he queried.

'She's almost as excited about Kate as she is about Becca.'

'And how is Kate coping with that?'

'Oh, she's lapping it up,' I said. 'It's quite nice to watch, actually. It gives me a heightened appreciation of Mum, which is a good thing.'

He smiled and picked up his drink. 'I always thought you were hard on her.'

'I know you did,' I tutted. 'I remember you telling me off on a regular basis about that – as well as a multitude of other things. I can't help thinking that your relationship with me was primarily lecture-based back then.'

'I'm surprised you noticed,' he said, his eyebrows raised. 'You never gave the impression of actually listening.'

'I didn't get the tattoo, did I?' I argued.

'I always thought that had more to do with a fear of needles than anything I had to say.'

'It was fifty-fifty.'

He looked sceptical.

'Or perhaps sixty-forty.'

'I'll accept that on the basis that it's closer to the truth,' he said, smiling. 'But how is life beyond the pregnancies? How are things with Alistair?' he asked, glancing surreptitiously at his phone. He was, I thought, clearly conscious of the time.

'Great,' I said hurriedly, aware that the clock was ticking on our conversation, and determined to talk about Beattie before he had to go.

'Good to hear,' he said quietly.

'Yes.' I lowered my gaze to the memory stick, in order to avoid the eye contact which I feared might cause me to lose my nerve. 'Look, Felix, I think it's good that we can talk about Alistair, don't you?' I began tentatively.

'I guess so,' he said.

'I just mean that you can ask me how things are and you're not worried about putting your foot in it, which is great,' I smiled. 'But the thing is, when it comes to Beattie…' I looked up to find him frowning at me in a way which I refused to let myself even attempt to interpret; there was to be no inferring or reading between the lines tonight, I reminded myself. 'When it comes to Beattie, I'm completely in the dark, and I was just wondering,' I continued lightly, returning my gaze to the memory stick and pressing on, 'how things stand between the two of you, because it's a relationship which is obviously very important to you one way or another, and I don't want to have to tiptoe around the subject, or worry about saying the wrong thing.'

I looked up at him and he shrugged. 'That's fine,' he said, now looking and sounding completely relaxed. 'You don't have to justify asking. You were put in an awkward situation at Martin's party and I should have explained things there and then really. But I suppose I just wanted to forget about it and not let it become part of our weekend. I can see why you'd be curious, though.'

'I'm not just being nosy,' I said, with a hint of protest.

He shook his head. 'I know, and it's honestly fine. And Beattie and I are fine. We went out for dinner last weekend, in fact.'

'Oh, right,' I said, attempting a smile but hugely disappointed by his response. 'That's nice.'

'She wanted to discuss getting back together and so we talked it all through. Obviously it was quite an emotional evening. Thank God neither of us was on the Ribena.'

I looked up and he offered me a small smile.

'Oh yes,' I said quietly, forcing a laugh. 'The Ribena.' I sipped my wine and then made myself, in the interests of not reading between the lines, ask the obvious question. 'So you're back together then?'

'What? No,' he said emphatically, shaking his head and clearly surprised by the question.

'Really? Oh, I thought maybe…'

'There has never been any possibility of that,' he said, frowning. 'I was just sorry that Beattie thought that there was. If I'd recognised that, I would have been clearer with her about exactly what I did and didn't want. I remember you saying how much better you felt when there was clarity between you and Alistair and how important that was. Beattie and I needed that clarity too. Although obviously the outcome for us was very different.'

I nodded, briefly intrigued by what he meant when he said the outcome had been very different – maybe Beattie had been reluctant to accept what he'd had to say, or maybe she had thrown a plate at his head. But in the end, whatever the difference was, I didn't really care, because in that moment I felt more optimistic regarding a possible future for Felix and me than I had at any time over the past two weeks. He and Beattie were well and truly over. *And* he seemed completely at peace about it *and* it had been entirely his decision. Not only was their relationship dead in the water, it had been chopped into little bits by a motorboat propeller and then consumed by an enormous shark. The situation could not be more final.

'Yes, clarity is great, isn't it?' I said, smiling broadly and resisting an urge to leap up and buy everyone in the pub a celebratory pint. 'Whatever the outcome.'

'It is,' he replied, looking thoughtful and nodding slowly. 'I'm feeling so much clearer about everything and,' he added, 'ready to move on.' He looked at me and smiled.

My smile broadened even further and I felt myself blush. Felix was ready to move on and he wanted me to know it. The evening was just getting better and better. 'I'm so pleased for you, Felix,' I said.

'Thank you.' He raised his beer in salute to me and then took a sip. 'Yes, so I thought I might perhaps text our mutual friend Rosie.'

My grin, my gaze, and the hand I had just extended towards my own drink, froze immediately. 'Rosie?' I echoed, my mouth stretched to the max, in the manner of a life-sized ventriloquist's dummy. 'The policeman woman?'

'You gave me her number,' he said.

'I did? I did,' I murmured, my expression glazed as I pictured myself pulling a handgun from my bag, carefully removing my shoe and then shooting myself in the foot.

'And Mark likes her.'

'He does,' I agreed, now on emotional autopilot. 'Very much.'

'So,' he continued, 'I thought I might get in touch with her. I can't really see any reason not to.' He looked at me for a moment and then picked up his beer again. 'Can you? What do you think?'

I continued to stare at him whilst the two ego- and soul-destroying facts of the matter sank in, namely that: (a) Felix couldn't see any reason not to call Rosie, even though (b) I was sitting just a table width away from him and, at five foot seven, clearly visible to anyone not wearing a bucket on their head.

And now he was asking me what I thought about that.

I lowered my hand slowly to my lap, my smile remaining perfectly in place whilst I groaned internally at my own complete *lack* of thought to date. Ever since Martin's party, I had considered my relationship with Felix only in terms of his relationship with Beattie. She had been the sole obstacle I had identified on the road to our happily-ever-after. It had not once occurred to me that there might be a whole host of female potholes, roadworks and speed bumps to negotiate.

If it hadn't been a moment of such devastating reali- sation, I might have laughed at my own arrogance. Felix could have his pick of the bunch and I was hardly the best of that bunch. Hadn't my own mother told me how surprised her friends at the wedding had been to discover that we were a couple? And absolutely everyone – from

Nanny Flo and Auntie Dawn to all the single heterosexual women at Martin McGarry's birthday party – thought that Felix Davis was a catch. And what on earth would someone like him be doing with someone like me? It was laughable really.

'What are you smiling at?' asked Felix.

I blinked and shook my head. 'I was just thinking that you calling Rosie is a great idea,' I said. 'She's very attractive and would be more than capable of seeing you safely home on a dark night.'

'So I should go ahead?'

I glanced down at the small table between us and then back up at Felix. 'I'm like you; I can't see any reason not to.'

'OK.' He nodded, looking at his watch. 'I've got to go.'

'Right now?' I said, aware that he was pushed for time, but surprised nevertheless at the suddenness of his decision to leave.

He picked up his briefcase and stood up. 'You stay and finish your drink.'

'Oh… OK then.'

'And have a great weekend,' he said. 'I didn't get a chance to ask what you were up to.'

'I'm at a birthday party,' I said. 'They're like buses, aren't they?'

'So it would seem.' He glanced towards the exit, clearly now in a hurry to be gone, before his eyes darted back, somewhat anxiously, to the table.

I followed his gaze and picked up the memory stick, placing it in my bag. 'Don't worry. I'm not going to leave it behind. Against all odds, I'm actually quite on the ball when it comes to business.'

He hesitated for a moment and then bent down to kiss my cheek. 'I hope it's OK.'

'I'll text you tonight and let you know. Bye, Felix, and thanks again.' I placed my arms briefly around his neck and, in a moment which seemed suddenly familiar, remembered a goodbye years earlier. He had been preparing to go his way and I had been preparing to go mine, and the wrench of separation, together with a sense that the separation might be a lengthy one, felt just the same now as then.

'Bye, Dot,' he said, walking away.

'Bye,' I repeated quietly and pointlessly, picking up my drink and watching as he made his way through the increasingly busy pub and disappeared outside.

'Well, there was no reading between the lines necessary there,' I murmured to myself, aware of tears beginning to threaten. And as I gave in to my feelings, acknowledging a growing and painful sense of disappointment, only the sudden and insistent buzz of my phone saved me from a very public and completely humiliating display of grief.

I took the phone from my bag and, blinking at the screen through embryonic tears, read: *Felix Davis Office*.

Confused, I took the call. 'Hello?'

'Oh hi, Dorothy. It's Kevin. Sorry to bother you. Is Felix still with you?'

'Er, no,' I said, sniffing and dabbing a finger under each eye in an attempt to prevent mascara run. 'He left just a minute ago, Kevin. I assume you've tried to call him? Is there a problem?'

'Not really,' he sighed. 'It's just that the client has been trying to get in touch with him to tell him that the meet time has changed.'

'It's OK. He already knew that.'

'Really?' He sounded surprised.

'Yes, from eight to seven -thirty.'

There was a pause, during which I heard Kevin talking indistinctly, his comments interspersed with a succession of several, rather snappy, female responses. 'Sorry, Dorothy, I was just checking the time of the dinner with Linda because we've got some crossed wires here. It's been pushed back from eight to eight thirty. Are you sure he said seven thirty?'

'Yes, he rushed off a moment ago.'

'Really? Because seven thirty was never on the cards and the client said he was unable to reach him, so I don't know where on earth he got the earlier start time from.'

'Me neither,' I said, a slight resentment now mingling with the disappointment of Felix's unconscious rejection of me. If he had been so anxious to leave that he had to lie about the time of his meeting, then why arrange to see me at all? 'Maybe he just couldn't wait to get away from me, Kevin,' I said morosely.

At that, he laughed so explosively that I was forced to hold the phone some distance from my ear. 'Oh yes, that'll be it,' he guffawed. 'Dorothy says Felix obviously couldn't wait to get away from her, Linda,' he added at considerable volume. I returned the phone to my ear just in time to catch another clipped response. I had an increasing sense that Kevin lived his office life under the cosh that was Linda.

'But not to worry, Dorothy. Better that Felix is early than late for dinner, so no harm done. I'm heading off now, so I'll let you get on home to... er...'

At this point, I heard Linda shout impatiently and quite distinctly, 'Alistair. His name is Alistair.'

'Yes, that's right. Thank you, Linda,' said Kevin affably. 'I'll let you get on home to Alistair, Dorothy.'

I frowned into the phone. 'Alistair is my *ex*-boyfriend, Kevin. We haven't been together for over a year now.'

There was a pause and more murmuring before Kevin spoke audibly again. 'I'm so sorry, Dorothy. Felix told Linda that your relationship with Alistair had resumed.'

'Really?' I said, surprised to discover that Felix's day-to-day interaction with scary Linda was on such a personal level. 'When did he tell her that?'

I waited while Linda and Kevin discussed the point at the other end of the line.

'Well, Dorothy, I have just had it explained to me,' resumed Kevin, his tone now as conspiratorial as it had been when discussing Felix at Martin's party, 'that Felix didn't actually *tell* Linda that you and Alistair had reconciled. In *actualité*, it was information which she accidentally oversaw.'

'Oversaw?'

'*Oversaw* in the same sense as to *overhear*,' clarified Kevin. 'Linda accidentally *oversaw* the information when Felix inadvertently left his password-protected personal daily account open onscreen.'

I thought for a moment. 'You mean she read his diary, Kevin.'

At this point I heard Linda chip in again.

'Apparently Felix had popped down to reception and Linda unconsciously absorbed various details about your weekend together while tidying his desk for him,' explained Kevin.

'Various details?' I queried, appalled at Linda's shameless nosiness whilst, of course, desperate to know what else was in the diary.

'Right, well I really had better go,' said Kevin brightly, crushing my hopes of further gossip. 'Oh, but wait one moment. Linda has a question,' he added hastily before engaging in yet more muffled discussion. 'She says have a lovely weekend and wonders whether you are up to anything nice. Are you at home or away?'

I sighed and put a hand to my forehead, suddenly wishing that I was at home right now. 'I'm off to Exeter tomorrow morning to stay with my parents. It's my grandmother's eighty-seventh birthday and we're having a little party for her.'

'Well that sounds fabulous, Dorothy. I'll let Linda know and I hope you all have a wonderful time.'

'Thanks, Kevin. I'm sure we will. Bye.'

Ending the call, I threw my phone back into my bag and stood up, leaving the rest of my drink untouched and resolving to get into bed and go straight to sleep the moment I got home. I wanted to leave myself as little time as possible for reflection, either on my relationship with Felix, or on the frank conversation I would have to have about that relationship with my parents the next day. It was a conversation which even I realised could be deferred no longer, but that didn't mean I had to think about it tonight.

Chapter 33

The following morning, Dad was already outside and waiting for me as I stepped out of my car and onto the drive of our family home. 'I was reading the paper in the lounge and saw you pull in,' he said, opening his arms and enveloping me in the most welcome of welcome hugs. 'How was your journey?'

'No hold-ups whatsoever,' I said brightly, hugging him back. 'And how are you?'

'Very well indeed,' he smiled, watching as I opened the boot and took out my overnight bag. 'Here, let me have that,' he said, taking it from me, 'and come inside. Mum is upstairs sorting out Nanny. She had a birthday breakfast in bed and is now being pampered and preened, but they'll both be down in a minute.'

'No sign of Becca yet?' I asked, following him towards the house and checking the time on the grandmother clock at the end of the hallway as we stepped inside. 'She said she was aiming for around now.'

Dad closed the front door behind us and placed my bag at the bottom of the stairs. 'She texted me about ten minutes ago to say that they're running a little late. Apparently the traffic wasn't great as far as the motorway. Now, I'll take that upstairs for you in a moment,' he said, pointing at the bag over his shoulder as he began to walk down the hallway and towards the kitchen. 'But first of all, come with me and I'll make you a coffee.'

'Ooh, yes please,' I said, following. 'I went to bed early last night but still feel tired. Do you ever do that?' I pulled a chair out from the kitchen table and flopped down.

Dad glanced at me over the top of his glasses as he went to the sink and began to fill the kettle. 'I do – frequently. But then I'm nearly seventy, Dot. Are you OK? You're not under the weather, are you?'

'Not at all. I feel great,' I insisted. 'It'll just be because I've usually had three cups of coffee by ten thirty, and I'm two short of that target right now.'

He nodded but looked unconvinced. 'And how is Felix?' he asked, his back now to me as he switched on the kettle and reached for some mugs and the cafetière. 'I know you told Mum it was doubtful he'd make it today. I hope he's not overdoing it at work. It always amazes me how a decade of time-saving technological advances since I retired seems to have resulted in increased, rather than decreased, office hours.'

'Yes, that is strange,' I murmured, turning to gaze out through the patio doors behind me. 'I love your garden in autumn,' I said. 'Just look at those colours.'

'So Felix is well?' asked Dad. I turned to find him now sitting opposite me.

'Yes, really well,' I said, bending down to pick up my shoulder bag from the floor and opening it, simply for something to do other than make eye contact with my father.

'And everything is OK? Between the two of you, I mean.'

At that, I looked up and smiled, but discovered that I couldn't quite manage a reply. Dad looked at me for a moment and then nodded. 'Well, we can catch up properly later,' he said gently. 'Perhaps over a brandy when your mother has gone to bed.'

I nodded mutely, part of me dreading that conversation and part of me wishing that the pair of us could sit down on the sofa and have that brandy right now, so that I could get it all off my chest: the stress of maintaining a well-meant deception, the joy of a rediscovered friendship and the heartache of feelings unreciprocated.

'Lost something?' asked Dad brightly.

I frowned in confusion. 'What do you mean?'

He pointed at the open bag on my lap. 'In there. If you have, I'm not at all surprised, Dot. It's huge,' he laughed. 'You may as well be carrying a rucksack.'

I gazed into the bag. 'Oh yes, I just wondered where I'd put my... Drat.'

'What's wrong?'

I reached into the bag and took out the memory stick which Felix had given to me the night before. 'I forgot all about this.'

'What is it?'

I sighed and placed it on the table in front of me. 'Felix is going to look at Eat Fruit and help me think about what we can do if Kate's return is delayed, or if she decides not to come back to work.'

Dad raised his eyebrows in surprise. 'Is that likely?'

'She's insisting it's not,' I shrugged. 'But you never know how things are going to go, do you?'

'True,' he said. 'It's very sensible of you to think through the possibilities. So what's on there?' He pointed to the stick.

'I don't exactly know, to be honest. I think it's a list of the information Felix needs from me. Spreadsheets to complete, maybe? It must be quite a big file because he couldn't email it. He gave it to me last night and asked me to check that it was readable on my Mac. If there's a problem, he wants a chance to sort it before Monday. But it's OK,' I said, returning it to my bag, 'I'll look at it when I get home. I just feel a bit bad because I said I'd let him know last night.'

I replaced my bag on the floor. 'So, tell me about your holiday. It sounds like you had a great time.'

'We did,' said Dad, smiling. 'But why don't you go into the study while I make your coffee and check the stick on the Mac in there? Then it's done and you can call Felix and let him know.'

I hesitated for a moment, not wanting work to interrupt my visit, before deciding that it really would be best to check the stick now and let Felix know early if there was a problem. 'That's a good idea, if you don't mind,' I said. 'It will only take a minute or two.'

'Exactly,' he said, standing up. 'So off you go, and I'll bring your coffee in to you – if it's ready before you are. But you'd better hurry up, because those two,' he added, pointing at the ceiling, 'will be down any moment and then you'll not get a minute's peace.'

I rose to my feet and, after a minor detour to give Dad a hug, walked out of the kitchen, through a small lobby and into Dad's study, a relatively recent addition to the house and a haven in which he frequently snatched a few minutes' peace and quiet surrounded by his DIY manuals, gardening magazines, golf trophies and anything else my mother had deemed *man clutter*. Then I sat down, switched on the Mac and, as the screen came to life, I inserted the memory stick.

A yellow file entitled *DOT* appeared immediately in the upper right of the screen and I clicked on it. As expected, a second screen opened, on which was listed the contents of the stick. Everything seemed fine and I was just about to randomly select a file when it struck me that there was actually only one document on the list and that all the other files were images. I frowned, clicked on the lone document and began to read.

> Dear Dot,
>
> This memory stick is for memories. I spent most of last weekend rooting through my own and my mother's 'archives' for these. I hope you think it was worth it. I'll email you all the dull accountancy stuff on Monday. There's not much and we can discuss it whenever you're ready.
>
> Felix

Still frowning, I closed the document and opened the first of the image files. It was a photograph of the lower school choir, circa 1992, and it took me only a matter of moments to spot first of all Felix, giving it his all in the front row, and then myself, several inches taller and looking significantly less enthusiastic, a couple of rows back.

Gasping and then laughing out loud, I began to work my way down the list of images.

There were pictures of us at parties, first of all passing the parcel and then, as we grew, passing the beer. In one photo we were two twelve-year-olds on either end of a see-saw, laughing hysterically – me high up in the air with absolutely no chance of coming down until Felix got off. In another, we were sixth-formers on a field trip to the coast, standing on a beach, wearing wellies and holding clipboards, drenched and clueless.

I opened image after image, remembering and reliving every moment as we danced, ran, jumped, sang, sulked, climbed and most of all, it seemed, laughed our way through a decade-long friendship.

And then suddenly, as I clicked on a photograph and it filled the screen, I realised that although I was still smiling, I was crying too; the tears trickling unchecked down my cheeks as I leaned forward, eager to take in every single detail of the image in front of me. I gazed with enormous affection, tinged with undeniable regret, at Dot and Felix, standing side by side in Devizes market-place, his arm wrapped around her shoulders, her arms thrown around his considerable middle. Her face was tilted upwards towards him as she leaned against him, smiling broadly, her eyes hidden beneath a large bucket hat. Felix, meanwhile, wasn't looking at the camera either, but instead down at Dot, and he too was smiling. It was obvious, I thought, that they loved each other very much.

'Oh my goodness, is that you and Felix?'

I hurriedly wiped the tears from my face and half turned towards Dad as he placed a cup of coffee down next to me. 'Yes,' I said, somewhat huskily, before clearing my throat and adding, 'There were no spreadsheets on the memory stick, just lots of photos of Felix and me growing up.'

'Well isn't that marvellous?' said Dad, beaming. 'What a lovely surprise.'

'It was,' I replied, smiling. 'It really was.'

He laughed. 'What on earth are you wearing in this one?' he asked, pointing at the screen. 'Is that my old fishing hat?'

'You know, I think it is,' I nodded. 'And that dreadful orange skirt I made. Gosh, and those boots. Do you remember those? I never took them off.'

'I remember,' he smiled, pulling a chair towards the desk and sitting down.

'That was the night before Felix left for university,' I said, pointing at the screen. 'He'd brought one of those disposable cameras with him and we asked someone to take a picture. I had no idea he had this. I don't remember ever seeing any of the photos.'

'I love it,' said Dad. 'Can I see the others?'

'Sure,' I said. 'I'm just working my way through them.'

'Well you keep going. I can go back and look at the rest later.'

'OK.' I clicked on the next image. It was of Felix and me at Becca's wedding; a rather drunken selfie, the angle of which left no doubt that I was the photographer. 'Oh, we must be into the more recent ones now,' I said, a little awkwardly, staring at the image of me kissing Felix hard on the cheek as he screwed his face into a disgusted ball.

Dad laughed and stood up. 'Hmm, well, if we've reached the more recent ones, maybe you had better vet them before I look at them.'

'Dad!' I protested.

'I'm teasing, Dot,' he said, bending down and planting a kiss on the top of my head. 'You keep going and I'll look at them later with your mum and Nanny. Or maybe you can copy them for us.'

'I will,' I smiled, turning back towards the screen, and clicking on the next image as he left the study.

There were a couple more of the wedding, and then two or three of Felix and me at Martin's party. And I had just opened a night-time photograph of me lying flat on my back and shining a torch into a tree whilst pointing upwards in excitement – an event of which I had only a very limited recollection – when the doorbell rang.

I jumped at the sound, my thoughts immediately transported from happy midnight shenanigans in a rural back garden to the reality of my current relationship with Felix. A relationship which I would shortly have to redefine in agonising detail to my family, and one which was at this moment as lopsided as our adolescent selves on the see-saw: me up in the air and with zero plan as to how to get down; Felix perfectly grounded and ready to move on with PC Rosie.

'That'll be Becca and Mark!' shouted my mother at top volume. 'Can you let them in, Don? I'm just helping Mum down the stairs.'

'I'll come and help!' I called, taking one last look at the photograph onscreen before taking my phone from my bag and, after just a moment's pause for thought, texting Felix.

The memories are wonderful. I love them, and you, so much – then and now. Thank you.

And then, allowing myself no chance to change my mind, I pressed send, tucked my phone into the back pocket of my jeans and hurriedly made my way back into the kitchen. Even from there, I could hear my mother gushing over the new arrivals and demanding to know *where on earth* I had disappeared to.

'Yes, you pop outside and get it from the car, darling,' she was saying as I reached the hallway and saw her huddled with Dad and Nanny Flo in the open doorway, looking out onto the drive. 'And I'll go on a Dottie hunt,' she laughed, turning around.

'I'm right here, Mum,' I said, walking towards her and giving her a hug. 'I just had to check something on the computer. And hello, Nanny Flo, and happy birthday to you!' I added, releasing my mother and hugging Nanny, delighted and rather emotional to see her out of her wheelchair and standing unaided for the first time in six months. 'You look amazing! Did Mum use her heated rollers on you?' I asked, looking admiringly at her soft white waves.

'She did,' she nodded, putting a hand to her head. 'Nearly scalped me.'

I laughed. 'Other than that, how are you feeling?'

'I'm feeling absolutely wonderful, Dottie,' she said, smiling. 'And what a happy, happy birthday it is to have you and your lovely young man here to celebrate with me.'

My heart sank. 'Oh Nanny, I'm not sure that—'

'Here they are,' said Felix.

I turned to see him step inside carrying an enormous bouquet of flowers.

'Happy birthday, Flo,' he said, holding them out towards her.

'Oh my goodness,' said my grandmother, looking at the flowers but hugging Felix in preference to taking them from him. 'Look at those roses and peonies. And lily of the valley – my favourite. Aren't they the most beautiful flowers you've ever seen, Helen?'

'They are, Mum,' she replied. 'Here, Felix, give them to me and I'll find a vase and pop them in Mum's room. If we've got a vase big enough, that is.' She smiled at the flowers and then turned to me. 'What on earth's the matter with you, Dottie? Standing there catching flies. Aren't you going to say hello to Felix?'

I closed my mouth and forced myself to look away from him. 'Mmm,' I said.

'She's overcome,' said Nanny Flo. 'I know just how she feels. I fell in love with your father afresh every single day, Helen. And I can tell that our Dottie is the same. Neither of us might have much going on up top, eh, Dottie? But there's an awful lot going on in here.' She placed a hand on her chest.

'I think she's surprised to see him, aren't you, Dot?' beamed Mum. 'But I'm not,' she added, turning to Dad. 'Didn't I say he'd come, Don?'

'You did, love,' said Dad, smiling at her.

She beamed at him and then looked again at the flowers. 'Right, well, I'm going to go into the utility room and find that vase. Don, can you take Mum into the lounge, and Dottie, can you put the kettle on for a cup of tea for Felix? Then we can all sit down and have a good catch-up,' she called, the volume of her voice gradually increasing as she disappeared into the kitchen.

Dad watched her go, then turned to Felix. 'Good to see you,' he said, patting him on the arm. 'Dot's just been looking through those photos you gave her. I only saw a couple but I thought they were great. That must have taken you quite a while to put together.'

Felix smiled and opened his mouth to speak, but Nanny Flo got there first. 'What photos are these, then? Can I see?'

'I'm sure you can, Flo,' said Dad gently. 'They're photos of Felix and Dot when they were at school.'

'Ooh, that should be interesting,' my grandmother grinned. 'Do you remember what a roly-poly boy he was, Dottie?' she said, smiling up at Felix and placing an arm around his waist. 'And all that hair. Like a chubby little Leo Sayer.'

Felix laughed and Dad stepped forward, taking Nanny Flo by the hand. 'OK then, Flo,' he smiled. 'How about we get you settled in the lounge? Then I'll find the laptop and Dot can show you the pictures while you have a cup of tea.'

'That sounds lovely, Don,' she said, as he led her into the lounge. 'I really am having the most wonderful birthday.'

I watched them go, and then, taking a deep breath, turned back towards Felix. He was looking at me steadily, his hands in his pockets. 'I gather you haven't told them yet?' he said quietly.

I lowered my eyes to the parquet flooring and shook my head.

'I guessed that might be the case when your mother texted last night to say that she hoped I would be able to make it today and to ask if I was allergic to salad,' he said solemnly. 'Which was just before Linda texted to tell me that you are in fact still single and not, as I had thought, back with Alistair. I haven't quite got to the bottom of how Linda knew that might be of interest to me, but I may just let that slide.'

I continued to gaze at the floor. 'Sorry for not telling my parents yet.'

'I'm thinking maybe you should put that on a T-shirt.'

I nodded but didn't look up. 'OK.'

'Have you not told them because you're worried about upsetting your grandmother?' he asked gently.

I heaved a sigh. 'No. I mean, she would have been very disappointed and I hate the thought of that,' I murmured, 'but she's much better now and would have coped. The truth is…' I paused and took another deep breath, 'I haven't told them we're not a couple because I don't want that to be true. And the thought of it being true breaks my heart, because I don't think I'll ever find another Felix.'

I looked up to find him smiling down at me, his dark curls falling forwards across his forehead.

'Well, why would you ever have to?' he asked.

I returned his smile and, with Kate's regularly repeated advice to stop fannying around ringing in my ears, said softly, 'Felix Davis, will you go out with me?'

He looked at his watch. 'You know, I thought you were *never* going to ask.'

I took a step towards him and, reaching up, placed my arms around his neck, closing my eyes and pulling him down towards me. When he remained resolutely unbending, I opened my eyes and looked up at him questioningly. 'Don't you want me to kiss you?'

'No, I don't actually,' he said simply.

'Oh… OK…' My smile dropped and I slowly lowered my arms.

'What I want *this time*,' he said, taking my face gently in his hands, 'is for me… to kiss you.'

And then he did. And then I kissed him back. And then we kissed each other – for quite a while. Or at least for as long as it took my mother to find a vase large enough for his bouquet, which was in turn long enough for my hair to be released from the messy updo into which I had piled it that morning, and for a button on Felix's shirt to mysteriously come undone.

'Dorothy Riley!' exclaimed Mum, pausing in the lounge doorway on her return from the utility room. 'Put poor Felix down. He doesn't want you slobbering all over him like that, do you, Felix?'

Felix stopped kissing me and looked, I thought, equivocal.

'It's very polite of you to be so amenable,' said Mum. 'You always were such an uncomplaining little boy. But be firm with Dottie and get her to show you where to put your things.'

'You're staying over?' I asked, looking up at him.

'Dorothy, for goodness' sake,' sighed my mother despairingly, 'he is your boyfriend. Of course he's going to stay over. I sometimes wonder where your head is. His bag is by the front door. You can take yours up at the same time,' she added, at last disappearing into the lounge. 'And hurry up!'

I sighed and leaned my head against Felix's chest. 'I'd better take you upstairs.'

'I'm not resisting,' he said.

'Shush,' I replied, releasing myself from his arms and bending down to pick up my bag as he retrieved his own. 'Hey, and what did you mean, *this time*?'

'Sorry?' he asked, frowning.

'You said that you wanted to kiss me *this time*,' I said, starting to climb the stairs, Felix following.

'I'll explain later,' he said.

'OK,' I shrugged. 'Now, you do realise that we're going to have to share a room tonight, don't you?'

He stopped climbing and I turned to look at him. 'Is there a problem with that?' I asked.

'Do you have a waterbed?'

'No.'

He nodded and started to climb again. 'Then I'm OK with sharing a room.'

Friday 17 September 1999

I placed the pint glasses of water on the table and sat down next to Dot on the bench. 'Where did Chris and Ian go?' I asked, scanning the now almost empty pub.

She looked at me blankly for a moment and then tapped a thoughtful finger against her lower lip. 'Er… let me think. Ooh, now they did say something before they stood up and walked towards the door. Now what was it?' She hiccoughed quietly, causing her hat to fall down over her eyes.

'Which door?' I asked, pushing her hat up for her. 'Are you saying that they've left?'

She nodded slowly. 'I am, Felix. I am saying that. I'm just trying to remember what they said when they went. Think, Dorothy, think,' she murmured, placing her fingers on her temples and rubbing.

I picked up my glass of water and sighed. 'It doesn't matter. I'm just surprised that they went without saying goodbye.'

'That was it!' she exclaimed. 'That was what they said! They said goodbye! I remember now.' She beamed triumphantly at me.

'Well done.'

'And they had to go cos Chris's dad was waiting outside in the car and they asked if we wanted a lift, but I said no thank you very much indeed ever so.' She put a hand to her mouth and sniggered.

'Well done again,' I sighed, shaking my head.

'What's this drink you've bought me?' she asked, pointing at the glass in front of her.

'Tap water.'

She frowned, looking confused. 'But it was last orders and I asked for a cider.'

'I know, but you're pissed and we haven't got enough cash for a taxi, so we're going to have to walk home, remember?'

'Oh yeah,' she said, picking up the water and taking a sip, 'that's right. So why did we say no to a lift with Chris?'

I shrugged. 'I'm not sure. That was weird of us, wasn't it?'

She returned her glass to the table and leaned her head against my shoulder while wrapping her left arm around me, resting it on my stomach. 'Thanks for looking after me, Felix.'

'Pleasure.'

'How many drinks have I had, do you think? I reckon I've drunk seven or eight pints tonight, don't you?'

'You've had three halves, which is two more than you usually have. And I seriously think you may be allergic to alcohol,' I said, putting down my glass.

She laughed and sat up, pushing the enormous bucket hat out of her eyes for a second time. I smiled down at her. She was so pretty – even in that bloody stupid hat.

She stopped laughing and turned away, staring at the bar, where Tony the barman was busy stacking empties.

'What is it?' I asked.

'Shh, shh, shhhh. Listen,' she whispered, holding up a hand.

'What? I don't hear anything.'

'Tony's got the radio on under the bar and I love this song,' she said in a murmur.

I leaned forward and listened. 'The Cure?'

She nodded. '"Friday I'm in Love". And the thing is,' she said, turning back towards me, 'it is Friday, our last Friday together in ages, and…' she offered me a slow smile, 'well, this could be our song, couldn't it?'

I looked at her, wanting to tell her how much I loved her. 'You are so pissed,' I said, laughing and reaching again for my water. But before my hand got there, she had taken it in hers.

'Listen, Felix,' she said quietly, leaning closer until her face was just inches from mine, 'you're funny and fun and kind and clever and I love your hair and I love your eyes and I love being with you and I'm going to miss you more than I'm going to miss anything else and that's all true.'

'Long sentence,' I said, trying to be cool and not to take her seriously.

And then suddenly and without warning, she pushed my hair back from my face and kissed me. Not the way she usually kissed me. Not just a quick peck on the cheek. This was her mouth pressed hard against my mouth and then her teeth on my lower lip. And for a second, just a second, I put my arms around her and I kissed her back. And it felt like the best second ever.

And then I did the right thing.

'Stop it, Dot,' I said quietly, gently pushing her away.

She stared at me for a moment before slumping back on the bench and folding her arms. 'I've fancied you forever,' she said grumpily.

'You have not.'

'Have. But I keep it in here.' She made a fist and banged it dramatically against her chest. 'I don't admit it… to myself or anyone else… cos you're always going on and on about… girls who like… maths,' she said, pausing several times to hiccough.

'I am not.'

'You are.'

'I am not.'

'You are'

'I am not.'

'OK then,' she said, sitting up and glaring at me defiantly, 'go out with me then.'

'What?' I laughed.

'Felix Davis, will you go out with me?'

She looked up at me unblinkingly.

'No, I will not,' I said.

'See.' She leaned forward, collapsing her upper body onto the table. 'I knew you wouldn't,' she mumbled, her face pressed against the sticky wooden surface. 'It's because I'm thick.'

'For God's sake, Dot, you are not thick.'

'I am compared to all the Tefal-heads you fancy. And I'm too plain to make up for being thick.'

I frowned down at her and placed my hand gently on her arm. 'I'm saying no for two reasons, and neither has anything to do with you being thick or plain. One, I go to London tomorrow and you go to Sheffield on Sunday, and two...'

She sat up and looked at me blearily. 'Two?'

'And two, you are as pissed as a fart. You don't know what you're saying and you won't remember any of this in the morning.'

'I will, I will, I will,' she insisted.

'OK, well in that case,' I said, 'ask me again another time, when you're sober and we're not about to spend three years living at opposite ends of the country, and then I'll say yes.'

Her face lit up. 'Promise?'

I smiled back at her, loving her and aching at the thought of leaving her behind.

'I promise,' I said, as she placed her arms around my middle and rested her head against my chest. 'Now let's try and get you home.'